DARK ASSET

DARK ASSET

A Marc Portman Thriller

Adrian Magson

Severn House Large Print
London & New York

This first large print edition published 2017
in Great Britain and the USA by
SEVERN HOUSE PUBLISHERS LTD of
Eardley House, 4 Uxbridge Street, London W8 7SY.
First world regular print edition published 2017 by
Severn House Publishers Ltd.

British Library Cataloguing in Publication Data
A CIP catalogue record for this title is available from the British Library.

ISBN-13: 9780727893031

Severn House Publishers support the Forest Stewardship Council™
[FSC™], the leading international forest certification organisation. All
our titles that are printed on FSC certified paper carry the FSC logo.

MIX
Paper from
responsible sources
FSC® C013056

Typeset by Palimpsest Book Production Ltd.,
Falkirk, Stirlingshire, Scotland.
Printed and bound in Great Britain by
T J International, Padstow, Cornwall.

To Ann. My best, bright and only asset.

Acknowledgements

My thanks to David Headley of DHH Literary Agency. Equal thanks to the team at Severn House for their continued confidence in my writing. A special thanks to the real Colin Doney, teacher, world traveller, inspiration and jolly decent chap, who generously donated his name for my story. Note the description, Col; chiselled . . .

One

I was six floors up in an abandoned office project with a dead man for company when I heard the sound of engines. Two at a guess, driven hard and sliding to a stop nearby followed by the sound of doors slamming, running footsteps and a lot of shouting.

A corner window gave me a grandstand view of the surrounding area, which included a collection of clearance sites once marked for re-building that never happened, a dense spread of squalid residential housing running out to the old port of Mogadishu and the choppy inshore waters of the Indian Ocean.

The new arrivals had stopped about eighty yards back in the parking lot. Two grey Mitsubishi pickups with tinted glass, disgorging six men in combat uniform, armed and ready for a fight.

Al-Shabaab, Somali troops or African Union? It was hard to tell. Al-Shabaab were well-versed in passing themselves off as regular army so they could slip into the capital to carry out regular bombing campaigns. Dressing the part had worked well in the past and served as useful propaganda, proving that they could go wherever they pleased while making Mogadishu one of the most dangerous places on the planet.

Whoever these guys were, arriving right now made an already hazardous situation a lot worse.

1

This building, part of a dead dream of commercial growth several years back, had long been stripped of anything useful, especially hiding places and secret portals to somewhere safer. The elevator was lying in a heap at the bottom of its shaft, and every sound of movement echoed the length of the stairwell like a boom box. If I could have chosen a bad place to be, this had to be high on the list.

I watched as the men spread out across the parking lot. The way they moved told me all I needed to know: they were committed, armed with modern weapons, and looked too well-drilled to be extremists. Worse, they looked ready for trouble and I got the sense that they weren't expecting to take prisoners. Not surprising in a country where the rule of law comes mainly out of a gun and dissenters have a habit of disappearing.

My only professional criticism might have been that they should have approached more cautiously, rather than running across open ground with no cover like they were going to the chuck wagon for coffee and donuts.

Even as I thought it, someone down there showed the same line of thought. There was a shout and three of the men in the centre dropped to their knees and sprayed the front of the building at ground level with automatic gunfire. After the near-silence that had greeted my arrival, save for a few bird noises and the distant flap-flap from a piece of loose fascia board on the front of the building, it was a brutal invasion, the thump of shots impacting on the walls downstairs and echoing upwards like a trip hammer.

2

That told me they were serious. Always good to know.

Then they upped the ante. The three other men took their place and began firing at the other windows, moving up floor by floor and stopping only to change magazines. While they did that the first three men took over, leaving no window untouched. It was a murderous assault geared to kill and intimidate. From my perch I saw a shower of cement and cinder-block fragments raining to the ground, and could feel the snapping ricochet of shells bouncing around the inside of the building as the shockwaves moved up inside the structure. If I'd been on one of the floors below, I'd have been dead meat.

It was time to move out and I only had seconds left to do it. I figured any locals hearing the sustained gunfire would ignore it and stay out of the way. Mogadishu was well known for bursts of random fighting, and it was wise not to get involved. Being killed for a specific reason or by accident can be explained away as bad karma; getting shot because you were dumb is not so easy.

I moved back from the windows and considered my options. I had no valid reason for being here and in any case I didn't think the men downstairs would care a whole lot for chit-chat or due process. They'd obviously been sent in on a clearance exercise and that was what they were going to execute. Flushing out whoever they were after was probably secondary to making sure their target didn't leave the building alive.

A deeper thump sent a faint tremor through the

building and an acrid smell drifted up the stairs. Smoke grenade. It was followed by another, this time higher up. Any second now the men would be ordered inside to clear the building floor by floor.

A much sharper bang was an indication of how they intended to do that: fragmentation grenade.

The dead guy on the floor nearby was André Masse, a Frenchman. Outwardly a consultant engineer based in Djibouti to the north, he was actually a deep cover operative for France's main intelligence agency, the General Directorate for External Security, or DGSE. Put in place to keep an eye on the situation on the Horn of Africa, he'd sent an urgent message to his bosses in Paris requesting a come-and-collect. It meant he had something important to hand over but couldn't leave the country himself or trust anyone local to handle it.

For reasons I hadn't been given, the French had hired me to play pickup instead of one of their own. Not that I was questioning their tactics. The French intelligence community was well known for doing whatever was required to protect the country and its overseas territories, often using unorthodox methods when called for. That didn't make them so different to any of the others on the planet including the UK and US; they were simply less bothered by any fallout if and when caught.

In short, hiring an outsider like me to go into a potentially lethal situation was one way of keeping their hands clean.

4

I hadn't been told what kind of information Masse had gotten hold of, only that it was on a hard drive and vitally important. So, meet, collect and carry back.

Unfortunately, Masse was now beyond caring what happened from here on in and had been for a while; he'd been knifed in the abdomen and there was a nasty open gash across the palm of one hand, showing he must have tried at the last second to ward off the attack. His face was a mess, too; he'd been savagely beaten to a point beyond recognition. The smell of infection and death were already heavy in the air, and I could only hope for his sake that he'd died before enduring the beating.

It at least explained why he hadn't been in touch since we last spoke.

I'd got his cell phone in my pocket along with a hard drive I'd found tucked into his sock minutes earlier. It was an electronic biscuit, slimmer and smaller than a pack of cigarettes. He had no ID and nothing that could lead the authorities to his family, friends or contacts. There was nothing else I could do for him but get out of here with the information he'd been trying to get to his bosses, along with a snapshot of the scene. It would be up to them what they did with it. While giving his body a final pat-down I'd found a semi-automatic pistol under his hip. It was a French PAMAS 9mm, a variant of the Beretta, and hadn't been used in a while, going by the dust on the inside of the barrel. But it worked fine and looked ready to go, with a full clip. Maybe it had been his intended way out if he'd got caught; unfortunately his killer had trumped that option. I was carrying a similar weapon, and after what I'd just seen downstairs I had a feeling I might need the spare firepower.

I stepped across to the elevator shaft and looked down. Six floors doesn't sound a lot if you think of an average office building. Eighty feet or so as near as makes no difference. But that's still a lot of feet if you fall. Not that I was planning on it. Masse must have checked out the building previously ready for the handover – or maybe he'd used it before and had planned for all eventualities, because a coil of thick rope lay by the shaft doors. It was tethered to a length of steel pipe jutting from the wall, offering a quick way down and avoiding the stairs.

I could see a pool of light down below on what looked like the fourth floor, where I'd noticed one of the elevator shaft doors was open. All the others were closed and threw the shaft into darkness save for another faint glow on the ground floor where the doors had been blasted open moments ago by one of the grenades. They'd been partially closed when I arrived, although I'd been able to see where the elevator had crashed after the cables had rusted through and finally given up the strain of holding it up.

More shouting and shooting and another grenade blast that sent a tremor through the floor. So, it was this way or no way. Going down the outside would leave me open to target practice by any of the men waiting in the parking lot. And with no other way down save for growing a set of wings, I had to trust to the gods of vertical travel.

I looped the rope through a sturdy bracket on the inside of the shaft walls for luck, then threw the coils over my shoulder. Dropping the heavy hemp down the shaft ahead of me would be like sending up a flare saying, *here I am, guys!* With a quick breath, I kicked out from the open doors and began my descent, feeding out the rope as I went.

There's always one eager beaver who wants to spoil the party. I was approaching the fourth floor and sliding nice and quiet in the dark, hoping to avoid unseen obstacles, when the firing stopped as if a switch had been flicked. The sudden silence was intense, and I stopped dead. Then I heard a shout and the thump of feet coming up the stairs. Some poor duck had drawn the short straw and been sent up as a decoy.

He was ignoring any idea of stealth, his boots crunching noisily on the layer of grit and filth on the stairs and landings, each sound filtering through the fourth floor elevator shaft door. I hung there in the dark, spinning slowly. The foot-steps stopped. He must have heard something; maybe a fragment of debris I'd inadvertently kicked loose on my way down. Whatever it was, I was hoping he got moving soon; I wasn't going to be able to hang here for long and my shoulder muscles were already beginning to pop with the strain.

Then I got lucky. He poked his head through the elevator door just as I spun that way. He didn't see me at first because he was looking down the shaft. He was a big guy with a shiny head and huge shoulders, and I could hear his breathing coming in short, ragged bursts. I was barely ten feet away from him and it was only a matter of time before he sensed my presence and reacted.

He was carrying what looked like a bullpup, which was lousy news. A bullpup is a shortened military-style shotgun designed for close-quarter fighting, for taking down doors and conducting building clearance operations in confined spaces. The idea is, you send in the man with the bullpup and wait to see what comes out. If he's good, he'll either blow away any opposition or frighten them into giving themselves up when they see what they're facing.

When this guy finally looked up, it took a couple of seconds for him to compute what he was seeing. Then he snapped his jaw shut and began to bring up the gun. The barrel looked huge and menacing even in the poor light. If he got even a single pull on the trigger, he'd fill the shaft with hot lead and I'd be dead before I hit the bottom.

Two

I grabbed my gun. I had no option but to take him out; nothing wild, just a straight head-shot. Going for the centre body mass with the kind of weapon he was holding risked my bullet hitting the gun or simply wounding him. This had to be a one-time thing and no mistakes.

He stood for a second, and would have probably looked shocked if his brain were still active. But he was beyond all that, his body pinned momentarily against the elevator door frame until his legs got the message that it was all over and done. As he began to crumple the shotgun slid out of his hands and fell to the floor by his side. It bounced a couple of times, and teetered towards the open shaft with nightmare slowness.

I was already swinging, kicking off the shaft wall and releasing my grip just enough to drop level with the man and kick him and the shotgun away from the shaft. As I swung away again, a shout echoed up from below, asking what was going on. If the gun or the man had gone down the shaft, they wouldn't have asked twice; they'd have come up on the run, firing as they advanced to keep my head down until they were in a position to overpower or kill me.

'*Rat*!' I shouted back as I swung back towards the doors, and got a burst of derisive laughter from below. Rats are detested by most people,

9

even soldiers, but you have to be a wuss to admit it. I dropped the rest of the rope and slid down the shaft as fast as I could, hearing more footsteps pounding up the stairs. It was going to be a close call. Then came another shout, this time from above me.

They'd found the man I'd shot.

A split second later the shaft was full of the hammering noise of gunfire as whoever was up there opened up in the hopes of getting lucky. Elsewhere I heard the sound of running feet and more shouting and it was clear the ruse hadn't lasted long enough.

I was now the rat and on the wrong end of the chase.

I hit the remains of the crashed elevator, feeling the sting of a close shot scorch my back, and let go of the rope. I was effectively standing on a pile of noisy junk with my feet level with the half-open door. All I had to do was step across and out of the shaft.

Easier said than done; they'd left a man on guard while the remainder of the assault posse thundered up the stairs, eager to be in on the kill. He was dressed in camouflage uniform, boots and hat, and carrying an assault rifle. He looked lean, sinewy and quick on his feet, and was now turning to see what the hell all the noise was from the dead elevator, especially the sound of gunfire coming down from above.

When I stepped out of the darkness it took him by surprise, but only for a moment. He began to move so I slapped him with the pistol and dropped him to the floor, then checked out the rest of the small lobby. Nobody. He was on his lonesome while the rest of the group played commando.

Through the filthy lobby windows I could see the two Land Cruisers out in the parking lot, and a guard standing by the front of the nearest vehicle, toting a rifle. He looked nervous; a driver, probably, and the least experienced. But the distance between us was too great and he looked ready to start shooting if anybody other than his comrades stepped out of the building. It gave me an idea.

Tucking the pistol into my waist I stripped off the unconscious guard's camo top and hat and put them on, then bent and pulled the man up onto my shoulder and grabbed his rifle. Tugging the hat down over my face I made sure my head was shielded by the body and stepped outside. Hurrying across the parking lot towards the nearest pickup, I waved the rifle and called for the guard to help me.

The blatantly unlikely is sometimes the best way of fooling somebody. He wasn't expecting anybody to exit the building, not with all the men checking out the upper floors and having such a banging time, so his thought processes were a little off. The gunfire alone would have convinced him that the man they had come here to arrest was trapped on the upper floors. But seeing a figure emerge carrying one of his colleagues, probably wounded in the first contact inside, looked close enough to be plausible. It helped that he couldn't see my face, only the camo top and hat.

I was ten steps away when he must have

remembered that his colleagues were in uniform. He began to swing up his assault rifle and open his mouth to shout a warning that the bad man was on the outside, when I put on as near as I could a sprint and threw the man off my shoulder right at him, knocking him over. His head hit the side of the Land Cruiser with a vicious thump and he dropped his rifle. I followed it up with a tap to the head to make sure he stayed put.

As I jumped aboard and turned on the engine, I heard a shout from way up in the building, followed by a volley of shots hitting the ground around me and a couple punching through the pickup's thin bodywork. Somebody had been admiring the view and seen me come outside.

I hit the gas and accelerated out of the parking lot, pausing long enough to put a couple of rounds into the tyres of the other pickup on the way by. I had no idea what these men's tyre-changing skills were like, but unless they'd all been recruited from a Formula One pit crew, I'd gained myself several minutes' advance on any pursuit.

I got to where I'd left my own vehicle tucked behind a derelict workshop a couple of hundred yards away and dumped the pickup, tossing the keys into a hole before heading out to a road called the Corso Somalia. It was crowded with trucks and small cars, and if I got lucky it would take me to the city's Aden Adde International Airport. As I drove I got on the phone to the man who'd hired me. The name he'd given me was Victor Petrus. He answered immediately and didn't sound happy when I gave him the news.

'Dead? How dead?'

Like Masse, Petrus's English was good, if formal, which suited his professorial appearance. I figured he'd been thrown a little by the bad news, so he probably meant how was Masse killed, not how much was he dead. 'Knifed in the gut,' I told him, 'probably by somebody he knew.'

'How do you come to that conclusion?'

I explained about the defensive cut to Masse's hand. Somebody had got close enough in front to take him by surprise, and he'd tried to parry the thrust. He'd either known the killer or been fooled enough to let his guard down.

Petrus didn't sound convinced, but neither did he allow the death of his operative to get in the way of pursuing his agenda. 'Did you find anything of interest?' He didn't ask about any other problems I might have encountered, either, such as people trying to kill me, but I let it pass. Caring fella.

'I did. I'll see you at the airport. Be there because I won't wait.' I clicked off, then sent him the photo I'd taken of Masse's body. I figured it might stop him asking pointless questions and prick his conscience a little. Or maybe not.

I dropped the cell phone on the passenger seat and focussed on driving. I'd told Petrus I'd be at the airport, but that wasn't where I was flying out from. Mogadishu's Aden Adde International airport was too dangerous and would be the first place the soldiers back at the office building would aim for. A white face in this city was already easy enough to find, and being boxed in inside the terminal would make it even more so. With that in mind, I'd arranged an air-taxi flight

13

from a smaller field ten miles away. As soon as I was sure Petrus was clean and I'd completed the hand-over, I was out of there with a hop across the border into Djibouti and away.

I had no idea why the assault on the building had been made, but my every instinct told me that it had been too well-timed for my arrival to have been an accident.

I'm a close protection specialist. I run security, evaluate risks in hostile situations and, where needed, provide hard cover. To do my job I have to look ahead of where a principal is going to be at any one time, checking details, terrain, routes in and out – most especially out – and providing the best possible solution for a happy outcome. If it works the principal won't even know I'm there and will go home happy. If it doesn't, I step in.

And that's where the hard cover comes in; it means I have to take a more direct course of action and fight back.

With this one, the job had appeared simple enough – on the surface. I'd been hired through a cut-out agency for freelance contractors based in Paris, who'd told me it was an easy in-out collection job in north-east Africa and paid good money. I should have known that 'simple' and 'good money' are rarely good companions in this game. But I'd agreed on a meeting that same afternoon with Victor Petrus, an officer with France's DGSE. He was in his late forties, tall and slim with receding grey hair and a neat goatee beard. He wore frameless glasses and the way he peered at me over the top of the lenses put me in mind of a college professor about to give a student a bad grade. He also wore the attitude of a man who didn't want to get his hands too dirty beyond giving me my instructions.

Our talk didn't take long. He described my main task was to tag along with a man named André Masse through Mogadishu in Somalia, to make sure he stayed clean, alive and functioning. Masse, he said, was their man in that neck of the world and he'd been sent in to collect some information from a contact in the capital. It was a big deal, Petrus said; a very big deal. All I had to do was ride shotgun and get the package and Masse over the border to Djibouti to the north. Well, two borders if we took a direct line of flight. The first would take in a stretch of empty land in Ethiopa's top right corner, unless we went round the long way. Like I say, simple enough; what some refer to as a milk run.

But every now and then that's when circumstances throw in a twister.

Following the briefing I'd met up with Masse at a small hotel favoured by freelance reporters in the centre of Djibouti. There was sufficient traffic to help our meeting pass unnoticed, just another couple of media hounds among many, shooting the breeze while waiting for the next assignment.

The snapshot Petrus had given me was accurate and useful; Masse would have been easy to miss in a crowd, especially in this neck of the woods. He was of medium build, with close-cropped dark hair and large, slightly bulbous brown eyes. He had a deep tan and could have passed as a Gulf Arab, which I guessed he probably did a lot

15

of the time. You'd walk by him in most city streets around the world and not look twice.

Masse had just returned from a trip across the border into Somalia, and confirmed what Petrus had told me – that he'd got a line on some information which he had to get back to his bosses in Paris. He didn't say what the information was, just that it was important and had to be contained as quickly as possible. I was to accompany him to the rendezvous in Mogadishu as soon as he got word that it was ready to collect, and make sure the handover went according to plan.

'It sounds as if there might be some opposition over there. Who exactly are we dealing with?'

'You were not told?' He looked guarded and I figured I knew why: I was an outsider and a stranger on his turf. Maybe he didn't like the idea of having a nursemaid along.

'I wasn't. But I'm sure you can fill me in.'

He hesitated, and then said, '*Bien*. The information comes originally from a member of al-Shabaab – but it's not terrorist-related. I can't say more than that.'

He was either ingenuous or taking me for a cupcake. Everything connected with al-Shabaab is terrorist-related, and brings with it all the dangers that an organisation like that implies. But I could see by his face that he wasn't going to open up any more than he had done, so I decided to try again later before we got over the border. That way he either gave me something to go on or I backed out and left him to it.

'I'll need a weapon.'

'Of course. That is already arranged. Do you have any preferences?'

16

'A semi-automatic but nothing too heavy. Will I need papers?'

He smiled as if he wasn't quite sure whether I was joking or not. 'This is the Horn of Africa. Everybody has a gun . . . but papers not so much.'

I had a question. 'If the information your contact has is on a hard drive, why can't he send it to you online? We could save ourselves a trip.'

'It would be nice,' he said, 'but not possible. The communication network over there is very bad and always dropping out, and I believe the quantity of data contained might be substantial. Besides, I need to see this man face-to-face. He gives me the hard drive, I check it out and if it's good I give him the money we promised.' He shrugged and added, 'I may need to use him again, so it will be good to get to know him a little more.'

I nodded. Standard tactics when building and maintaining a network; keep your assets close and keep them happy. 'What does this man do?' I like to know who I'm meeting with. If the contact was part of a group, he might turn up with heavy fire-power and a bunch of pals. If that happened the exchange could be strictly one-sided.

'He's a Somali army officer. He works in their intelligence section. Believe me; over there he has more to lose than we do if he's caught. He'll come alone, I promise.'

We talked about routes – by air taxi in and out was the simplest, according to Masse – and where to meet in Mogadishu, along with cell phone numbers and fall-back message drops if we couldn't meet as planned. Masse seemed relaxed about the whole thing which, considering Mogadishu was

17

billed as the current murder capital of Africa, showed considerable *sang-froid*. But he was French, so I guess it was in his veins.

'I've been working this region for twenty years,' he explained, scanning the room as he had been doing ever since we arrived. 'I know how things work.' He didn't sound boastful, just matter-of-fact. He finished his drink. 'But in another three months, I'm out of here for good. It will be good to get back to the Loire, where I was born.' He stretched and stood up, then hesitated, his eye on the door. A man had just entered and lifted a hand in recognition before heading towards the bar. I glanced at Masse and he looked unsettled.

'Friend of yours?'

'An acquaintance. He's a teacher from Malawi.'

'That's quite a hike from here.' At a rough guess, about 1,800 miles of hard travel.

'He's a freelance. He works for a number of schools and was transferred up here on loan after a number of foreign teachers rotated out. He's a good man, don't worry.'

I'm paid to worry, especially about people who turn up at a meeting out of the blue. It could be a coincidence but I wasn't taking chances. The fact that this new guy was a teacher made no difference. One thing you try not to do in this business is to involve innocents. There's too much at stake and they don't know the rules. 'I'm guessing he doesn't know anything about what you do?'

'No, of course not.' He blinked as he said it. Big mistake.

'You're lying.'

There was a long silence while he figured out whether to tell me another lie to cover his incompetence or to come clean. He settled for somewhere in between. 'I told him I'm in construction.' He shrugged. 'It's been my cover for a long time, if he wants to check.'

Check? If this teacher did any such thing, it would prove he was no teacher. 'Did he buy it?'

'Of course. Why would he not?'

'Because the big thing down here is the war on terror, not construction, and there are bound to be people here who already wonder what you do for a living. Nobody stays secret forever. One careless word from him in the wrong company and your teacher friend could find himself in trouble.'

'That won't happen. Anyway, you're here with me; do you feel threatened?'

'Not yet. But I'm just passing through. By the time anyone connects any dots I'll be long gone.'

By now the newcomer was walking towards us. Masse clamped his mouth shut and stood up to greet him, then made introductions. 'Colin Doney, Marc Portman.'

Doney was medium height and stocky, in his forties with a growth of stubble around a chiselled jaw. Dressed in standard light cotton pants and shirt, he was holding a whisky in one hand. He looked fit and relaxed, with a deep tan; a genial looking guy at ease with himself and the world around him.

We chatted for a few minutes, and if Doney was hiding anything, he was a very good actor.

While Masse excused himself and went to the bathroom, Doney confirmed that he was a teacher on assignment, and as far as I could determine lacked any guile. He didn't even ask what I did, which showed either good manners or a carefree lack of interest.

When it was polite to do so, I gave Masse a nod and stood up. It was time to get moving and on our way across the border.

Three

Now, as I was approaching Mogadishu airport I began seeing uniforms – lots of them. With the likelihood of an attack by al-Shabaab on a daily basis, an open display of force was the customary approach. It worked more days than it didn't. But today I began to worry. It was like they'd called in every spare cop and soldier in the city, and I gave up counting after seeing about thirty armed uniforms wandering around checking vehicles in and out.

I drove by with my head down and found a parking slot sandwiched between two small trucks, with a good view of the terminal building and a short run to the exit if I had to bug out in a hurry. I knew Petrus would be waiting inside, but the one thing I wasn't about to do was waltz in there like a tourist. That was a quick way of sticking my head in a noose.

I dialled his number, and he answered in a rush, his voice low. 'You took your time, Portman. Where are you?' If he was trying to be cool and polite, it didn't work; he was way too tense and his question came out like an accusation.

I said, 'Trying to avoid trouble, if you must know.'

'What do you mean?'

'Like I told you, Masse was dead when I got there. But just minutes after I arrived I had company. A bunch of uniforms came in hard and hosed

21

down the entire building. They weren't looking to take prisoners.'

He didn't ask what building or how I'd got out. Instead he brushed it aside by saying, 'A coincidence, that's all. Masse would have been most careful. You must have been the one followed.'

I let the insult to my professionalism go by because it was a waste of time arguing. The one thing I always make certain of when going to a meet is to shake off any possible tails. If the other party brings one, that's different. But I'm usually far enough back to check out that possibility and deal with it.

This time there had been nothing. And judging by the length of time Masse appeared to have been dead, I knew the soldiers hadn't been waiting around close by on the off-chance somebody might show up; they'd been primed and timed and told to go.

'You must come in and complete the handover,' Petrus continued. If he felt any grief at the loss of his man, he was hiding it well. 'Come through the main doors of the terminal building and look to your right. I'll be waiting by the coffee franchise.'

As I switched off and got ready to move, a Magirus army truck full of troops arrived in front of the terminal, followed by a shuttle coach. The troops dropped out and scattered across the entrance and approach road, while a Hilux pickup stopped further back and dropped off more troops, who jumped down and stopped any other traffic from approaching and pushed people away from the entrance. The result was chaos and near panic.

22

Before things got completely out of control an officer gave a signal and the coach doors opened. A dozen passengers, a mix of African and Europeans, each carrying briefcases and wearing suits, scurried out and disappeared inside the terminal.

Government or African Union officials, I guessed, maybe even European observers leaving another of the many places on earth now drawing the growth industry of fact-finding organisations worldwide with a mission to make things better.

I leaned over the back of the seat and picked up a briefcase of my own. It's like a passport to normality in this part of the world, and while I knew it wouldn't stop me running into trouble forever, it would give any ordinary trooper or cop pause for thought before demanding a look at documents or making a body search.

I crossed the parking lot and approach road and walked up to the first trooper I saw and held out the briefcase, the top open. It held papers, a road map and a book. He glanced at the contents and waved me through in a distracted manner, one eye on the area behind me for signs of danger.

It was my pass into the building. I found the coach party hadn't gotten far beyond the entrance, in spite of their army escort. They were milling around impatiently, throwing nervous glances at the entrance behind them and trying to push through the already crowded terminal away from all the activity outside. But that simply added to the frenzy. The interior was already crowded with noise and bustle, with everybody seemingly shouting at each other, at airport officials or into cell phones. I slipped into their midst and looked

23

towards the coffee franchise Petrus had mentioned. It was an open trolley with an array of snacks out front and a coffee machine behind, operated by a single man juggling mugs and materials like a professional.

No sign of Petrus, though. I felt a tingle of alarm; he should have been here.

I was going to give it a count of ten, then leave. Not being at an arranged meet in a hostile environment like Mogadishu is hardly like standing up a hot date at a restaurant. It happens, but only if you're blown, incapacitated or dead. If you think you've got a tail, you make sure to let your contact know and stay clear. And in a crowded place like this, there was too much room for danger to be hiding; the kind of danger Masse's killers represented if they were looking for me.

Then I spotted Petrus. He was standing at the far end of the terminal by a recess in the wall. He had two obvious security guys with him who were keeping the crowds away, giving him a clear safety zone of several feet. Petrus himself was in a lightweight suit with an open-neck shirt, while the two others were dressed in tan pants and soft boots, with their hands inside sleeveless protective jackets. I could feel the tension coming off them all the way over here, and their style of dress and prickly attitude was pulling far too much attention from passengers nearby.

I didn't like it. Petrus was supposed to be keeping a low profile, the same as me. Instead he was making himself stand out, especially with the two goons on show. Anybody eyeballing them would spot me the moment I stepped towards them. In covert terms I'd be lit up like a Christmas tree.

A hefty, perspiring Frenchman nearby was spitting into a cell phone and asking why they weren't getting processed a lot quicker out of this place. He didn't use the words shit-hole, but it was there on the tip of his tongue. I didn't blame his anger; if anything kicked off here in the terminal, he and his buddies would be a lot safer airside.

I used the Frenchman as cover to dial Petrus's number and watched him snatch up his phone.

'Portman – where are you?' He sounded pissed, but in that cold, regal way that French officials have of letting you know you've dropped the ball. I guess it's a skill they learn in the *École Nationale d'Administration* – the civil service school that pumps out the suits who end up running the country.

'You said to meet by the franchise. So why aren't you there?'

'A precaution, that's all. There are too many people here. Where are you?' He was scanning the crowd and signalling to his men to put their eyes to good use. It wasn't going to do any good unless they could identify me, and I was already moving away towards the outside using other travellers as cover.

'I'm leaving,' I told Petrus as I stepped through the entrance. I didn't like the feel of the whole set-up and his change of position; it was too obvious that he was no ordinary passenger waiting for a flight. As far as I was concerned I'd accomplished what I was paid to do. Hanging around to criticise his lazy trade

25

craft wasn't going to help me any. 'See the crowd of Europeans near the main doors?'

'Yes, I see them. So?'

'The big shouty guy with the loud voice and the red face? He's French so you should get on fine. Have one of your guys check out his left-hand jacket pocket. I'll be in touch.'

'Wait!'

I walked back across the access road, which was now back to normal. The military truck, coach and pickup were gone, leaving behind a dense cloud of blue smoke. I got into my car and checked my surroundings. It would take me thirty minutes to get to the airfield where my taxi flight was waiting, and then I'd be out of here and on my way home.

I really should stop thinking thoughts like that. It always leads to trouble. A couple of hours later I felt the seat shift beneath me and opened my eyes. I was sitting behind the pilot of a single-engine Cessna C208b Caravan, along with a press group of reporters who'd got hazed into leaving Mogadishu in a hurry when a colleague had been shot by a sniper. The flight had been a quiet one, and I'd been glad of the chance to catnap and avoid answering questions about what I'd been doing in Somalia.

The pilot was on the radio to the tower at Djibouti's Ambouli International airport, talking in the flat tones of what sounded like a South African accent and shaking his head wearily at the answers he was getting. Through the window ahead I could just about make out the airport through the heat haze, dwarfed by the large military Camp Lemmonnier, the US Africa Command (AFRICOM) site stretching across the south of the city. From this angle I could also see in the distance the busy sea port and the lines of cranes towering over the boats below.

The pilot was beginning to make a wide turn to the east, so I leaned forward and asked, 'What's up?'

'They told me to circle and wait,' he muttered, his voice flat. 'Every day it's the same here in Djib; we have to give way to American and French military.' The way he sucked his teeth showed which side his allegiances lay, although I was willing to bet most of his passenger income came from ferrying around press personnel from both those countries.

To be fair it wasn't only the French and American forces who'd taken up a semi-permanent and heavy residence in the country; a number of other nation's armed forces had joined them in the fight against terrorism, and it meant a lot of extra flight movements in and out and more congestion in the skies and on the ground.

As we drifted out over the blue waters of the Gulf far below I got a buzz on my cell phone. At first I didn't recognise the voice over the roar of the plane's engine, and missed the name he gave me. Then he repeated it and I felt a chill touch the back of my neck.

It's not every day that I get a call from a dead man.

'It's André. André Masse,' the voice repeated. 'Please, I need your help.'

Four

'We have a problem.' Victor Petrus was staring out at the evening sun from his room in Djibouti's Hotel Kempinski and trying to hide his irritation at the day's events. He hadn't been looking forward to making this call but there was no way round it. His superiors in the Boulevard Mortier in Paris's elegant 20th arrondissement, barely a hop and a spit from the city's famous Père Lachaise cemetery, were not known for their patience, and he was expected to come up with a positive report on his mission to Mogadishu.

'This is not being recorded,' the voice on the other end said softly. There had been no introduction but he recognised it as Alain Degouvier, one of the operations directors. 'Go ahead but keep it brief.'

That didn't help Petrus's state of mind. He said, 'The meeting with Masse did not go as expected. The courier arrived and found Masse dead at the rendezvous, an abandoned building close to the port in Mogadishu. It appears he was knifed and robbed – probably in a random mugging.'

'That is unfortunate. What about the package?'

'The courier recovered a hard drive hidden on the body. The contents are on the way to you as we speak.' Petrus glanced at his laptop on the table nearby, currently buzzing softly as it transferred the contents of the hard drive to a zip file ready for sending. Once done, he'd be able to give a sigh of relief and leave this godless place; it would then be somebody else's headache.

'So, not really a problem, then.' Degouvier's voice carried a faint tone of sarcasm. 'Once we assess the information received, we can get on with business. What about this courier – does he know not to talk about this?'

'I think so.'

'You think?' Degouvier's response was sharp. 'It's your job to read people. If he had just found a dead body he must be wondering what happens next. You briefed him, saw him at the handover, did you not? How did he look?'

Petrus hesitated. 'I didn't actually have eyes on him. He made the handover by a drop through a clean third party – a passenger at the airport.' He went on to describe the situation at the airport and the phone call from Portman; how his men had retrieved the hard drive from the angry French traveller, who had expressed outrage at having his pockets searched until Petrus had pulled strings to get him processed immediately through departures to the safe comfort of a small lounge.

A huff of impatience came down the line. 'Did you check the drive before sending it?'

'No. I thought it best to get it on its way for evaluation.'

'So you have no idea if it carries anything of value.'

'I'm sure it will be as promised,' Petrus insisted quickly. He took off his spectacles and rubbed his eyes. 'I have faith in Portman having done

29

what he was hired to do. He would have had no benefit in making a switch—'

'So why did he not show up in person for the handover? It was a clear break in standard operational procedure, was it not?'

Petrus didn't want to mention that it was probably his own lapse in procedure that had driven Portman away, or that one of the reasons for hiring an outsider like Portman was because he was free of such restraints and able to act as he felt fit. Besides, he already had a problem in being the man who had hired the American to begin with. Instead he said quickly, 'I agree. But I think he was probably spooked by finding Masse dead and then finding an unusually heavy military presence at the airport. There had been another attack in the city centre and the authorities were on high alert. I gather from local reports that Portman had to use force to extricate himself from the building after finding Masse.'

'What did that entail?'

'He killed one man and injured two others. They were government troops – I have no idea why they were there.'

'So he's no ordinary courier, is he? Portman, you said?'

'Correct. He's a freelance and came recommended by sources in the United States.'

'An American? Was that wise, in view of the . . . situation?'

'You said not to use any of our own people. I checked through another source and they verified his credentials. He has worked in this region before so it seemed an advantage to use his experience.'

'Very convenient. Talking of Americans, have you heard from our new cousin?'

'He is arriving tomorrow.' He shook his head at the lengths some of his colleagues went to avoid saying certain names. This 'cousin' was Clay Lunnberg, a senior operative working for the Defense Clandestine Service (DCS), a new elite espionage group run by the US Department of Defense. Created as a smaller rival to the vast Central Intelligence Agency, it was already running its own operations across the world and forming partnerships where few had existed before, in this case with new elements of the French DGSE. Lunnberg was responsible for a specific operation in this region of North Africa, and was going to brief Petrus on the next stage of a joint Franco-American initiative that had the highest security clearance possible.

'Very well. What about Masse's body? We cannot have anything rebounding on us.'

Petrus winced at his superior's cold approach, but he knew he was right. 'Portman said there is nothing to identify him. I should perhaps arrange for recovery—'

'No.' Degouvier's voice was sharp. 'It's too late for that. It's regrettable but there is too much that can go wrong if you send anybody else over there. We'll let the Somalis deal with it. It's their problem now.'

'Were the Somalis sent in to intercept the package?' Petrus asked the question before thinking, the suspicion coming from some deep, dark corner of his subconscious. He'd been alarmed at the idea that the soldiers had gone in on orders from

Paris while his own man was going to be there, but also conscious that the Somali military might have stumbled on something themselves and launched a raid without telling anyone. Whichever the situation, it was out of his hands. Neither did he have any regrets about Masse's death. It had become clear to him over time that the man had been on his way out; he'd spent too long in the field in this part of the world and in Petrus's opinion had lost a lot of his edge.

'I'm sure you would know more about it than me,' Degouvier replied smoothly. 'Whatever the Somalis choose to do is not in our control; it's their country, after all. We also do what we have to in the best interests of ours.'

Petrus listened to the terminal click on the line and breathed deeply. As convoluted and impenetrable answers went, that one had to be world class. But at least he had survived another day. The worrying thing was that there were questions being asked about Portman. The American had been his choice going on what he'd considered reliable information. If Degouvier found anything dubious about him, then Petrus himself would be in a very weak position. And in this game, that could be fatal to one's upward mobility.

Ten minutes later, as he emerged from a cool shower, his phone rang. He snatched it up.

'You were wrong about your man.' Degouvier launched straight into the attack, his voice glacial. 'The data has been checked; it's worthless rubbish. File after file of nonsense culled from the internet.'

'What?' Petrus's towel slipped to the floor as shock took over. 'I don't understand . . . he would not have been able to do that – and why would he?' He clamped his mouth shut, aware that he was gabbling. This was a disaster. And it would all fall on him.

'I don't care how or why it was done. Either Masse failed to get the information he was promised or somebody tampered with the hard drive before it reached us. From the chain of events you describe, if you trust Masse implicitly, the only other person who could have done that is your man Portman. The question is what is he going to do with the original information, assuming he still has it?'

Petrus swallowed, the repeated emphasis on 'your man' a clear indication that this talk was being recorded and would be used against him in any subsequent evaluation. As would Masse's failure. 'I'm not sure what you expect me to do—'

'Simple. I want you to find him and rectify the situation.'

'Pardon? I don't see how . . .'

'That is up to you to sort out. It is now even more important than ever that this situation is cleared up before the information you were promised gets out and goes viral. Lunnberg has been advised of this development and a team is on its way to assist. I suggest you prepare for their arrival and arrange to give them whatever support they might need.'

'A team? To do what?' But the phone was already dead. He recovered quickly and dialled the number of Portman's phone. He should have done this earlier, but there had seemed no need. There was no answer.

He sat down on the bed, sensing his future teetering on the edge of an abyss.

Five

I'd worked with the French before, although not in the same way as this. A few years back I'd been part of a special ops training group on attachment to the French military – the 13th Demi Brigade of the Foreign Legion in Djibouti. It had been an illuminating experience and given us an insight into working in this part of Africa. After two weeks of hard training and a couple of anti-piracy sorties, the attachment had ended badly, with the loss of a legionnaire named Lameuve. I hadn't known him well but he'd seemed like a nice guy. We'd run into a crazy dust storm while tracking a suspected extremist group and Lameuve, who was on point, had gotten separated from the rest of us. We were already very close to the border with Somalia, and he must have become disori-entated and turned the wrong way. It was easy to do when there were no landmarks and radio signals in the area were unreliable. By the time we found him a couple of days later, after some arguing with the brass, it was too late. He'd been staked to a tree and left as a clear warning to the 13th Demi Brigade and others: *don't come back.*

By group agreement and against orders, we had done the opposite and tracked down his killers. Sometimes you just want to leave a warning of your own, to even up the score.

The air taxi didn't land at the main Djibouti

airport, but was diverted to a small airstrip outside the city. At least it avoided any awkward questions from customs officials, and I was able to catch a ride from a mechanic who dropped me in the city centre. As soon as I was checked in, I called the number Masse had given me on my way in.

'Last time I saw you, you weren't looking so good,' I said. 'Care to explain what's going on?'

He gave a dry chuckle. 'That's very good, Portman. You want proof I'm actually breathing and not lying stabbed and beaten to a pulp on the sixth floor. I get it.' His English was good and colloquial, if overlaid with a definite French accent.

'Something like that. First, tell me what was by the elevator.'

'A rope. I put it there in case . . . well, you know why. The elevator was smashed at the bottom of the shaft. Always have an escape plan, right?'

'Correct. Where are you right now?'

'Here in Djibouti. I got out of Mogadishu as soon as I could. I tried for hours to get hold of you to stop you going to the building but I couldn't get a signal. The African Union troops were running an operation in the suburbs clearing out suspected al-Shabaab cells, and had requested the Americans put a block on all communication networks. I also sent a messenger to your hotel to warn you but he didn't show up.'

It sounded plausible; although I wasn't too sure how hard he'd tried to contact me. If at first you don't succeed in a critical situation and the life

36

of an asset or colleague is involved, you try again. And again.

Going into details over the phone was too risky, so I suggested we meet up, and named another hotel I'd scouted earlier a few blocks away. It was small and busy and had a garden courtyard out back with access from the street.

'I know it,' he said. 'Say, eighteen-hundred?' He disconnected without waiting for my reply.

I left the room and made my way to the meeting point. I'd be early but I wanted to check out the area before meeting Masse. The streets were noisy and brash, which was fairly normal, and crowded with a mix of locals, traders and new military arrivals, the latter easily spotted by their buzz-cuts and raw sunburn. A group of young male Asians in civilian clothes, possible Japanese or Chinese military, were looking around like tourists on vacation, eyes wide but cautious. In among the German, and US-accented English, I heard a lot of French, and wondered if any of the speakers were men I might have worked with the last time I was here.

The hotel looked clear, but I circled the block a couple of times before going in. If Masse was still on somebody's radar I needed to avoid being caught up with him. And the only way to do that was to stay in the background as much as I could. Whatever had happened to him in Mogadishu, he now had a sizeable question mark hanging over him: who was the dead man I'd found on the sixth floor?

I entered the courtyard through an alleyway at the rear and checked out the clientele before showing myself. There were several tables dotted around an ancient fountain that spouted water in a haphazard fashion, with a narrow overhead walkway running around three of the walls giving access to the rooms. The air smelled of cooked meat, spices and tobacco smoke.

Masse was sitting alone with his back to the main building, alongside a narrow doorway. I had no idea where it led, but I was willing to bet it was an escape route. He watched me approach and flicked a finger at a grey-haired waiter, who brought two cold beers and placed them on cardboard mats in front of us as if he was on a wire.

'I'm sorry about what happened,' Masse said, once the waiter moved away, and launched straight into an explanation. 'But it was unavoidable. I was scouting the route to the building a couple of days ago when I realised I'd picked up a tail in the city centre. I led him on a tour to try losing him.'

'Why didn't you wait for me to go with you? That's what I'm here for – to watch your back.'

'You're right, and I should have done that. But I know Mogadishu and thought it would be a small matter to get out of the way. I wanted to make sure the building was safe before we got there, and one person would be less obvious than two.'

'Why that building?'

'It was my asset's choice of rendezvous. I knew of it but I hadn't seen it before.' He shrugged. 'It was a mistake. My tail came, too. He was very good – I couldn't shake him.'

'Who was he?'

'I have no idea. I suspect America . . . CIA, a

contractor, perhaps, or maybe one of their black ops people. Who knows? It's a hunting ground for all sides over there and we occasionally cross paths. All I know is that he shouldn't have been following me. Until that moment I'd been absolutely clean and clear.'

'What happened?'

'To him? I can't tell you. I watched him check out the area around the building, then he went inside. It was too open to wait around to see what he did next so I decided to head back to my room in the city and wait for my asset to call me. I was planning on suggesting an alternative rendez-vous, but if he didn't agree I was going to check out the building again later so we could still meet there. As it turned out, he insisted on another RV because he was being posted to the south and wanted to complete the exchange earlier than planned.'

If it had been me I'd have hung around to see where the tail went next. It's standard procedure if you pick up a watcher to at least try to identify them, because anybody taking such a close personal interest spells danger. Masse was supposed to be experienced, according to my briefing, but maybe he'd lost a bit of edge over the years. He looked tired and seemed to be having trouble focussing. But there were still a couple of questions I needed answering and I was waiting for him to come clean. Recovery could come later.

'Yet you went back to the building. Why?'

'I wish I could tell you.' He lifted both hands, palms up. 'Call it instinct, but I wanted to know who the man was, and maybe he'd left a clue in the building. Anyway, I returned in the evening and found him on the top floor. He'd been dead a while by then.' He shrugged. 'You saw how it was. He must have hung around too long and got noticed by a local gang. He'd been stripped clean of any ID and valuables. The killers had obviously taken everything.'

'So how come he had a hard drive in his sock?'

He shifted in his seat. 'I left it there. I panicked.' He hesitated and took a long drink, which made him look all kinds of guilty.

'Why?'

'A security precaution. As I told you my contact dropped off the packet as arranged, but I didn't get a chance to check it out. It was too dangerous carrying the drive around with me, and I couldn't shake the feeling that I was being watched. I knew the body had been searched, but I figured you would still look and find it.'

'And this?' I took the cell phone I'd found on the dead man and dropped it on the table. It was Masse's, as I'd discovered by checking through the contents earlier, but it held very little that would have been of interest to a third party. 'Why leave this behind?'

He didn't even hesitate. 'The same thing. The man was about the same build as me, so I thought it would be a way of putting off anybody looking for me if they thought I was dead. It wasn't clever, I admit, but I was reacting to events as I found them.' He picked up the phone and checked it still worked, thumbing through the icons on the screen.

His explanation was too slick for my liking. If Masse was as experienced as I'd been led to believe, his trade craft had holes you could drive a bus through. However, I knew what it was like to stumble on a shifting pattern of circumstances in a live mission with no immediate way of getting advice or back-up, so I decided to let it go. I might give him the benefit of the doubt now, but I didn't have to believe him all the way.

'Do your bosses know you're alive?'

'No. I haven't told anybody yet. If the man who followed me was part of an organisation, I think it's better to stay below the radar until the job is completed.'

'Don't you trust your own people?'

He looked conflicted, and I wondered if it was part of the stress he was under. 'I trust them, of course. But I cannot guarantee some of the people they're working with.'

'Like who?'

He shrugged. 'They're using outside sources – people I've never met before.'

People like me, I thought, but let it hang. Trust was a commodity hard-won but easily lost in this game. Lose even a hint of it and you were left not knowing who you could truly rely on. Masse evidently knew more than I did about the people working with his own organisation, but wasn't about to elaborate.

I said, 'What exactly do you want from me? I've handed over the hard drive, so my job's done.'

He gave me a shifty look. 'Not quite. The one you found was a blank. It contains nothing of any use.'

41

I wondered if I should just take out my gun and shoot him. Playing games like he'd done had put me in jeopardy and all for no reason. He must have seen something in my face because he added, 'I'm sorry, Portman – but I had no guarantees that either of us would get the hard drive back across the border. It was all I could think of . . . on the hoof, as you Americans say. Besides, if you had been stopped there was nothing incriminating on it that would have led to your arrest. Eventually they would have let you go.'

'You still haven't told me why you need my help, or why I shouldn't just walk away now and go home. And what is so hot about this information that you're risking our lives to get it?'

'I can't tell you that. All I can say is that it's of huge strategic importance to your country as well as mine, and it's vital we get the information to Paris.'

Terrorism. It had to be. Or oil. They were the only two growth industries in the region, although with the constant terror threat from al-Shabaab and other groups, I'd have put oil very much in second place to bombs and guns.

'Presumably you have the genuine hard drive, so where's the problem?'

'Unfortunately, I don't.'

'Say again.'

'It's still in Mogadishu. On the way back to my hotel I saw the same two men on three occasions. It was too much of a coincidence and I couldn't take a chance of being stopped with the original hard drive, so I headed straight for the airfield and got a plane back here.'

If I'd had any bad feelings before about this, they had just gone into overdrive. 'So what am I supposed to do about that?'

'I need you to come back over there with me and get it back.'

Six

'You're kidding me.' I could see he wasn't but it was an instinctive reaction. Going back into a hot situation like Mogadishu was a definite no-no until the heat died down. Masse was already a known face having been there for several days, and probably many times before that if he'd been operating in this region for so long like he'd said. If anyone had got a good look at me as well, they would have an easy time picking up either one of us.

'I wish I were. The fact is we have to do it.' He shrugged. 'Petrus expects it and we haven't completed the job until we get that hard drive. You know the rules.'

As if I needed reminding. A good reputation in my line of work is gained by finishing what you start and bringing home the cookies. Short of random interference from the opposition or a slip-up in procedure that led to calling off an operation, you stuck with it to the end. Anything else is failure, and that's bad for business.

It made me wonder about Masse's skills background. He undoubtedly had some nerve and courage, working and living out here the way he did, and would have had some weapons training with the DGSE, if only for defensive purposes. But how would that translate into meeting a heavy confrontation head-on?

44

'What did you do?' I asked him, 'before you joined DGSE?'

He hesitated for a second, then said, 'I was in Naval Intelligence. Is that a problem?'

'Not at all. I take it you've had combat training?'

'Some, naturally. We all do the courses. Is that what you are expecting – that we will have to fight?'

'I hope not. But I prefer to be prepared for anything; it's Somalia, not the Champs-Élysées.'

He shrugged. 'It's dangerous for some that is true. But only those who go looking for it.'

I ignored that. For a man in his line of work he was either very naïve or putting on a brave front. 'Petrus is your immediate boss, right – your controller?'

His eyes went a bit opaque at that, like curtains being drawn. He clearly didn't like my line of questions. 'One of them. Why?'

'Because I'm going to call him and ask the same question I asked you: what is this mission really about?'

He looked alarmed, as if I'd suggested spray-painting the Élysée Palace with the Stars and Stripes. 'No. You should not do that. Please.'

'Why not?' Actually, as a freelance I could do what I wanted; I wasn't part of the French or the US intelligence apparatus and if anybody had a degree of latitude in not following orders blindly without question, it was someone like me. I didn't have the same need-to-know restrictions as flagged-or-badged field operatives, so I could walk away if I really felt this was an uncontrolled situation with a dead-end outcome.

'Because he will not tell you . . . and if he thinks we are not in harmony he will recall me.' He hesitated then said, 'I need to finish this assignment. Recalling me will be the end of my career.'

So he had a hard-line boss who'd yank him off the mission if he thought things weren't going well. It wasn't unusual in this profession and made practical sense. But Masse looked genuinely worried. 'OK. But one of you had better fill me in. I was hired to escort you into and out of Mogadishu to retrieve a piece of electronic hardware, and we already have a dead body, a bunch of trigger-happy soldiers and you've switched the real deal for a fake. I'm not asking what's on the hard drive, just the background to it. You owe me that much.'

He gave it a good try, but in the end he caved. I think he could tell I was about to walk and he knew it was with good reason. I didn't doubt that he'd find a way of going back in without me if it looked like he was going to get canned. Bring home the prize; that was the only thing he could do.

'It's about oil.'

Oil. So much for my expert analysis. I should stick to shooting people.

'The Somalis are desperate for oil revenue,' he explained, 'but they face huge obstacles, such as continued threats from al-Shabaab and similar groups, and a real danger of tankers moving in and out of the area being targeted by pirates. In addition they have a problem with negotiating contracts because the central government does not have a defined regulatory system in place to do that. There are too many different regional bodies involved, and any energy companies signing up to an agreement would be facing years of protracted negotiations and high costs.'

'But somebody found a way round that?'

'Yes. My country and yours. At least, commercial organisations within both countries along with the assistance of the Somali government. But it requires the cooperation of all sides. Without it there would be nothing.'

Al-Shabaab. He hadn't included them in the list but he'd mentioned them before; it was where the information on the hard drive had come from.

'Don't stop there.'

He sighed but relented. 'The various . . . discussions that have gone on have involved very few people – for obvious reasons. One of the main stumbling blocks was al-Shabaab and their affiliates. We managed to get to a man named Hussein Abdullah, a deputy *emir* in the region, and included him in the discussions. He was in charge while his leader is in hospital . . . but that man has since died, so the leadership situation is up for grabs.'

'How did you get to him, exactly?' It's not as if you can simply walk up to a senior al-Shabaab member and ask for a private chat.

'I don't know how. That was accomplished by others working through back-channels. All I do know is, without his cooperation, the talks would not have begun. If successful, we would have had his guarantees that there would be no attacks on exploration and drilling sites in the region and free movement of oil.' He gave a wry smile. 'Everybody benefits.'

47

'I'm sure they do. What does this Abdullah get out of it?'

'He would have been paid a lot of money . . . and possibly other benefits – if he had survived.'

'Survived?' I realised he'd been talking in the past tense for a while, but I'd put that down to language.

'His base was targeted in error by an American drone strike. Abdullah was killed and everything was destroyed. At first that was not a problem; all we had to do was find the next person in the chain of command and start again. Then it was revealed that Abdullah had been a student of information technology . . . and had probably recorded all the proposals and video discussions on a hard drive.'

'They spoke to him on-line?' Jesus, how naïve was that?

Masse shrugged. 'I know. Fortunately I was approached by a man who said he had been to the site of the attack and found a computer and hard-drive inside a strong box. He offered to sell them to me.'

'And you said yes.'

'Of course. At first I thought it was a scam. But as soon as I took a brief look at the hard drive I knew it was dynamite. If ever it became public that we were talking with a terrorist group for commercial reasons, without a full programme of explanation and benefits beforehand, the fall-out would be colossal. Enough, I think, to bring down our governments.'

I wasn't sure that was true; modern governments aren't that fragile or honourable anymore, and soon find the means to spin their way out of sticky situations. But it would certainly raise an outcry and any potential commercial gains would be outstripped by the political and public fury. No wonder Masse and his bosses were keen to retrieve the information.

It made me wonder if anybody outside the three countries involved knew anything about it; like the Russians, the British or the Dutch, to name three. Maybe they had decided they didn't want to dirty their hands with terrorist-assisted oil money.

'What will happen to this information once we get it back?'

He shook his head. 'That is above my head. All I have been told is that if it gets out it will be a disaster.'

I stood up. Pity nobody had thought of that before. I was tempted to walk, but a part of me knew that there was enough political trouble in the world already; adding another scandal of this proportion wouldn't help anyone. 'If I do agree to help, where do we go from here?'

He looked instantly relieved, and smiled. 'I'll arrange everything and call you. We'll fly in with the same pilot you used already. He makes lots of cross-border trips so he knows the best places to land. For an extra fee he'll drop us close to Mogadishu and make sure we have transport waiting. Where are you staying?'

I didn't answer but he didn't take offence. We'd exchanged phone numbers and that was all we needed for now. I left him to it and took a cab out to the airport to check on flights out and book a couple of seats at different times over the next three days. I figured we would need to be in Mogadishu as short a time as possible before we got noticed, after which we'd have to bug out fast. And that included not spending any longer in Djibouti than was necessary.

It was getting late and the desks at the airport were quiet, so I got served quickly and efficiently. I picked up my confirmation stubs and began feeding in the details to my cell phone. As I finished doing that I turned to see a flush of passengers coming through from the arrivals hall. Those not dragging baggage carts and wheeled suitcases were hurrying through with the brisk step of the seasoned traveller heading for a lead position in the cab rank before all the available rides disappeared.

One of them was Victor Petrus. He was busy talking and had his head turned the other way, so he didn't see me. He looked all business, with one hand guiding another man by the elbow, and indicating a young guy in tan pants and shirt and a double-short haircut waiting the other side of a rope barrier. This one looked familiar and I soon realised why: it was one of the security guys I'd seen with Petrus at Mogadishu airport.

Without thinking about it I lifted my cell phone and took snaps of all three men.

When in doubt about anything you've seen, heard or been told, the simple rule is to check and double-check because your life and liberty may depend on it. Right now I had a bundle of facts I wasn't sure about and no easy way to verify them. But something about the guy with Petrus had me puzzled. He was in his forties, with broad shoulders and the brisk walk of a fitness addict . . . or a military man. He had close-cut brown hair with grey flecks and the eyes of somebody unaccustomed to taking prisoners. As they passed by, I heard him say something about making a phone call from a secured landline.

He wasn't talking French, either; his accent was pure American.

I watched them walk through the exit, the security guy leading the way and another sweeping in behind out of nowhere to watch their backs. They all climbed aboard a black Lexus 4WD with tinted windows parked outside in a no waiting zone and it took off as soon as the doors closed, heading away from the terminal at a brisk clip.

It didn't take rocket science to figure out why an American was cosied up with a French Intelligence officer right here and now, not if what Masse had told me was true. I know Djibouti has a large military presence from both countries, but I was pretty sure that had nothing to do with it. Still, experience told me it would be good to know who the American was. If Petrus had put himself out to meet the man off an incoming flight, it wasn't simply to show fraternal greetings.

I thought about calling Brian Callahan. He's a Clandestine Service Officer with the CIA and we'd worked together a couple of times. The intelligence community in Washington, as big as it is in personnel numbers, is tight, and I figured he might know who the American was. People in the trade tend to mix with their own kind, and although I had no proof, this one had all the hallmarks of a spook.

In the end I decided against it. If it turned out to be somebody Callahan knew, maybe even respected and liked, I'd be putting him in a difficult spot. He'd either tell me who the guy was, but with reluctance, or tell me to mind my own business. Either way my card would be marked and we might have trouble working again in the future.

I figured instead that it would be safer to go to somebody outside that immediate circle, and opted to call Tom Vale. A British intelligence officer with MI6, Vale and I had worked together in the past and had got on well; mostly, I think, because he was a former field operative from way back and knew the score. If I was treading on anybody's toes he'd soon let me know without rancour.

I checked the time difference and figured he would still be at his desk. It took a while answering pointed questions from security personnel, but I finally got through to Vale's extension. He sounded relaxed but with a definite hint of interest.

'Marc. Good to hear from you. How can I help?'

I gave a vague explanation without revealing details or names, and said that I'd come across somebody who seemed vaguely familiar, and I needed to know if I should stay out of his way.

'I see. Of course, I'll help if I can, but shouldn't

you call Callahan or Jason Sewell? If he's one of theirs, they'll probably know more about him than I do.'

Sewell was Callahan's CIA boss in Langley and probably not the person to go to for information. He would have justifiably strong reservations about giving out details about colleagues or assets, even though I'd done work for the agency in the past. 'I'm sure they do, but they might see a conflict of interest and refuse to tell me.'

'Good point. OK, it's a long shot but do you have a name or a description?'

'No name, but I do have a photo.'

He chuckled. 'Of course you do. Send it over and I'll get back to you as soon as I have anything.' He finished by giving me a cell phone number. I thanked him for his help, and two seconds later sent him the photo of the mystery American.

I made my way back to my hotel and had something to eat, then put my head down. If Masse got himself organised, we would have to move quickly and sleep might become a luxury. Some hope. I was an hour into it when my phone rang.

It was Tom Vale. 'I ran the photo you sent through our files. Interesting company you've got there. If you meet him and shake hands, make sure you count your fingers afterwards.'

I sat up, suddenly wideawake. 'Do tell.'

'His name's Clay Lunnberg. He was a promising big hitter in the US military a few years back, rising to colonel and serving as an assistant to

General David Petraeus in Afghanistan. He moved with him to the CIA in a similar position. After Petraeus lost his post as director, Lunnberg dropped out of sight. Some thought he'd become collateral damage as a result and had been sent to drive a training desk somewhere. Others said he transferred into special operations, which seems more likely.'

Petrus, Petraeus. Fate playing name games with Colonel Lunnberg? 'I agree,' I said cynically. 'He doesn't walk like a desk man.'

'He plays at it when it suits but he certainly isn't that. The last data we have on him is that he was recruited to a senior operating position with the Defense Clandestine Service, after which he really did disappear into the undergrowth. But I suppose you know all about them?'

Vale was fishing and I smiled. Once a spy, always a spy, on the lookout for information and trade gossip. But it confirmed my earlier feeling about Lunnberg being a spook.

The truth was that I didn't know much about the DCS beyond what little had been released into the public domain. Operating under the umbrella of the Defense Intelligence Agency, they'd been set up a few years back in what some suspected was a rival spying operation to the CIA, only more secretive. Their brief, though, now I thought about it, was interesting: their area of operations covered, among others, North Africa.

I told Vale as much, but I doubt it added anything new for his files.

'So where did you come across him?' he asked casually.

I could have lied, but that would have been to insult his intelligence. He would only have to click his fingers and one of his researchers would have Lunnberg's current location pinned down, with flight times, current agenda and change of clothes for the next two weeks.

'Djibouti,' I told him, and added, 'he was inbound through the airport.'

'Djibouti? Of course . . . you were on attachment to the Foreign Legion down there, weren't you? Catching up with old desert hands, I suppose? I thought the French had all decamped to Abu Dhabi.'

He was fishing again and I figured he knew more about the movement, operating bases and locations of friendly nations' military forces than most people. It's called checking known facts.

'I'm not here to see them. It's a private thing.'

'I see. Forgive me for being nosey, Marc – it's a bad habit.'

He didn't sound the least bit sorry to me, but as he'd given me the information I needed, I could hardly hold it against him. And I trusted him more than most people in this business. But now I knew a little more about this new man, Lunnberg, and his shadowy background, it gave me a plausible explanation for his being here and mixing with a member of French intelligence.

'Thanks, Tom,' I told him. 'I appreciate the information.'

'My pleasure. Always ready to help. Watch your back down there, won't you – it's dangerous territory. Call me if you need anything.'

I disconnected, trying to read behind Vale's last comment. Everybody knew the Horn of Africa was a dangerous place, so why the warning? Did he know something I didn't?

Seven

By the time Lunnberg and Petrus arrived at the Hotel Kempinski, where they were both staying, Petrus had given the American a full report of events so far. Lunnberg listened in silence, absorbing the facts without comment. If he had any opinions on the way things had been handled, he kept them to himself.

After a moment or two of thought, he said, 'Where did you find this Portman guy?'

'I was ordered to bring in a protection specialist from outside. I asked around.'

Lunnberg grunted. 'By outside you mean not French.'

'That's correct.'

'Do you often use outsiders to do your grunt work?'

Petrus frowned at the implied criticism. It was rich, he thought, coming from a man representing an intelligence network that relied heavily on non-attached personnel and private military contractors to do their 'grunt' work. 'We do whatever we have to. But this . . . issue is highly sensitive; we wanted no links back to France if anything went wrong.'

'And yet you used this French national . . . what was his name – Masse?'

'That was unavoidable. It was Masse who first discovered that there was information out there

57

that could be damaging to both our countries if it became public knowledge.'

'How?'

'How what?'

'How did he find out? Has he got second sight? Don't get me wrong, I'm not doubting him. But I am interested in how he got access to something as remote as a file of information kept by a senior member of al-Shabaab. That's pretty amazing, if you ask me. Or are you going to tell me he had family connections inside the organisation . . . maybe a girlfriend's brother or the husband of a mistress, something like that?'

Petrus kept his voice level. 'Masse was very good at what he did, colonel. He had built up a number of contacts over many years. He knew the region, the people and the way things work. He blended in. He had assets here that – with respect – your people do not have. It was one of those assets who came to him with the information.'

'If Masse was such a hotshot, why did he need somebody riding shotgun?'

'Because it was important to recover the information and Mogadishu is a very dangerous place. It was decided by my superiors that we could not risk losing it.' He shrugged. 'I suggested sending a team but their response was that one man providing protection would be less noticeable than a team.'

'How many do you have here?'

'Three men, all former *Legionnaires* and highly experienced. They know this region very well. I have them on stand-by.'

'Good to know.' Lunnberg walked over to the

window and stared out. 'Did your Masse guy have a reach inside al-Shabaab, or did he buy the hard drive from a camel-boy who happened to find it out in the desert?'

'Of course not.' Petrus's response was snappier than he intended, his patience beginning to wear thin. He didn't know much about Lunnberg's status, only that he was highly-regarded, with a distinguished military career behind him in Iraq and Afghanistan, and now occupied a vague but important position linked to the US intelligence community. A troubleshooter, Degouvier had called him, when tasking Petrus to work with him and provide whatever support he needed on a joint venture between the US and France that was beyond secret. But he was starting to resent the man's arrogant and overbearing attitude. 'This is not how we should be working together, colonel. I find your insinuations about our methods insulting.'

Lunnberg turned and waved a conciliatory hand. 'Don't get your britches in a twist, Victor; I'm just trying to clean up the back-trail. If my rough manner offends you, I apologise. I'm a soldier by training and inclination, so I might lack a few of the diplomatic touches here and there. Thing is, I have to make sure that this stuff wasn't planted on Masse to get us running around like a bunch of girls, wasting time and resources. We know al-Shabaab has access to computer-savvy people, so it's not beyond reason that they might have done this to throw us off-course for their own reasons.'

'It's possible, yes. But from what Masse saw on

the original when it was offered to him, it contained details of negotiations, proposals, times, dates . . . and names. That is why we needed to get it back.'

Lunnberg turned and smiled. 'Right. You're absolutely right. See, it's the names and details that concern me the most. Let's jump back a pace here: at what point did Masse get hold of the information?'

'After Deputy Emir Hussein Abdullah was killed by one of your drones, his office was looted before his followers could secure the site. As you know he was their leader in this region while *his* emir is recovering in hospital from a sickness.'

Lunnberg gave a humourless chuckle. 'Beats everything, doesn't it? One of the world's top terrorist group leaders can take time off in some clinic to be ill, just like ordinary folks. I bet he's even got health insurance and a convalescence plan, too. Sorry – carry on.'

'One of the looters found a laptop computer with a hard drive attached. His only interest was to sell the computer to somebody who could use it. He has a cousin in Somali military intelligence and this man approached Masse and gave him first refusal. The computer was damaged but the attached hard drive was good. As soon as Masse saw what was on it, he realised its significance.'

'And got it for a song, I bet.'

'He paid enough. He realised that it was too important to risk having his contact try to sell it on the open market. There are no patriots down here, colonel. Everybody has an angle, even, as you discovered, senior members of al-Shabaab.'

Lunnberg shook his head and murmured, 'Abdullah. Now there was a prime nut job. But he was a useful guy; you could talk to him. Pity he didn't keep us informed of his movements, though; he might have lived a lot longer and given us vital help in this project before we decided to dispose of him later. Still, couldn't be helped.' He eyed Petrus speculatively for a second. 'Or does your organisation not agree?'

'I have no idea what my organisation thinks. All I know is that Abdullah was an important link in our joint plans to regenerate oil exploration in the region. He guaranteed a safe pathway for our companies and we promised him a great deal of money and a possible seat in a reformed Somali government in return.'

'Ambitious little bastard, wasn't he? Thing is, he would never have made it into any kind of government; I don't know about your side, but we don't do that kind of deal with terrorists. He'd have suffered a fatal accident before we'd have let him anywhere near decision-making powers in this region. However, that's by the by.'

'As you say, history.' Petrus took off his glasses and studied the lenses, and blew off a fragment of dust. 'The issue right now is that we no longer have a link inside al-Shabaab.'

'Well, that's not quite correct.' Lunnberg tried not to look superior, but failed. 'In getting what we wanted from Abdullah, we also got the goods on his deputy.'

'Goods?'

'Leverage. You've heard of Liban Daoud?'

Petrus lifted his eyebrows. Who hadn't? Daoud

was a known firebrand in the terrorist organisation, his origins being in the former Union of
Islamic Courts before al-Shabaab took over.
The idea that Hussein Abdullah had given the
Americans some form of leverage over Daoud
was hard to believe. On the other hand, they
had suborned Abdullah himself, who had once
seemed untouchable, so where was the truth
anymore?

Lunnberg must have read his mind, because he
explained, 'We believe Abdullah felt threatened
because Daoud had more backing than he did
within the organisation and was looked on favour-
ably by the rest of their council. Whatever the
reason, we now have Daoud like that.' He
clenched his fist and made a squeezing motion.
'It means he'll play ball as long as he gets something out of it.'

'And what will that be?'

'Hard cash in a Swiss bank account. Daoud's
a realist in a tough world, Victor. One day he'll
trip up because they all do. His people will
discover what he's been up to and if he's lucky
he'll get out before they come calling. He
thinks a bunch of money will help him stay out
of their reach, but it won't. They have long
memories.'

'You have been busy,' Petrus said drily, and
wondered if Degouvier and those above him
knew of this development. The Americans, it
seemed, had been working away quietly in the
background down here and he was willing to bet
it was without informing Paris. If so, it was a
troublesome hint about how solid the new

'relationship' was between Washington and the Élysée Palace and their combined search for oil.

'That's what I'm paid for, to stay busy and on top of the game. So, this guy, Portman. Why use him?'

'Because like you we are trying to keep a sanitized zone around this business. Using freelance operatives, cut-outs where possible and the fewest possible ears and eyes involved on the ground. That is why we do not wish to have our local forces involved.' He hesitated, then forged ahead, unable to resist giving a dig back at this arrogant man. 'As for Portman, we asked around and he came with strong recommendations . . . from your very own CIA, as it happens.'

Lunnberg's eyebrows shot up but he recovered quickly. 'Well, that was your first mistake, Victor. The CIA does not have the solution to every problem, believe me. In fact, it wouldn't surprise me if Portman is their man. Do you have a lead on his current location?'

Petrus ignored the barbed criticism. 'He's here in Djibouti, but I don't know where. He prefers to remain in the background. All I have is a cell phone number.'

'Doesn't matter. It shouldn't take too long to track him down in a place this size. I'll get some guys on it.'

'Men at Camp Lemmonnier?'

Lunnberg shook his head. 'Hell, no. I'm not going anywhere near our special forces unless I'm forced to. I'll use my own people.'

'They are with you now? I didn't see them.'

'You weren't supposed to.' Lunnberg gave him

a cool smile. 'They're always with me . . . or close by. It saves time if I have to deal with a situation and keep things contained.'

Petrus felt the first stirrings of disquiet. Until Masse's unfortunate death, he and Portman had had the situation in their hands. So why did Lunnberg think he needed his own men – men he must have arranged to have standing by already? It made him wonder who was really calling the shots here.

'You do a lot of that – keeping things contained?'

'When I have to.' The American's face was empty of expression. 'We do what we have to, right?'

Petrus didn't answer. Lunnberg had already made it clear that he regarded Petrus, and by association the DGSE, of lesser importance than his own organisation. But fighting him was a waste of time and emotion. And he still had a job to do.

'So what are you planning now?'

'It's simple. If the information Masse was sold is genuine, it's still out there and we need to retrieve it. Nothing else counts. For whatever reason, Masse – or more likely, Portman, now Masse is dead – made a switch and dumped you with a dummy. We have to get hold of Portman and the original hard drive. With me so far?'

'I understand.' It reminded Petrus that they were both treading a very fine line here. It would be bad enough if al-Shabaab found out that their leaders had cooked up a private deal with members of the French and American oil industries; but the fallout would be as nothing compared with the international reaction if the wider world learned the same information. While there had been a few high-profile advocates of talking to terrorists in the past, it was rarely discussed openly and never with the media.

Just then a phone on the bed began buzzing. Lunnberg picked it up and checked the screen. 'I have to take this call. Let's meet again in the morning.' He walked over to the door, the cell phone in his hand, and opened it. The signal for Petrus couldn't have been clearer; he was dismissed.

As soon as the door closed behind the Frenchman, Lunnberg opened the connection and pressed the hands-free button, before tossing the phone on the bed and beginning to pace around the room. It was his favoured method of taking calls and allowed him to think freely.

'Go ahead. We're clear to talk.'

'What's the situation down there, colonel? We're getting vibrations from the French and they're not sounding very happy.' The speaker was a man named James Warren, one of the many glossy and wealthy inhabitants of Washington's inner circle of power brokers and key influencers. For years he had occupied a conveniently vague position somewhere between the government community in the capitol and the corridors of Wall Street – most especially building connections with the big hitters of the energy industry.

'It's all good, sir,' Lunnberg replied smoothly. 'There was a little trouble with a freelance operative the French hired for the pickup, but I'm on top of that. I'm talking to their people right now, in fact. Give me a couple of hours and he'll be out of the picture.'

'Well, that's your responsibility, colonel. Who is this operative?'

'His name's Portman, but that's all I have so far. Seems the French asked around and the CIA gave him a solid reference.'

'I see. That makes this matter even more urgent. We don't want Langley getting wind of it. I'll leave it to you to do whatever is necessary. Do you have eyes on the hard drive?'

'Not yet. I've just got here and still getting the situation clarified. Petrus is working on his contacts to find the man and the hard drive and we'll progress the situation from there. It shouldn't be too difficult to get this wrapped up quickly.'

'I would like to share in your optimism, colonel, like a few others around here. We need to control this situation or the French will be jumping all over our collective asses and starting to call the shots. We can't have that; there's too much riding on it.'

'I understand, sir. But I thought we were equal partners on this venture.'

'Working with them, colonel. But you won't find anywhere in the agreement between us that says we're equal partners – and that's strictly between you and me. It's all about using their knowledge and history of the region to get the best out of this situation. Once we're in and operational, who knows? Partnerships change all the time. Folks fall out, right?'

In other words, Lunnberg thought, the French are going to get stiffed. He wondered if that was going to be as simple as Warren seemed to think. He had no close knowledge of, or love for, the French, but he didn't think they'd roll over quite that easily. Their history in this region had been brutal and hard-fought, and they wouldn't give up any part of it without a fight – and that included getting access to any of the oil deposits if the situation offered. It was an attitude he could respect more than words from some back-seat driver in Washington, who had probably never seen this part of the world in his life.

'Are you sure there's nothing else I should know about, colonel? Nothing that could lead to embarrassing headlines?' Warren's voice was gentle, almost liquid, hinting at a degree of knowledge that instantly had Lunnberg on his guard. What the hell did the man know?

He hesitated before answering. Had Warren acquired a back-channel to the DCS in Washington and somehow discovered that one of his men had gone missing while on a covert visit to Mogadishu? Working separately from any of his other team members, Joshua McBride, an ex-special forces vet, had travelled to the capital on the papers of an aid expert. Since checking in once on arrival several days ago, nothing had been heard from him and there had been no replies to repeated calls. While it was possible McBride had gone silent due to poor communication channels or a decision to go into deep cover, he should have been able to get a message out by now. Lunnberg hadn't mentioned it to Petrus for the simple reason that he didn't entirely trust the man. But there was another reason for secrecy: there had been an express agreement with the French not to take any unilateral action, which included sending in operatives without a nod from both sides. And McBride's mission had blown that agreement wide open.

'Sorry about that, sir – just checking an incoming email. To answer your question, no, there's nothing else you need to know.' And that, he thought, was how it was going to stay.

There was a click at the other end and Lunnberg was left staring at the phone. Typical Washington, he reflected. High-minded pricks didn't know the first thing about fieldwork and assumed it was no more complicated than hitting buttons on a game console. As for their manoeuvring of foreign individuals for national gain . . . well, that was what he was here to oversee. And nothing could be allowed to get in the way of that goal.

He dialled another number, this one to a member of his support team back in Virginia. Paula Cruz was a tough-minded former lieutenant in Army Intelligence who knew how he operated and could work information systems like nobody else he'd ever met.

He relayed what Petrus had told him about Portman. 'The guy sounds like a pro to me. It's probably not his real name but ask around, will you? And keep it low-level. I don't want the wrong people getting to hear we have an interest.'

'Yes, sir.'

'I want to know who we're dealing with here. Somebody in Langley gave him a nod of approval. I can't ask Petrus who that was in case we have to take the hard option.'

'I understand, sir. What's your plan on that?'

'We have to find Portman and get him out of the picture. If he sees any part of what I hear is on that hard drive – I mean, really sees it and decides to go public with it – we're in a shitload of trouble. Same if he gives it to the French; they'll keep it in their back pocket and it would be years before we could rest easy with them again.' He paused, thinking about his missing man. 'Have you heard from McBride yet?'

'No, sir. Nothing. I think his cell must be dead by now.'

'Right. Stay on it in case he surfaces. In the meantime I want you to check all flights and passenger manifests into and out of Djibouti and Somalia over the last ten days. Portman had to get into Mogadishu and back out somehow. He doesn't have special powers and he would have left a trail. Everybody does.'

'Copy that.'

'Good. Look for non-attached Europeans first, anyone who isn't press, government or military. Then drill down to aid agencies and commercial representatives.'

'Understood, sir.'

He cut the connection and paced the room, planning his next moves. He had a few logistical problems to deal with, mostly off-the-book kind that Warren didn't need to know about. But they were solvable given the right application of pressure and persuasion. He had a name he could call at a secure and secretive inner compound within the huge base that was Camp Lemmonnier, but he didn't want to make contact there unless it was absolutely necessary. The trouble with running unauthorised operations was that certain details too often managed to find a way of getting out; and when they did, they inevitably came back to bite you. Most were containable even then, with a little of what he liked to call management control. But as far as the vast majority of people at Lemmonnier were concerned, he was never here and it would help if it stayed that way. In the meantime, the sooner he could locate Portman and the hard drive without anyone else being the wiser, the sooner he could bury them both so deep nobody would ever remember their existence.

Eight

The following morning I met up with Masse to discuss plans. He'd arranged our flight into an airstrip near Mogadishu and transport into the city for later in the day. Until then we had to stay below the radar. Neither of us could be sure that the man who had died in his place in the office building hadn't been found by now by his colleagues. If so, they might have slipped into Djibouti to make certain of the job. He didn't mention the soldiers who had nearly been the end of me, or who might have set them on me, but I let that slide. There would be time for that later.

'Are you going to tell me where this hard drive is stashed?' I asked him. If I was going into Mogadishu, I needed to know where he'd left it in case anything went wrong and we got separated. We'd likely only get one chance at this and I didn't want to waste time going into a situation where the odds of moving unnoticed were slim to nil.

He played cute for a while before acknowledging that it made sense to share what we knew. I guess he was wary because he saw it as his responsibility to retain some control over what happened to the drive. Eventually, he named a small hotel on the west of the city. 'It's in the room I had there, behind an air vent by the bed. Room five, on the first floor. I have used the place for many years. The device is identical to the one you found on the body.'

'And you'll be handing it to Petrus?'

'Yes. Those are my orders.' His face looked tight while he spoke, and I wondered what was going on behind his expression. The cold, hard fact was that Masse was a field operative for an intelligence organisation and had been abandoned, presumed dead by Petrus, his controller. It had been me who'd erroneously reported him killed, but the fact was his body should have been recovered and identified. It's what organisations do for their people. In Masse's case they hadn't even tried. I guess he must have mulled it over at length by now; otherwise he'd have called Petrus already and told him he was still alive. Occasionally things do go wrong on missions, with agents or operatives in the field getting isolated and sometimes caught. But nobody expects to be ignored and not given a second thought.

I wondered if he had some career power play in mind, getting the hard drive back to France and using it to swing a better position at home. If so he was playing with fire; organisations like the DGSE don't like their staff using blackmail tactics on them. But that was his decision. Had it been me, I'd have been more intent on having a quiet talk with Petrus for leaving me hanging. Perhaps Masse was more forgiving.

We split up and I returned to my hotel and got some rest ready for the trip. The biggest danger in the field is a build-up of mental fatigue brought on by stress and assuming you can stay on the case no matter what. Every operator feels it, no matter how experienced, and that's where mistakes can happen. Even deciding to get some fresh air and go out for a stroll can lead to a chance encounter and disaster, when staying inside would be the better option.

I slept for a while, and woke up feeling drugged. It was mid-afternoon and the air in the room was heavy. I splashed water on my face and thought about having something to eat before going to meet Masse. I didn't know when we might get the chance later, and it made sense to stoke the boiler now.

As I bent to pick up my jacket, I heard the door open at the end of the corridor. It had a high-pitched squeak each time it opened and again on the return. I knew the door led onto the emergency stairs at the rear of the hotel. I'd got used to it very quickly, and learned to look for a pattern. It was a habit ingrained from a long time ago, a habit that had given me an edge on a couple of occasions since. I'd heard the door a number of times and on each occasion it had been a single guest or a member of staff going about their duties, the footfall light and short-lived.

This time it was different. The squeak came once, but with no return. There was more than one footfall and a whispered exchange of voices, and I figured at least two people trying to be quiet with the door held open for more.

I stepped past the bed and across to the window just as somebody knocked on my door and mumbled something about room service. It was a good try bit didn't quite work. In this hotel there wasn't any room service unless you went looking for it yourself.

I'd already scouted ways out of here in case I needed to make a quick exit. Like having a plan B, you had to ensure you had a back door out of any given situation. The obvious route for me would have been the rear stairs, but that was now out. A glance down at the courtyard below showed me that was also a no-go; three men were standing by a white Toyota Land Cruiser with tinted windows. They were looking up at me without expression and it was clear they knew exactly where to look. I couldn't see any weapons but I wasn't betting on the men being here for a friendship call.

I was in a tight spot. The two automatics I'd brought over from Mogadishu were wrapped in a plastic bag in a tin flowerpot on the ledge outside the window. I'd put them there because the room had no other places to hide anything larger than a postage stamp. But getting at them without the three men seeing me was not an option.

As I turned away from the window, wondering who they were and how they'd found me, there was the sound of a key sliding into the lock and the door was kicked open. Two men stepped inside. They were armed with semi-automatics and looking casual enough to suggest they knew how to use them.

'You Portman?' said the man in the lead. He had an American accent, was about six feet tall and heavy across the chest. Just to make sure I didn't try anything, his pal stepped off to one side and stood smiling and ready. I stayed very still. They had clearly worked together before and knew all the moves.

'No,' I said. I'd registered under the name of Challenor, but something told me they must have already trawled the city and narrowed me down to a shortlist of possible individuals to check out. The name being used really didn't matter, they already knew who they were after.

'Wrong answer.' The second guy oozed scepticism. He was thin and pasty, with the dark-eyed look of a snake and spoke with a trace of a Latino accent. Puerto Rican, maybe, but out of the same stable as his colleague. 'You need to come clean with us, Mr Portman.' He grinned at the sarcastic use of title and lifted his pistol. 'If you don't like it we could always shoot you instead. Right, Ratch? We'll still get paid no matter what.'

He looked cold enough to do it, so I nodded. The reference to being paid was interesting; it confirmed to me that while they might once have been military, they were now something else altogether.

His pal Ratch appeared not to care either way. 'Makes no matter to me,' he confirmed, and prowled round the room, looking in the wardrobe and bedside table and up-ending the mattress and pillow. Whatever he was expecting to see didn't materialise, and he turned back to me. 'Is this it? You got anything stashed away with the manager for safe keeping?'

'Like what?'

He gave a slow shake of his head. 'Smart ass, huh? I mean like a hard drive – you got one of them?'

'No. Why would I? I don't have a computer with me. Who the hell are you?'

He stepped up close, bringing a whiff of body odour and stale coffee. 'The name's Ratchman, since you ask. Not that it'll do you any good. Now, I didn't ask about a computer. Do. You. Have. A. Hard. Drive?' He accompanied each of the six words with a prod in the chest from his pistol.

'I told you, no. What the hell is this all about?'

He didn't respond, but stepped back. 'OK. We'll see how long you can hold out, shall we? Let's go.'

'Wait. Is this a military thing? Are you army cops? Only I think you've got the wrong guy. I'm here on business, so if you can tell me who sent you we can get this cleared up and I can go back to bed.' The idea when being picked up like this is to try and forge some dialogue with your captors. Ask questions, drop your shoulders, assume a non-threatening manner, and smile a lot – basically, anything to make them relax their guard. If they give you any information, all to the good; if they don't, well it's worth a try.

He didn't even flinch; it was like talking to the wall. So I pointed at my jacket. 'Can I take that? It's gets cold out at night. You might like to check it out for dangerous items. I think the pen in the inside right pocket contains a grenade launcher.'

Neither of them saw the joke. Ratchman picked up my jacket and checked it over before tossing it to me followed by another poke in the chest from the barrel of his weapon. This time he wasn't sparing the horses, and it hurt. He was close enough and if his pal hadn't been watching me

76

and waiting for a wrong move, I'd have taken his gun and made him eat it.

'I'm gonna let you have that one wisecrack, Portman,' he said coolly. 'One more and I'll shoot you in the leg.' He nodded at his pal and said, 'Dom, get his stuff.'

We waited while Snake-Eyes, or Dom, threw my few possessions into my bag, then Ratchman stepped aside with a gesture towards the door. 'Now, move. Hang a left along the corridor to the back stairway and down to the rear door. Don't attempt to run or you will get shot. Try to fight back or call for help and the same applies. There are more of us outside so don't play clever. Make it an orderly transition and you won't get hurt.'

Orderly transition. Only the military could adopt such a banal term and make it sound so final.

I led the way out into the corridor and wondered if they'd picked up Masse, too. I guess I'd soon find out.

As we stepped out of the back door into the open, two of the three men I'd seen waiting by the Land Cruiser moved away to block any chance I had of making a run for it. The third opened the rear passenger door and nodded at me to get in. Three other men were already waiting inside the vehicle, two Europeans and an Asian, I figured Japanese. They were dressed in plain clothes and watched me approach without comment.

'I'm touched,' I said. 'All you guys to welcome me? Let me tell you, your unit is either over-manned or you've been spun some wild tales about me.'

'Do not talk.' This from the man in the front passenger seat. He was big-framed but wiry, and what flesh I could see on his arms, face and throat was burned deep brown by the sun. He spoke with a French accent and looked downright unwelcoming.

'Hands on the seat in front of you,' said the man next to me, the Japanese. He slapped the seat back for emphasis. He wasn't big but he was all muscle in tight bunches, like a bag of coconuts. A weight freak, I guessed.

I did as ordered and a pair of handcuffs were slipped over my wrists and shut tight. At the same time, Ratchman tossed my bag into the rear compartment before leaning in and giving me the benefit of his coffee breath again.

'Portman, you're about to go for a ride with JoJo here, and his men.' He nodded at the Frenchman. 'Now, you get maybe twenty klicks to give them whatever you know about a hard drive, or you won't be coming back. You get me?'

Twenty klicks, kilometres. It wasn't far, although with the state of the roads here, that could mean I had an hour to come up with an answer. But the fact that he'd already given me his name told me I wasn't going to be coming back.

He slammed the door in my face and walked away, followed by the other men. As I thought about what was likely to happen, the man in the front, JoJo, grabbed my wrists in an iron grip while Hirohito alongside me dropped a cloth hood over my head.

I'd just become the filling in a handover sandwich.

The driver took us out of the parking lot and into the street, hitting the horn to clear the way. I could hear voices and laughter outside, then the noise of other vehicles, but other than a flicker of light around the lower edges of the hood, I was blind. Then even those outside noises were lost to me when one of the men turned on a radio and blasted the inside of the car with loud rock music. French rock music.

That was plain vindictive. I was relieved when JoJo turned it off again. Maybe he was a classical music buff.

I forced myself to sit back and relax. I figured this was all part of a softening-up procedure, designed to disorientate and intimidate, rendering me sightless and in a world where I couldn't fight back. They'd effectively taken me out of circulation with nothing left behind and nobody the wiser as to where I might have gone. It had been slickly done and all I could do was wait and see what they had in store for me and, if offered, take my chances.

The American group I figured were contractors; they didn't have the stitched-up, ready-to-go-now but controlled attitude of current serving troops or special forces. But the glimpse I'd gotten of this second group told me they looked and sounded like Foreign Legion. They were trimmed down and lean, as if they'd been left out in the sun like lizards, every ounce of spare weight burned away to muscle and sinew.

If this was a joint effort between US and French forces, it told me who but didn't tell me why. If what Masse had told me was correct, we should have all been working to the same ends, but right now it didn't feel like that.

It didn't take long to reach the relatively dead sound of empty streets then even emptier roads, moving from the city into the suburbs, then open country. At first I had a sense of travelling vaguely north. Then the light around the lower edges of my hood shifted as we began to turn left and we were moving in a westerly direction. That made sense because driving north from the city centre would eventually have put us in the waters of the Gulf of Tadjoura. I summoned up a mental map of Djibouti the country. If we continued going west we would be heading into the country-side away from the main areas of population. The road surface so far felt good beneath the wheels, no doubt courtesy of western governments to help troop movements in the area. I figured we must be on the RN1 which, if we turned north would take us into a range of low hills or, if we kept on going west, would eventually lead to the border with Ethiopia.

But that was way further than twenty klicks. We'd either turn off before very long, going directly north, or south into more hills. And both options were one-way trips for me.

Nine

André Masse stood in the cover of a stall full of cheap leather goods and watched as the Land Cruiser holding Portman swept out of the parking lot and made its way along the street. It had taken time and a large stroke of luck, but he'd finally picked up a lead on where Portman was staying, and had decided to check things out for himself. Portman had played his movements very carefully, which Masse could respect, but in a city he'd been working in for so many years, there were easier ways of searching for a man than visiting every hotel or guest house in the city. He'd put the word out and been rewarded with three possibles, all recent arrivals. They bore similarities to Portman, but he'd quickly discounted two of them.

He watched the three men in the parking lot at the rear of the hotel and recognised the type immediately; he'd seen enough of them around. They were Americans with the cold-eyed, purposeful attitude of special forces troops or private military contractors. As for the men inside the vehicle, if they weren't legionnaires they hadn't long been out of the service and still bore the lean, honed look of their kind.

Whoever they were, he didn't want to meet them; he had enough problems already.

He debated what to do next. The normal

procedure would be to call Petrus. But while he might enjoy letting the high-minded snake know that he hadn't died in Mogadishu after all, a timely reminder that he had made no attempt to mount any kind of recovery mission, the satisfaction would be short-lived. As for telling him about Portman's kidnap, he doubted Petrus would care one way or another. Portman was a hired hand and a disposable one at that.

He could go after the vehicle holding Portman to find out what was going to happen to him. Knowledge was power and it could prove useful if he came head-to-head with Petrus and needed an edge. But he dismissed it as too high-risk to be worthwhile. In spite of the heavy traffic throughout the city there was every chance the men would identify him as a threat. And with former legionnaires that meant taking extreme measures to stop him. It would prove pointless on two fronts: the first in his death, obviously, and second, in retrieving the hard drive from Mogadishu and taking it back to his bosses.

His ticket back to France.

Then everything changed. He watched the five men who had taken Portman out of the hotel climbing into two pale 4WDs. Without thinking why, he decided to follow them. He had a good idea who they were but at this point any intelligence was better than none, and he needed to find out if they were in any way connected with the dead man in Mogadishu. If they were, it meant he wasn't out of the woods until he got the hard drive back and sent it on its way.

The journey was brief. It took in a series of

narrow streets and ended out by the airport, at a nondescript single-storey building at the far end of a cul-de-sac. Other buildings nearby were given over to small business premises and cargo warehouses, but none of them was positioned close enough to allow Masse easy access to overhear anything that might be going on inside. The building itself was surrounded by mesh fencing and unhelpfully devoid of useful cover on either side.

Masse pulled into the side of the road behind a haulage truck where three young men were transferring packages to a smaller vehicle, and gave them a friendly wave. They stopped what they were doing and waited while he asked directions to a shipping company he'd seen earlier. While they discussed the location and route at length between themselves, he eyed the building where the men in the two cars had stopped before entering a small door at the front. The last one in had paused to look around under cover of lighting a cigarette, and it was clear he was checking for signs of surveillance.

He thanked the men for their help and drove back to the city centre. The building the Americans had entered looked like a short-term rental unit, with no signage, weeds growing around the edges and a general air of despair. Although surrounded by a fence, it was a lot smaller than many others in the area and was probably of little interest to the majority of larger businesses needing storage and shipping facilities. That said, if the Americans were using it, it had to have some kind of function and instinct told him he needed to know what it was. Was it simply their base of operations, or something more?

Even as he thought about it, he knew he was subconsciously delaying going back to Mogadishu to recover the hard drive. As he'd admitted to Portman, it had been a bad idea conceived in panic. If he'd kept his head, he'd already have the information and be in a position to use some leverage with Petrus. But that was too late now and he was going to have to scramble hard to play catch-up.

He stopped at a busy bar he favoured and walked inside. He had a couple of hours to go before it would be dark enough to go back and scout out the building, and he needed a drink while considering his next move. First, though, he rang his contact with the plane and told him to cancel the pickup at the airfield tonight and schedule it the following afternoon. It was too late to worry about Portman, who was probably in a hole somewhere, but that was tough luck. He'd have to get across the border and finish the job himself.

As he took his first sip of a beer, he saw Colin Doney step through the entrance and look around. The English teacher spotted him and waved before wandering across towards him, pausing to greet a couple of other obvious pink-cheeked expats on the way. For a second Masse felt a wash of doubt; was Doney's arrival right here and now a coincidence . . . or something else? He forced himself to relax. Djibouti wasn't a big place and there were just a few bars where incomers found common ground and could meet others in the same position. Besides, he'd introduced Doney to this place himself.

'Hi, André.' Doney was relaxed and affable as usual, comfortable, as the French would say, in his skin. He ordered a beer and swallowed half in one go. 'God, I needed that.'

'Busy day?' Masse gave the expected response, but with one eye on the door.

'Busy enough. Chasing around after expat kids who should be studying. It's like herding cats. You?'

'Same thing, only my kids are building contractors who don't stick to their agreements.'

They switched to mundane matters and were chatting about a new French restaurant rumoured to be opening just down the block when the door opened and two men stepped inside. Masse felt his gut tighten.

He recognised two of the Americans who had taken Portman out of the hotel.

He turned away, but not before one of the men caught him looking. It was enough to nail him. He leaned close to Doney and said urgently, 'I'm sorry – but I have to go. You should leave immediately, my friend, and not talk to anybody.'

'Why? What's up?' Doncy looked around, sensing trouble, just as the two Americans focussed on him and Masse.

'Don't argue, please. Go home and do not use this place again. It's for your own safety.' He clapped a hand on Doney's shoulder before turning and walking away past the end of the bar towards the washrooms in the rear. As he turned at the corner, he caught a brief reflection of Doney in the bar mirror, looking confused. Then his view was blocked by a bartender moving to serve a customer.

The short corridor ran past the washrooms and kitchen to the back door, and acted as an amplifier for the footsteps hurrying after him. He put on speed and pushed through the door into a darkened side street, where he merged quickly with the crowd.

Inside the bar, Doney looked around as a new customer eased his way through the crowd to stand alongside him and called for a beer. The man was of medium height and broad across the shoulders, with cropped hair and a dark tan, and wore light cotton pants and shirt. He turned and nodded a friendly greeting to Doney and said, 'Man, is this place always so full?' He had an American accent and a genial face and gestured at Doney's glass. 'Can I get you another one of those? I hate drinking alone.'

'That's very kind. Thank you.' Doney finished his drink and placed the glass on the counter, already forgetting André's oblique warning before he'd disappeared.

'My name's Carson,' the American said. 'You a regular here?'

'I'm Colin. And yes, I suppose I am. You?'

'I've been here a while and it's already way too long. You know what marks out somebody who's overstayed their time in Djib?'

'Go on.'

'They don't spend all their time staring at their cell phones because they know the signals are

86

shit and getting drunk or high is better. Am I right?'

Doney smiled, wondering how much this man had already drunk. He'd heard the saying a lot and it was true. In fact he'd already given up carrying his cell phone because it was added weight he didn't need in 100 degree plus Fahrenheit of heat.

A figure appeared down the corridor from the washrooms. Doney looked up, half expecting to see André coming back, but it was another stranger. He was tall and well built, with a distinctly military look about him. The man was shaking his head as if in frustration and appeared to be looking at Carson. He eased through the crowd until he stood the other side of Doney, effectively crowding him against the bar.

Carson put his glass down before leaning in close to Doney. 'What say we go find somewhere quiet for a chat, Colin? My friend Ratch, here, would like to talk with you.'

'With me? Why?' Doney began to feel the first twinges of alarm, and made to move away. Before he could do so, he felt his elbow gripped tight from behind by the newcomer.

'Make a sound,' the man said in his ear, 'and I'll break your arm.'

Carson took his other arm and steered him away from the bar as if they were best buddies. Seconds later they were in a side street and Doney was being pushed inside a battered Mercedes saloon and wedged in tight against the far door by Carson. The other man, Ratch, slipped into the front passenger seat and said to the driver, 'Go. Get us out of here.'

'Hey – what's going on?' Doney tried to push back, but it was futile; Carson had hands like steel clamps and the car was already moving fast along the street, the driver clearing the way by leaning on the horn. The man named Ratch made a softly-worded phone call that lasted less than thirty seconds.

Twenty minutes later the Mercedes stopped in a deserted street in the suburbs. Ratch turned and stared at Doney with the coldest eyes he'd ever seen. He was holding a gun which looked huge.

'So now . . .' Ratch paused and looked at Carson. 'What's his name again?'

'Colin.'

'Colin. People call me Ratch and I'm probably your worst nightmare. I'm also in kind of a hurry so you don't wanna piss me off. I have one question: what were you and the frog talking about back at the bar?'

Doney's mouth had gone dry as dust and he badly needed a drink. 'Frog?'

'Masse. The Frenchie.'

'What – I don't know . . . I mean, why are you asking me? I only just met him.'

The gun barrel came up and stared Colin in the eye. 'Now that's the kinda thing that annoys me, Colin. Y'see, I ask the questions and you give me some answers. It's a simple procedure and if we stick to the programme, you'll get to go home before lights out. Now, again, what were you talking about?'

Colin wished he could tear his eyes away from the gun and that the man's voice would go away. But that clearly wasn't going to happen. 'Is this about the corruption thing?' he managed to say. 'He didn't tell me the details, just that he'd stumbled on something.'

Ratchman pursed his lips. 'Corruption. Well, I guess that's a kind of answer. But it ain't the one I was looking for.' Without warning he leaned over and punched Colin hard in the face. The pain in his nose was unbearable and he felt a flood of warm blood spreading down his face and dripping onto his chest and knees. 'Did the frog give you anything . . . anything to keep for him?'

Colin coughed, spitting blood onto the seat and floor. 'No. Noth – nothing. We hardly know each other!'

'Well, that's a real shame.' Ratch slapped his cheek. 'Come on; don't go soft on me now. Tell you what, Colin, we're gonna get ourselves a change of vehicle because you've just messed this one up and I hate the smell of blood. Then we'll drive to whatever shithole you live in and you're gonna let us search the place, during which we'll smash and tear every item you hold dear unless you come up with something useful. After that I'm going to get seriously pissed. Understand?'

Colin tried to protest but his throat was clogged with blood and mucous and his head was spinning. He wanted to resist, to fight back and tell these morons where to get off, to show them he wasn't afraid. But the truth was, he was more terrified than he'd ever been in his life.

Ten

JoJo ordered a stop after about an hour of listening to his driver cursing about the state of the roads, the indiscipline of animals and pedestrians, and having had to negotiate the mess around two bad traffic accidents. Both times JoJo had prodded me with what was clearly a gun and told me to put my head down between my knees and stay quiet until we got clear.

The reason for this latest stop was simple: the driver said he needed a break. JoJo had grunted assent and told him to make it quick. Minutes later the car slowed and bumped over a patch of rough ground before stopping. The engine was turned off and the driver climbed out, letting in a rush of heavy air.

The silence after the engine noise was intense. Seconds later the hood was removed and I screwed up my eyes ready for strong sunlight. But it wasn't necessary; we were parked in a small depression beneath a jumble of large rocks, and whatever sun there was had dropped behind them, throwing the car and the surrounding area into shadow. Darkness couldn't be far off and would come quickly. Maybe that would be my one opportunity.

'Can I take a comfort break, too?' I said.

JoJo turned and stared at me. 'Is that a joke? You a funny man?'

'No. It's just that I have a thing about pissing my pants.'

He didn't say anything for a few moments, and I wondered if this was as far as we were going. Why else would they have pulled so far off the road if it wasn't to dump me here where nobody would find me?

I began to psyche myself ready for whatever might happen next. They and the rest of the snatch squad had been too practiced so far to have given me even a hint of a chance to do anything, and I didn't see these three relaxing any time soon. But when the next minute looks like being your last, you begin to think in terms of all-or-nothing, because doing nothing is not an option.

'Let him out.' JoJo turned and jumped out, while Hirohito opened his door and dragged me roughly across the seat so I could swing my legs out and stand up.

The air here was still very warm, trapped between rocks which were acting like storage heaters. The driver had walked off a few yards to relieve himself, while the other two stood watching me. JoJo was holding a semi-automatic by his side.

I held up my cuffed wrists. 'It would make things easier if I wasn't wearing these.'

'Forget it.' He pointed with the gun to a large jumble of rocks piled nearby. 'Get on with it. Hurry.'

I nodded and walked over to where he had pointed. A faint breeze was being channelled between the rocks and brushing my face, and I could hear the cry of goats in the distance, and high overhead the drone of an aircraft. If this was where they were going to do it, there were worse places in the world to go.

I did what I had to, which required some major concentration, then turned to head back. JoJo hadn't moved, but was staring at me and scowling. He said, 'You have been to Djib before, no?'

'Me? No.' The last thing I was about to do was admit anything, especially that I'd been in the country previously. Somewhere there might be a record and they'd only have to find it and they would know who I was. As desperate as things looked right now, I preferred to keep my identity secret for as long as possible. 'Do you have any water?'

He didn't answer but gave me a searching look, so I walked back to the car and climbed in. Logic told me I was safe inside the vehicle; if they had intended to kill me outside, they would have done it the moment I walked away.

JoJo stuck his head in after me. 'So what's so special about you, Portman? Are you a traitor or something? Somebody's got the hots for you sure enough, you know that? What's this hard drive you're supposed to have?'

I braced myself for another jab from his handgun, but it didn't come. 'Like I told the other crew, you must have me confused with someone else.' He didn't even blink. 'But what say you take me back to my hotel and we'll forget all about it? Put it down to an honest mistake.'

The driver re-joined us, zipping his pants, and stood ready to take over while one of the others took a break. '*Alors, on fait ca ou non?*' he said, and pulled a pistol from under his shirt. *Are we doing this or not?*

Maybe he had a hot date and didn't want to miss out on some action. Whatever the reason, it confirmed to me that this was a one-way trip.

'No. Not yet. We wait.' JoJo shook his head and walked away, muttering under his breath, so I sat back and did the same while Hirohito played statue and watched me. The brief exchange between the other two had given me a bit more information: they had snatched me without knowing the full picture and were now awaiting instructions from somebody higher up the food chain.

Moments later JoJo took a cell phone from his pocket and answered it. He listened for a few seconds, spoke briefly, then cut the connection.

Five minutes later we were off again, bumping back onto the road and putting on speed until we reached a turning north and a wind-battered sign saying ARTA. Hirohito hadn't bothered replacing the hood and now I knew time was running out. They were no longer concerned about keeping me subdued and disorientated because it no longer mattered.

They'd had orders to end it.

Ironically, just as I realised where we were.

I'd been up this same road a few times. About ten miles further up in the hills from here there was a barrier manned by an armed guard whose sole job was to turn back unauthorised visitors. The reason was simple: the Legion had a facility on the coast near here where they put trainees and invited guests through their own special kind of hell. I'd been up there with the rest of my group before the Lameuve incident, and had vivid memories of lots of water-based exercises under the rough command of French instructors, doing their best to break us down. It hadn't worked, and it was a place I hadn't planned on seeing again, ever.

As we drove up a narrow canyon between rocks, the driver switched on his lights but seemed unconcerned about where the road stopped and the long drop down the hill began. It had been a feature of the legionnaire drivers to take visitors up and down this stretch of road at breakneck speed to test their nerves. Sitting in the back of an open truck and seeing that drop go by so close had been no joke, and this was as bad. But for me it confirmed the origins of these three men.

JoJo turned at one point and said, 'You know where is this hard drive? Last chance.'

I shook my head. 'No. As I already told your American pal, I have no idea what you're talking about.'

He turned away, shaking his head, leaving me to go over memories of the landscape up here. The road was narrow and twisting, with a steady climb through bare, rocky hills, with a few passing places where vehicles could squeeze by as long as both drivers held their nerve. I figured the driver was probably familiar with it, but even so, the higher we got the more he had to concentrate and work hard through the gears to control the vehicle on the rocky surface, especially in the fading light. Off to the right the ground fell away sharply, leaving us looking out over a dark void, and I hoped he didn't get cocky and take us over the edge.

I'd already tested the cuffs but they were tight and offered no room for manoeuvre. Whatever I did was going to have to be two-handed. Against three armed men, the odds weren't great.

Up ahead I could see we were approaching a sharp bend in the road, with a spill of rocks and shale jutting out just before it where there had been a recent landslide. We were going to have to go round it and there wasn't a lot of room. The driver muttered under his breath and JoJo told him to take it slow, throwing a look at the drop on his side. For once, Hirohito took his eyes off me and hissed through his teeth. He was clearly thinking the same as the rest of us: the bottom, wherever it lay, was a long way down.

The engine was whining in low gear and I could hear pieces of stone snapping away under the tyres and bouncing beneath the bodywork like a jackhammer. The interior of the vehicle was thick with the smell of hot oil, metal and sweat, and the front of the hood was wavering as the left-side front wheels touched the landslide and lifted, giving us a birds-eye view of what was the deep gulley below. If we went over, none of us would walk away from it.

I looked down at the door lock. The button was up. They'd forgotten a basic rule: always secure the prisoner so he can't kick off or throw himself out of the vehicle.

Their first mistake. Breathe easy.

The rear left-hand wheel lifted as it touched a large stone, throwing a lot of the vehicle's weight outwards, until the back end shifted into what felt like an irreversible slide. For a second the car teetered right on the edge, the outer wheel dropping alarmingly as the unstable ground began to give way.

'Allez, putain!' JoJo swore, and banged his hand on the dashboard. Hirohito joined in, screaming something in Japanese and moving across the seat towards me away from the drop.

The driver did the only thing he could, which was to slam his foot down and hope to launch the car clear of the edge before the rear wheels slipped all the way over. For a second nothing happened, just the roar of the engine and the clatter of dirt and stones being fired into the underside of the bodywork by the spinning tyres. But it worked. With a sudden burst of speed, we bumped over the layer of stones and hit firm ground, and the Land Cruiser shot forward towards a wide turn in the road – and a solid wall of rock.

It seemed to take the driver by surprise. He still had his foot on the pedal and was pressed back in his seat by the momentum, his arms straight on the wheel as he focussed on getting us back on the road. Sitting directly behind him and free to move, I could feel the heat from his shoulders and see the flush of stress across the back of his neck.

Their second mistake. Get ready.

I lifted my hands and placed them on the back

of the driver's seat. If Hirohito noticed he didn't say anything; I think he was still living that dizzying drop into darkness. It put me well within touching distance of the man in charge of the car.

Their third mistake. *Go.*

As we approached the rock wall, I clenched my hands and slammed them into the side of the driver's neck. The cuffs connected first just behind his ear and he let go of the wheel and slumped sideways, his foot slipping off the gas. The car immediately lost speed. It was the best chance I was going to get and I swung my fists the other way and connected with Hirohito's nose as he tried to grab me. The double fisted blow knocked him back against the door. But he was made of tough stuff and shook his head, spraying blood across the seats, and tried to make a knuckle-strike to my throat. Wrong move. I snapped my arms back, blocking the strike and drove my elbow into his face, pushing with my other hand for extra power. He gave a grunt and his head lolled back, out of the game.

JoJo was caught on the hop. He started turning in his seat and bringing up his gun, aiming at me through the seat back, so I grabbed Hirohito by the shirt and dragged him across in front of me just as JoJo pulled the trigger. The gunshot was deafening. Amid the burst of fabric thrown up by the blast, and the flicker of flame as it caught fire, I felt Hirohito's body jump with the impact. Before JoJo could fire again, I pushed Hirohito away and shouldered the door open, hitting the ground on my feet but rolling with the momentum with my arms over my head. I came up on my feet, groggy but mobile, just as the Land Cruiser hit the rock wall with a loud crunch and the engine stalled.

I didn't need to look round to know that there was nowhere for me to run. If I tried, JoJo would shoot me in the back and there was no way he could miss. I had to disarm him now or I'd never leave this place alive. I ran towards the car just as the front passenger door opened and he almost fell out, a splash of blood showing on his forehead where he'd impacted with something inside the vehicle. But no gun.

I launched myself at him as he got to his feet and turned to face me, shoulder-charging him into the vee of the door hinges. He roared with pain and tried to push me off, but this was going to be a one-way fight and I wasn't about to lose. Besides, I knew what he'd had planned for me and that was sufficient to channel every ounce of aggression I could muster.

I grabbed the door and slammed it against his body, then again, and he finally slumped to the ground and lay still.

Inside the car Hirohito and the driver were unmoving. The driver's eyes were open but he wasn't breathing, and the position of his body against the wheel told me he'd taken a fatal hit. Hirohito's eyes were fluttering but he'd been hit in the mid-section and I doubted he would last long. I pulled him and the driver from the car, and rolled all three of them off the side of the road into the gulley. It was no worse than what they had been planning for me and I didn't have any regrets. Then I jumped behind the wheel and started the engine, and taking great care, turned to face back down the hill.

Eleven

Lunnberg was about to leave his room in the Hotel Kempinski for a progress meeting with Victor Petrus when his phone buzzed quietly. It was his comms and research specialist, Paula Cruz, calling from Washington.

'Sir, you requested details on Marc Portman.'

'Go ahead.' Lunnberg sat down by the window to listen. It was probably too late to be concerned about Portman now, but you never learned anything by ignoring information.

'Sir, he's buried deep, even by Washington standards. The first people I spoke to had never heard of him. Then I picked up some gossip via a contact in the private contractor sector, and his name rang some bells. He's good, apparently. Very good. He's primarily a close protection specialist and has an impressive reputation among those who know of him.'

'Jesus – a bodyguard?' Lunnberg immediately began to lose interest. Contractors hired for protection duties were a dime a dozen. Many had specialist skills to sell such as Delta, Ranger or SEAL backgrounds, but a vast number did not, merely claiming experiences they had never gained. This Portman might have done that, and had played a good tune to sell himself into an assignment for the French in return for a good cash payment, no questions asked. God knows, the US intelligence community had used enough men like him over the years in conflict situations all over the globe.

'He's more than that, sir. A lot more.'

Lunnberg took a little more interest. Cruz sounded impressed, and that didn't happen often. She must have picked up something worth knowing. 'Tell me.'

'Yes, sir. Nobody knows his full background, so a lot of what I've heard has to be taken at face value. But in my opinion and going on the people I spoke to, it's pretty solid.'

'I understand.'

'The general feeling is that he's highly regarded in Langley and other intel agencies, such as the UK's MI6 and now France's DGSE. But an interesting take on him came from a contact in the DEA, who said he's a specialist in providing protection for undercover personnel. In short, he goes into a theatre of operation even deeper than they do and watches their backs to make sure they don't get compromised or caught.'

'Like our own Special Activities Division?' Now Lunnberg was more intrigued. The CIA and its newer sister agency, for which he worked – at least nominally – the Defense Clandestine Service, had their own teams of ex-military specialists whose job was to reinforce operations in hostile areas. Indeed, some of his men came from a similar background.

'Yes, sir. But he's not a team player. Portman works absolutely solo so as not to compromise himself and stays below the radar. It's why he's been so successful according to my contacts.

He's thought to have worked in various hot areas such as Iraq, Iran, Afghanistan, Russia and Ukraine – where he rescued a State Department officer from extremists and brought him home.' She paused, then added, 'That was a CIA operation. He's also worked in Somalia.'

Lunnberg stood up. He was beginning to get a feeling of unease the longer Cruz kept talking. He had no personal knowledge of specialists like Portman working inside Russia, although he guessed it must have happened over the years. That alone was bad enough. But what concerned him most was to learn that Portman knew Somalia. 'Whereabouts?'

'In the far south, sir, along the border with Kenya. The story is that he pulled a couple of British operatives out of a kidnap situation involving al-Shabaab and local pirates. He pretty much destroyed that operation and is rumoured to have killed the local leader, although that's not been confirmed.'

'Christ—' Lunnberg's voice was savage – 'does he wear a cape as well?'

Cruz took a moment to reply, then said, 'He's also thought to have had special forces experience with the Foreign Legion . . . in Djibouti.'

'What?' Lunnberg sat forward. Christ, where was this going?

'Yes, sir. I hear it might have been a training exchange, but I have no details on how long he was there. Please bear in mind, none of this comes from official files. But I have no reason to doubt my sources.'

'I understand. That's good work.'

'Thank you, sir.'

Lunnberg ended the call. If he'd entertained any thoughts of talking to this Portman to find out more about why he was here and who else knew what his assignment was, Cruz's information had rendered it pointless. He'd encountered enough specialists like Portman in his time to know that any information they might impart would be difficult to obtain without resorting to force, of dubious value – and messy. If Portman wasn't already dead, he soon would be, and would take any secrets he possessed to the grave.

He rang Petrus. 'Meet me downstairs. We need to talk.'

Victor Petrus stared hard at Lunnberg, who he'd joined at a corner table away from other guests and just outside the spread of lights on the terrace of the Hotel Kempinski. He was wondering if he'd heard correctly. The American had revealed that instructions had been issued for Portman to be terminated.

'Is that absolutely necessary?' Petrus muttered. 'He could have been useful in helping find the hard drive. He might even know where Masse left it.'

'Doesn't matter if he does or doesn't. He's a loose end and needs to be silenced.' He flicked at a piece of lint on his knee. 'A bit like another loose end that's just come to my attention. Actually, two loose ends.' His eyes glittered with some inner amusement, and Petrus felt a shiver of alarm go through him. He hadn't known Lunnberg long but he had already deduced that the man rarely showed anything approaching levity unless it was at somebody else's expense.

He was about to hear something bad. He could sense it.

'I don't follow.'

'It seems your man Masse had a friend here in Djibouti. A Brit named Doney. Did you know that?'

'No. How could I know all his friends? He probably had many – he's been here a long time.'

'Well, this one seems to have been a drinking buddy . . . and who knows what else.' His lip curled and he added, 'Was Masse married?'

'Once, yes. His wife asked for a divorce some years ago. Is it important?'

'It might be. Why did she divorce him? Did she find out he was playing away . . . maybe for the other team?' He shrugged. 'I mean, it happens, right?'

'No! It was nothing like that. She did not like the climate or his work and wanted to go back to France. He did not.'

'Well, whatever the reason, what's the likelihood that Masse confided in this Brit about this hard drive? Perhaps a little bit of boasting to impress his new friend.'

'Impossible.' Petrus flushed red with anger at the suggestion, and realised that Lunnberg was deliberately trying to unsettle him. The more he got to know this man the more he realised he was a serial manipulator, looking for an edge with every person he met. It made him wonder if he had any genuine friends, or whether only those who could be useful were accorded a temporary status until they were no longer of value. 'He would not have done such a thing – he was too professional.'

'Let's hope you're right, Victor. Let's hope. I wonder if Doney would tell the same story.'

'What do you mean?'

Lunnberg hesitated for a moment before saying, 'My men tell me that Masse and Doney were seen in a bar right here in Djibouti.'

'So? That was then, this is now.'

'Now is what I meant. They were seen just a few hours ago. Care to comment on that?'

Petrus felt his mouth drop open but no words came out. He was in deep shock. It was a mistake – it had to be. A ghastly error. If Masse were alive, then who was the dead man Portman had found inside the building in Mogadishu?

'You didn't know, huh?' Lunnberg was almost smiling, a tight twist to the side of his mouth.

Petrus finally found his voice. 'I don't believe it. Masse is dead. If he were alive he would have called me the moment he was able to do so.'

'You know that for sure?'

'Pardon?'

'That he's dead. Have you seen the body and verified loss of life?'

'No. I received the information from Portman.' Petrus stopped speaking as he realised how that sounded; his admission that he had not bothered to check up on his missing operative's location, but had left him out there. There were also the questions that would arise in the suspicious minds of people like Lunnberg and his own superiors. What if Portman and Masse had conspired and

105

lied about the hard drive? What if the two men had checked the contents and decided to return a dummy drive instead, planning to use the real one for . . . He felt a dead weight settle on his shoulders at the thought. Surely not. Why would they?

He put that last question to Lunnberg, followed by: 'Why are you asking such a thing, anyway? Portman wouldn't lie about it.' Suddenly he remembered the photo of Masse's body he'd received from Portman. He hadn't done anything with it yet because he was still debating what to tell Degouvier and those above him in Paris. But now was the time to use it. He dug out his cell phone and switched it on. 'Here . . . Portman sent me this.' He tapped the photo gallery icon and handed the phone to Lunnberg. He didn't need to look at the photo again; it showed the body of a white man with a splash of red on the torso. He'd automatically taken it to be Masse. Yet if what Lunnberg was saying was correct, he'd been wrong.

The American studied the screen for a moment without expression, then handed the phone back. When he looked up, Petrus felt a cold chill go through him. The air seemed to crackle around Lunnberg as if he were charged with electricity.

'Well, Victor, somebody's telling untruths – and I know it isn't my guys. They say when Masse saw them coming he took off like a jackrabbit.' He shifted in his seat and tilted his head to one side. 'Now, why would he do that, do you think . . . unless he had something to hide?'

Petrus had no answer to that. Instead he asked, 'Where are they now?'

'Well, Masse's away in the wind, so no telling where. As to the other two, the clock's running down on them as we speak. Portman's room was a blank but that was expected; he's a skilled professional.'

Something in Lunnberg's voice as he said it made Petrus look up. 'I think we knew that. Do you have information I do not?'

'It means, Victor, that in hiring Portman, you and your colleagues got hold of a tiger by the tail.'

'What do you mean?'

'He's more than just a – what did you call him – a protection specialist? He's got skills that go way beyond your average bodyguard. In fact, in different circumstances, I'd probably hire the man myself. But that's not an option. The sooner he's gone the safer I'll sleep at night.'

'I see.' Petrus didn't like the look the American was giving him, and decided he didn't want to know more about Portman than he did already. Sometimes ignorance really was to be valued. Instead he said, 'And this Doney person?'

'Oh, he's a genuine article, all right – a teacher. My men checked his room but didn't find anything there. They're currently making sure he didn't have another rabbit hole somewhere else, although my guess is he didn't. Still, they'll find out for sure soon enough.'

Petrus didn't like to think what that entailed. He had no doubts that Lunnberg's men would be thorough in their methods, and would go to whatever lengths were needed to get what they wanted. 'What will you do with him?'

'That's not your concern. My decision, my moves.'

'Forgive me,' Petrus said coolly, 'but if it threatens the security of this operation, then I think it is my concern. You cannot go leaving dead bodies around, especially in this part of the world. With all the troops stationed here, questions will be asked and somebody will have seen them.'

'Them?'

'Your men. And Portman, Masse and Doney.'

'Let me worry about my men. They'll be gone soon, anyway, once this is over. As to the others . . . well, beyond tonight that won't be a concern.' He stood up and straightened his jacket. 'A piece of friendly advice for you, Victor. You've got a man gone rogue on you, you know that? He didn't report in to tell you he was still viable, and you should be asking yourself why. What's he hiding? You might want to get that situation clarified before your bosses in Paris find out, don't you think?'

Petrus didn't respond, but stared at the wall.

Twelve

Two hours after leaving the hills I was back in Djibouti and heading for the city centre, where I dumped the car. Being caught with it would connect me to the two bodies, possibly three, in the hills, and I didn't need any more aggravation than I had so far. My job was a long way from done and as far as I knew André Masse was still out there. I dialled his cell phone a couple of times on the way in but there was no answer.

When in doubt about a missing person, check out the most obvious places first. I headed for the hotel courtyard where Masse and I had met up previously. It was late when I got there, with decorative lanterns casting soft pools of light around the courtyard, and there were only a few tables still occupied. I recognised one of the waiters as the grey-haired man who had served Masse and pulled him to one side. 'Do you know André Masse?'

He shook his head, slapping a table with a damp cloth. 'Masse? *Non, m'sieur*. French?'

'French, yes.'

'No. There are many French here. I do not know this name.' The way he spoke told me he was lying, although I guessed it was an instinctive wish not to get involved rather than trying to protect Masse.

I remembered the snapshot Petrus had given

109

me. It was still in my pocket and I took it out and showed him. He barely gave it a glance then turned and called another waiter over. 'This boy might know.'

His colleague was in his teens, a slim young man with a ready smile. He nodded a greeting and stared at the photo. 'Ah. That is *M'sieur* André.' He pointed at the building. 'He was here but is gone.'

I handed them both some money, then had a thought. I said to the young man, 'Can you show me his room? He had a book of mine and he may have left it behind.'

He shrugged as if foreigners did that kind of thing all the time. 'Of course. Come, I show you.'

Five minutes later I was back on the street holding a postcard-size leaflet for a nightclub a few streets away. Masse's room had been empty and I figured he either travelled light, ready for a quick move, or had cleared out altogether. I wasn't interested in the nightclub on the postcard but there was a telephone number written down one side, the sevens crossed through in the French manner. It was snatching at straws but in the absence of any other clue leading to the Frenchman, it was worth a try. Maybe he'd bugged out for somewhere safer.

I tipped the youth again and thanked him for his help, then dialled the number.

A woman answered. She told me she ran a small guest house and gave me the name of a street on the south-western suburbs of the city. I went round there straight away. I figured I didn't have much time to wander around the city before

I bumped into Ratchman or one of his heavy brigades, so I had to move quickly.

The Residence Ashmir was an elegant building, cream-painted and decorated with moulded balustrades set in a wide street of houses and small shops, some still showing lights in the hopes of picking up some last-minute trade. The owner was a large woman in a voluminous green gown and headscarf. I mentioned Masse's name but she gave me a blank look before saying in French, 'No, *M'sieur*. I do not know this man.'

'It's important that I find him,' I told her. 'I work with him. He has some papers which I need urgently.'

That didn't impress her much. She shook her head and began to close the door. Then I had a lightbulb moment. What if the phone number on the card hadn't been for Masse but a contact number for Doney? I said quickly, 'Colin Doney. Is he here? He's a teacher.'

She confirmed that Doney was a guest but she hadn't seen him since earlier that day.

'Do you have any idea where he might be?'

She gave me a look that told me I was asking the impossible and how would she know where her guests went at night? When she saw I wasn't giving up she turned and shouted something over her shoulder. A young girl appeared from the back of the building and I heard Colin mentioned. The girl had big brown eyes, and looked at me for a moment before rattling off a whispered reply to the owner and pointing over her shoulder. 'He was here earlier,' the older woman translated.

111

'The girl saw him with two men. They came in but did not stay long. I did not see them as I was visiting my sick mother.' She scowled at the girl at this point and I guessed visitors were not encouraged to go to guests' rooms.

I asked if I could see Doney's room in case the papers were there, and she agreed and took a key from a hook on the wall above the reception desk. She led the way through to the rear of the building where the air was cool and fragrant, and unlocked a door. Then she stood aside and let me in.

The room was a wreck.

Whoever had searched the place had done a comprehensive job. The bed had been taken apart, the pillows slashed and the mattress gutted, the soft innards spread over the floor like grey snow. A single wardrobe stood open and empty, and by the knife marks in the wooden sides, had been tested for concealed spaces and loose panelling. A couple of floor tiles had been taken up, but that had been abandoned after a couple of attempts. Even a line of hooks mounted on a strip of wood had been ripped off the wall and tossed in one corner.

Whoever the two men had been, they had taken his possessions with them, probably to search later. I didn't waste my time looking; there was nothing to show Doney had even been here.

The owner took one look and pushed past me, uttering a low cry of alarm when she saw what had been done. She shouted something I couldn't understand, and the young girl arrived on the run, sandals slapping on the tiled floor. She looked equally stunned at the state of the room, her hand to her mouth and her eyes like cue balls. There was a snappy exchange with a lot of head shaking before the owner turned to me and explained in full.

'The two men came with *M'sieur* Colin. They were here a short time only and came to this room. The girl was here alone and did not like the look of the other men. They frightened her and she did not want trouble with the police, so she went to visit a friend in the next street. When she came back she saw them all getting into a big car in the street. They drove very fast that way.' She waved a hand towards the window, which faced south-west.

'What didn't she like about them?'

'They were angry and she thinks one man had a gun.' She said something to the girl, who patted her hip to demonstrate that he was carrying the weapon under his shirt.

'What about Mr Doney? Did he say anything?'

She hesitated for a moment, then said, 'She says he did not speak, but there was blood on his shirt. When the men were not looking he waved at her to go away, which she did.' She said something else to the girl, then said, 'She liked *M'sieur* Colin – he was always kind and polite and made her laugh although she could not understand his language very well.' She shrugged and explained, 'She is my niece from the town of Galafi in the Dikhil region and does not speak much French.' She rolled her eyes in a what-can-you-do expression of apology for a helpless case in the family.

'Did she hear or understand anything the men said?'

Another quick exchange and she said, 'They spoke American but she could not tell what they said.' She looked disdainful and added, 'They were soldiers, she thinks. There are many American soldiers here.'

It sounded like the same men who had taken me from my room, but without a name it was only guesswork. The added worry was that they hadn't lost any time in using violence on Doney. 'What lies that way?' I asked, pointing at the window. I had a good idea: south-west was open country for a long, long way. But maybe she had an idea.

She thought about it for a moment, then confirmed it. '*Pas beaucoup.* Some villages, settlements, people . . . and *chévres*. Lots of them.' She gave a faint wrinkle of her nose as she used the French word for goats, one of the region's main herd animals. 'After that, the town of Ali Sabieh, but after that I do not know. A long way is *Ethiopie.*' She glanced at the wreckage and seemed to recall what had happened here, and began to build up into a wail of anger, with her arms in the air as if the real shock was just hitting her.

I calmed her down before she went off like a siren by taking out my wallet, thanking her and the girl for their help and paying for Doney's room rent with extra to repair the damage.

It had been the same kind of clearance operation they'd used on me. Only they must have figured I had nothing to hide, whereas they would have been primed to suspect Doney of being implicated with Masse and hiding the hard drive. With this kind of wreckage it was less a method of hiding tracks and more about intimidation and control.

One thing I was certain of: Doney wasn't coming back.

I left the two women to clear up and found a room in another small guest house nearby. The manager pointed me to an auto-rental down the street where I was able to hire a battered but serviceable Mitsubishi with a full tank of gas and tinted glass, and from a store two doors down, I stocked up for a trip into open country. As the likelihood of me getting at the two guns I'd left back at the hotel where I'd been captured by Ratchman and his buddy was remote, I waved some banknotes and got hold of a serviceable SIG Pro semi-auto and a spare clip, no questions asked.

Now I was ready.

I wasn't sure what was driving me, but if the men had taken Doney south, there had to be a reason. In the morning I would follow my nose and see where it led. The last thing I did before sleeping was to call Masse's cell phone. No answer.

Thirteen

The soft cover of darkness was sliding over the city as Masse pulled off the road and reversed into a shadowy alley between two warehouses and cut the engine. He climbed out and walked back to peer round the corner of the metal siding. Two hundred metres further along stood the building where he had seen the Americans. He stayed there for a good ten minutes, watching the front windows for any signs of light and listening to the night.

Nothing. No movement and no vehicles in sight and the only noise was of a distant aircraft engine over towards the vast military camp. The building had all the feel of a space deserted. Satisfied that he was unobserved, he walked past his car down the alley and reached the rear of the warehouses, where he turned left.

He stopped every few paces, slowing his breathing and listening for anything which didn't belong. If he was walking into trouble he would likely get only a momentary warning before it hit him broadside. He continued this stop-start journey, and crossed a deserted space at the rear of the next warehouse, the air ripe with rotten fruit, then across a similar area next to it.

He stopped, looking at the fence surrounding the building he was here to see.

He took a metal flashlight out of his pocket

and waited, sniffing the air. Cigarette smoke hung heavy in this climate, trapped by the heavy warm layer close to the ground. If the men were still here, signs of the one he'd seen smoking earlier would be his first warning signal.

Satisfied he couldn't detect anything to concern him; he drifted along the mesh fence heading towards the rear of the premises, looking for a weakness. He didn't want to go near the front of the building because that was where the windows were located, and he could be too easily observed from the road. The fence wasn't new, but it had been here long enough to have suffered from previous attempts to climb over, with occasional dips in the structure where somebody had scaled it and dragged it out of shape.

Finally he found where a section had been cut through and pushed back into place. He unclipped the ends and slid through, pausing to check the shadows before moving swiftly across the open space and fetching up against the steel sides of the building. He touched it with his fingertips, feeling the roughened surface of weather-beaten paint, still carrying a degree of residual warmth from the day's sun. Locating a flat section, he leaned in close and pressed his ear against the metal.

Nothing. A couple of bird noises, but no voices, no electronic sounds or the cough of a security guard with a dry throat.

He checked the rear of the building first, and found a double roller door and a fire exit. Both were locked fast. It was time to take a chance. He walked towards the front of the building until he reached a side window a couple of metres from the corner. He peered round the edge of the glass, but all he saw was darkness and the oval of his own reflection. He glanced back towards where he'd left the car. If the Americans came back, he'd have to move fast. But first he had a job to do.

He pulled a roll of cargo tape from his pocket and ripped off four strips, stretching them in an H pattern across the glass. He then untied an old T-shirt from around his waist and wrapped it around the flashlight. Picking a spot on the window, he jabbed hard until the glass cracked and gave way. He peeled off the cargo tape, taking the broken pieces with it, and was able to reach in and undo the window and climb through.

He was standing in a short corridor running from the reception area at the front of the building to a door in a wall at the back. Beyond that must be some kind of small warehouse or workshop. A faint crackle of grit sounded beneath his feet as he moved, but there was nothing he could do about it; the building would be full of it, blown in through cracks and crevices every time a door was opened. He kept the flashlight wrapped in the T-shirt to reduce the glow and flicked it on, then moved quickly towards the front of the building.

He tested the handle carefully before opening the door. It revealed an open space, empty and smelling of mould, the floor layered in gritty dust and showing several sets of footprints. He peered through the front windows but nothing moved out there save for the vague shape of a dog scavenging in the gutter.

He turned away. A broken broom handle lay

on the floor, and he instinctively picked it up and closed the door, leaning the handle against it before moving away down the corridor. As he did so he felt a sudden sense of panic, brought on by not being able to see out of the building. A line of windows might have made his use of the flashlight more difficult, but at least he'd have had the faint comfort of being able to see any signs of movement outside.

He paused to open a door in the wall halfway along the corridor. This showed another room, also empty. Next he turned and walked to the end door.

He placed his fingers against the bare wood, hoping to pick up any sense of danger waiting for him on the other side. Was this building some kind of temporary logistical base for the American contractors? Would there be beds inside where they bunked down between operations? There was no way of knowing unless he took the next step.

He opened the door, subconsciously braced for an attack. But none came. Instead he saw a large shape in the centre of the space, gleaming in the flashlight.

A car. A pale Mercedes saloon, covered in dust. The two vehicles he'd followed from Portman's hotel had been *quat-quats* or 4WDs. But why was this one here? A spare, perhaps.

Beyond the car against the far wall was a line of sleeping bags on layers of carpet, and nearby a couple of small gas stoves and a box of supplies, like field rations.

This is their base, he realised with a rush of alarm. They might be back anytime soon.

He hesitated, fighting the instinct to run. Security first. He walked over to the back doors and released the locking bar on the fire exit. If anybody came, he had a way out of here. Then he returned to the Mercedes and peered through the windows. It didn't reveal much so he took a chance and opened the rear passenger door.

Blood. A splash of darkness down the rear seat and on the floor. More on the back of the driver's seat and some flecks on the ceiling and door panel. He sucked in a deep breath and caught the acid smell of it, and the heavier tang of urine. He backed out, confused by the evidence. This wasn't the vehicle Portman had been in with the three Frenchmen; that had been a larger, white Land Cruiser. The other two 4WDs had contained the Americans. So who had been in this one? And why the blood?

He recalled his flight from the bar when the Americans had arrived, effectively leaving Colin Doney behind to fend for himself. He felt momentarily guilty, telling himself that Colin should have been ignored, that he would not have got caught up in this business and—

He jumped as a sharp slap of sound echoed down the corridor from the front of the building. It was the broom handle hitting the floor. He turned and ran for the fire exit door, knowing he had only seconds to get out of here. Whatever else the Mercedes may have contained, he was sure it wasn't going to help him now.

He ran out of the door and headed for the hole in the fence. As he did so he heard a shout from inside the building and the slam of a door being kicked open, followed by other voices and running feet.

He didn't look back, but ran to the rear of the next building along and continued until he reached the alley where he'd left his car. Seconds later he was inside with the engine turning over and driving fast down the road towards the city.

Fourteen

I was on the road out of Djibouti early to take advantage of the cool air. But if I was hoping to beat the traffic I was in for a shock. This wasn't some western city with orderly queues of commuter traffic all going the same way; this was a packed North African community where daily survival depended on trade. Instead of gleaming family sedans there was transport of every kind, from donkey-and-carts to cars, pickups, flatbeds, buses and container trucks. I met them all in a seething, seemingly never-ending flow, interspersed with death-wish pedestrians and overloaded motorcycles, all keen to gain right-of-way and get to where they were going by proving they had the loudest horns and nerves of steel. Even overhead there was the constant buzz and clatter of aircraft, from small craft right up through choppers and the thunderous roar of a military transport C-17 Globemaster curving out over the bay. Sharing the sky with these noisy engines were dozens, maybe hundreds of crows, wheeling in dizzying circles overhead or clustering in trees and electric wires around the houses, waiting for their chance to feed.

Only when I got a few miles out did the madness reduce to a steady flow, and allow me to relax. At least, it would have done if I wasn't dogged by the feeling that I might be heading into a trap.

I was keeping an eye out for military traffic in particular. I was pretty certain that the Americans who'd taken me out of the hotel were contractors, and wouldn't be able to throw their weight around too much out in the open. But I didn't want to take chances. Nobody argues about a person's credentials at the point of a gun unless they have a bigger one. I didn't and I wasn't able to do much out here if anybody decided to stop me for a chat. All I could do was keep my head down and hope the sight of a bashed-up Mitsubishi pickup that had seen better days would get me past any random stop-and-search.

I stopped a couple of hours after leaving the outskirts of the city. It had been slow going so far and the heat was building to a point where the air-con was struggling to keep pace. Having to negotiate a dead camel and three accidents all being argued over with heated enthusiasm, while keeping my eyes open for white men in a suspect vehicle, didn't help speed things up any, and I saw the town of Ali Adde go by before deciding to take a break about a mile outside, away from prying eyes.

The town itself was a scattered collection of single-storey houses nestled around a group of rolling hills. Some of the structures had flat roofs; some were in whitewashed stone and clay, others of tin. There were no vehicles that I could see and the few people visible were outnumbered by goats, cows and a few camels.

I drank some water and tried to think where, if the men had brought Colin out this far, they would have taken him. And why. I didn't think

123

they would have gone too far, but the only reason for coming out here would have been to make sure they were unobserved. In a speeding car, few of the locals would have cared to notice any details about those inside other than, perhaps, their colour. But in this wasteland, who would dare question them?

I drank some more water and ate a couple of bananas while trying to tune in to the atmosphere and put myself in the place of Colin's kidnappers. If I was planning on doing away with somebody it would have to happen off the road – the same end that JoJo and his men had planned for me. The chances of a military vehicle happening along were too high and being stopped at random was a risk that they, like me, wouldn't want to take. That meant getting out into the hills where nobody could see them.

I finished my makeshift breakfast and continued driving. I was soon out in dead ground, with hills on all sides, covered in coarse scrub and stones and small herds of goats. On the slopes in between I could see the occasional portable roundhouse known as a *toukoul*, used by nomads and formed by making a frame of branches and covering it with woven material and bark.

I came to a fork in the road and slowed for half a dozen skinny goats to get out of my way. They were being watched by a young man sitting under the cover of a spindly bush with a thin blanket thrown over to provide shade. He gave me a wave so I stopped and got out, the heat hitting me like a giant hammer. I was expecting a communication problem but when I asked him if he could speak French, he nodded.

'What cars have passed this way?' I asked, and pointed towards the forks. I figured most of the traffic would have been trucks, but I needed to narrow down the possibilities.

He mulled it over for a moment, then said, 'Military?'

He was smart, and had guessed I was looking for something specific.

'No. A *quat'quat',*' I told him, using the French colloquial for a 4WD. 'Ford.'

He scowled and nodded. 'I know *quat'quat*. Yesterday, late. There was one, going very fast. It killed one of my goats.' He nodded behind him to a grass-covered bundle leaking blood. 'It did not stop. It went that way.' He pointed down the left-hand fork and flapped a hand to indicate that it had disappeared from sight. 'Then it came back.' He nodded towards a slope a couple of hundred yards away. 'I was up there with my goats.'

I gave him some money for the information and the goat, and got back in the car. It could be an entirely false lead, of course. But it was the only one I had and sounded plausible. I followed the road along a natural valley, climbing for a short while, then eventually emerging onto a plain dotted with trees.

It was like going through a portal into a different country. I stopped and checked for signs of life. Nothing. No vehicles or people.

Then I saw the crows. A couple of dozen at

least, darkly elegant against the sky, some moving in a circle over a small clutch of trees half a mile away off the road, others drifting higher on the thermals with an occasional descent to the ground below. As soon as one rose, another took its place, a natural display of raw nature's pecking order.

There had been crows in Djibouti city, but not like these. We were a long way from anywhere so I slowed down, scoping the area for others signs of movement. Out here you didn't have to come across danger up close and personal; it could hit you from a ridge a quarter of a mile away, the report reaching you only when it was too late to duck. But all I could see was a herd of small goats on the other side of the road, nosing for grass among a cluster of boulders.

When I was satisfied it was safe, I stopped and watched the birds for a couple of minutes, gauging their actions. It wasn't unusual to see carrion birds in a cluster, but something about the way they were moving portrayed a simple message: something had gotten their attention and it wouldn't be small, not with this many in one place.

I drove on and stopped again two hundred yards away on the edge of a clearing and got out. I reached under the seat and took out the SIG, then listened to the sounds around me. Other than the crows, I heard insects clicking and a faint hiss of breeze through the scrub grass. And far away the drone of a plane. I hadn't seen anybody on my approach here but I wasn't about to take chances. Out here people can disappear without a trace, lost to everything but the dusty surroundings and the creatures like these birds that eventually feed on what is left.

As I moved closer, the birds voiced their disapproval, filling the air with raucous protests. A few braver ones stayed in the trees overhead, but soon took off when they saw I wasn't going away. I was twenty paces off when I finally saw what had aroused their attention: it was a man's body, pale against the brown earth beneath. As I moved closer I felt the shock of recognition.

It was Colin Doney. He'd been stripped naked and staked out between two stunted acacia trees with thick, twisted trunks. His wrists and ankles had been wired to each one and pulled tight. In that position there was no way he could have gotten free. The remains of a small fire smouldered nearby, a faint hint of smoke drifting into the air mixed with something sweet and sickly, like burned meat.

I took a closer look, although it was obvious he was long dead. The crows and other animals had already started picking at the body, stripping away the soft flesh of the torso and under the arms. I couldn't tell precisely what had killed him, but his chest and belly were a mass of burned flesh and a pile of blackened sticks lay on the ground either side of him. In addition, his left wrist was broken and three fingers on his right hand had been snapped backwards against the knuckles. Somebody's sick idea of drawing out the pain.

Knowing too much – or somebody thinking he did – had caught up with Doney, and I wondered what he'd been able to tell his torturers before he'd finally given up and died.

I left him where he lay, but gathered a few rocks to cover him. I hadn't got the tools to bury him deep enough to prevent animals digging him up again, and taking him with me would have served no useful purpose. Instead I took a photo of the body before covering the face to record the fact. Petrus or the British embassy could sort it out when this was all over.

Walking back to the car I passed two sets of tyre tracks in the earth, figuring on one arriving and the other leaving. The treads were deep and heavy, of the kind used for rough terrain travel in these parts. I couldn't tell if they belonged to a Land Cruiser but I wasn't going to bet against it.

It was dry as dust out here and the sun was relentless, baking everything in sight, even beneath the sparse cover of the trees. I decided to make tea. It would give me something to do while considering my next move. I dug out the small spirit stove and filled the billy pot, both courtesy of the store in Djibouti. The water was already warm from the ambient heat and didn't take long to boil.

As the steam rose in the air, I heard a sound and turned to see an old man standing at the edge of the clearing a hundred yards away. He wore the traditional regional clothing of a sarong and shawl and was leaning on a heavy stick, its length gnarled and browned with age and marked with scars. He had a decorative cloth bag slung over his shoulder and looked as if he'd come up out of the earth itself. I certainly hadn't spotted any dwellings for a while since the *toukouls*, and the

128

reality was he'd probably walked many miles to get here.

Then I saw movement either side of him and two more men appeared. They were younger, dressed like the old man but carrying AK47 rifles.

They didn't look friendly.

I stayed very still and focussed on the old man, keeping my hands in plain sight. He was holding his free arm out to one side and it took me a moment to realize that he was signalling for the two younger men to hold back while he assessed the situation. There wasn't a sound save for the crows in the distance and the wind, sighing through the scrub grass, and it was easy to believe that we might be the last four humans on the planet.

I smiled. It was all I could do. I didn't want to alarm the old man's companions, because if anything kicked off they'd already got the drop on me and a quick squeeze on the trigger of an AK47 would be enough to turn me into chopped meat.

He evidently thought it was safe, though, because he moved forward a couple of steps and lifted his chin in greeting. The two men stayed close, guns levelled.

I made a careful gesture of welcome and he eventually decided it must be safe. He shuffled forward, leaning on the stick, until we were only a few feet apart.

'Would you like to share tea with me?' I said, and pointed at the billy pot.

He nodded and moved closer, settling into a

squat and waving his companions forward on either side. There was a certain etiquette to these things, and we were both keen to observe the rules.

I only had two small mugs but the old man solved the problem. He dug into his bag and produced two battered tin cups and placed them by the fire. I poured the tea and placed the cups on the ground, then took a box of sugar cubes out from my supplies. I knew the locals had a case of sweet tooth, especially with black tea, and this got them interested. I held out the box for them to help themselves. The old man went first. He very daintily picked out a single lump, which he dipped into his tea for a second, then sucked on it with a nod of enjoyment. The other two followed, after which we all took more sugar lumps to put in our tea.

'Are you French?' the old man said, the courtesies observed. He spoke carefully and softly, his French clear but the words lightly blurred due to the absence of teeth.

'American,' I replied in the same language.

He turned and said something to the two other men, and they moved away and stood watching the open countryside around us.

'I was a guide for the Legion for many years,' he explained. 'I learned their language and taught them how to track. It was a good time; I earned much respect and had many sons.' He looked proud at the thought.

I nodded at his two companions. 'Like them?'

He pulled a face. 'No. My sons are in school or working for the military. They will become doctors or teachers or engineers, if Allah wills it. These two fools are from my cousin's family; they are running from the *Mujahideen*.'

That meant al-Shabaab. 'What did they do?'

'They journeyed across the border to join them because they were promised money and thought it would also bring them respect. They found there was no money or respect and what they were told to do was only going to get them killed.' He shrugged and took another sugar lump and dipped it in his tea. 'Young people . . . they have no commitment. Now they must look over their shoulders all the time and pray the *Mujahideen* will forget about them.'

'They will need good luck for that. Are you far from home?' I couldn't figure out what these men were doing out here, but it wasn't to fight, not with the old guy along for company.

'Not so far.' He waved a hand at the horizon behind him. 'Over there – half a day's walk, near the border. I am looking for some of my goats; I have many but they are spread out all over this place. I must gather them in and have them ready for the meat buyer who comes around to collect them for shipment to the wholesale market. These two were supposed to be watching them but got distracted.' He turned his head and spat, then apologized with a soft smile.

'I saw some over that way,' I told him, pointing to the road. 'Among some rocks, maybe half a kilometre from here.'

He smiled, showing me his gums. 'Thank you. I know the place. I was about to turn back.' He turned his head and called out to the two men, and they put down their cups and set off at an amble towards the road. He shouted again and they upped their pace to a jog-trot, like a couple of reluctant kids, only carrying lethal weapons of war.

'Do you have sons?' he asked.

'No. I don't have the courage. I leave that to men like you.'

We sat in silence for a while after that, sipping our tea, then the old man looked towards the crows in the sky and said, 'I observed what happened to the white man. Was he your friend?'

'Not really. I only met him a few days ago. But he was a good man – a teacher.'

'Then Allah will take care of his soul. Is that why you came here – to find him?'

'Yes.'

He studied me carefully. 'This is not a safe area. You are either a brave man or a foolish one. Do you have a gun?'

I shifted slightly and revealed the SIG under my thigh, and he smiled. 'So. Not foolish.'

I nodded towards where Doney's body lay under the pile of rocks. 'Can you tell me what happened?'

'A big car from that way.' He pointed to the east, towards the capital. 'It stopped by the trees and three men got out. They talked for a while, then went to the car and took another man out. He was struggling and shouting so they beat him until he went quiet. Then they laid him on the ground and bound him to the trees. One of them made a fire while the others stood guard. Then they cut away his clothing.'

'These were all white men?'

'Yes. After a while one of the men took sticks from the fire and the man on the ground began screaming. He did it for a long time. Then he stopped. After that the men began to argue between themselves. They sounded very angry, I think because the man was no longer alive. Then they left him and went away.' He waved a hand back towards the east. 'That way.'

'Can you describe them?'

He hesitated before saying, 'They were not French. I know the French. Americans, I think, loud and angry.' He slapped his bony chest and puffed himself out to demonstrate how big they were. 'Americans here are bigger than the French.' He shook his head as if in sorrow and added, 'Too many Big Macs and soda.'

They must have been the same men who took me out of the hotel. The fact that they'd handed me over to the French had proved to be my lucky day.

Colin hadn't been so fortunate.

'And they went back towards Djibouti?'

'The city. Yes.' He nodded towards the body and gestured at the area all around it. 'This is a sacred place for my people from a long time ago. It is where we came from, from the earth and the rocks and the dust, and where we will go back. Bringing death is defilement.'

'I'm sorry.' It seemed painfully inadequate but was the only thing I could think of saying. I nodded at the fire I'd built. 'I didn't know. I hope I haven't offended you.'

He shook his head and leaned forward to lay a

133

wizened hand on my arm. His touch was warm, and light as a breeze. 'No. You have not. There are no stones or signs here because we do not need them, not like in the towns. Our people know this place because it is part of them.' He didn't look or sound angry but his manner had changed subtly, like a small charge of energy.

'You come here often?'

He nodded slowly. 'As often as time allows. I come to honour my family and the people before us and give thanks for what we have and what may be.' He looked at me. 'But what those men did to the man and to this place was something that should not be forgiven. I am old but I have a duty. It is better the ones responsible do not come back here. If they do they will not leave.' He lifted a hand and spread his fingers. 'That is my sacred promise.'

The way he said it was simple and final, and I knew he meant every word. There was nothing I could say. Whoever Colin's killers were, they would be back in the city by now, enjoying a cold drink, unaware of what they had done.

The old man sighed and gathered his bag to him, ready to leave. I noticed him glancing longingly at the box of sugar cubes, so I handed it to him. He tried to refuse but I closed his fingers over the box. They were dry and hard like sticks, brown and lined with age like the trees and the stones on the ground around us. He thanked me with grave courtesy and the box disappeared into his bag.

'Will you take the dead man back?' he asked.

'I don't know that I can,' I replied. 'Those men

might be waiting and there would be too many questions. I will arrange for somebody to come.' I felt guilty saying it, as if I was ducking the responsibility, but the old man took that out of my hands.

'Do not concern yourself. I will have these two fools bury him,' he announced. 'They will not like it but they will not refuse. It will be another lesson for them for losing my goats. We will come back later with tools.'

He collected his two tin cups and walked away, eyes on his two reluctant helpers as they herded a dozen skinny goats in front of them, one of them occasionally dashing off to retrieve a would-be escapee. It was a bizarre image, a man with an AK47 chasing a dumb animal.

I packed up the stove, billy pot and mugs, and when I looked next they were gone, the three men and their animals dissolved into the raw landscape as if they had never been.

Fifteen

It was late afternoon before I got back to the city. I was tired and angry and covered in a layer of gritty dust, and looking forward to a shower. Then my phone buzzed. I checked the screen. It was blank. I made do with a 'Yes?' aware that somebody I didn't wish to speak to might have located my number. I was hoping it might be Masse.

It was Tom Vale calling from London.

'I have some information you need to know,' he said without preamble. There was emphasis on the word 'need'. 'Are you anywhere civilized?'

'About thirty minutes out from Djibouti.'

'Good. One of my people has copped a ride on a German military flight landing in one hour. She will wait for you in the passenger terminal and give you a briefing. She's flying out again immediately but this is important enough to warrant a face-to-face chat. Can you do that?'

Her. A she. Well, it made sense; I figured MI6, like most intelligence organisations, was an equal opportunity employer. I said I would meet her. 'How will I know her?'

He gave a brief chuckle. 'Oh, you'll know her, don't worry.' Then he was gone.

I drove straight to the airport and left the car in the parking lot, then walked into the terminal building and through a couple of security checks.

When I was done, I looked around for an unaccompanied woman with a London tan – pale in other words – and spotted a familiar face watching me from a table at a small café in one corner.

Vale hadn't been kidding about me recognising her. The last time I'd seen Angela Pryce she had been stumbling out of the basement cellar of an abandoned villa on the coast of Somalia. She and a colleague, Doug Tober, had been held captive by a group of al-Shabaab pirates looking to make a trade after luring the two operatives into a negotiation for the lives of two UN personnel being held among a group of aid workers. The reality was, there was no negotiation and both MI6 officers were to have ended up in the hands of an al-Qaeda cell further north. The propaganda coup for the terrorists would have been huge and the hostages would not have survived the transaction.

I'd been hired by Vale to go in and pull them out if possible. I'd done it but it had been a close call.

She stood up as I approached and held out her hand. 'Marc. It's nice to see you again. Can I get you a drink?' She looked cool and relaxed, but her lightweight cottons were showing signs of a hectic travel schedule. I figured Vale must have snatched her in between assignments to come and see me. If so, it was a sign of how important this meeting must be.

'Soda, please – a double.' It was comfortable in the terminal but the tea I'd shared with the old man had furred my tongue. I needed the fizz of something cooler to cut through it.

We didn't speak until we had drinks in our hands and the waiter had moved away. There was nobody real close so we were good to talk.

'How are you?' I asked. The last time I'd seen her she wasn't looking too good after her incarceration, but holding up gamely all the same. She had guts and determination to spare, and Tom Vale rated her highly, which was good enough for me.

'I'm well, thank you.'

'And Doug?' Tober was one of MI6's hand-picked specialists in a unit called the Basement. They were not unlike the CIA's Special Activities Division. Seconded from the British Special Boat Service, Doug had been wounded on the mission with Pryce but had pulled through.

'He's fine. Still working underground. If he knew I was here he'd tell me to say hi.'

With preliminaries over, I said, 'Vale said you had some information for me.'

She nodded. 'I hear you're working with the French.'

'That's right. At least, I was. Things may have got skewed over the past forty-eight hours, though.' I gave her a summary of events involving Masse and Doney, so she knew the score and didn't have the wrong perspective on what was happening. The need-to-know rule of all intelligence organisations is well and fine; burden a person with details they neither need nor care about, and you have a potential leak if they fall into the wrong hands or talk out of turn. But there are occasions when the bigger picture helps explain a lot. In this case the fact being that there was more going on here than a straightforward fetch-and-carry job.

She listened in silence and showed no surprise at what I told her. Neither did she question that I might be being indiscreet in telling her what I knew about the focus on oil.

'We knew about the oil thing,' she said at last. 'It's been on the cards for some time but there's been a lack of companies willing to take the risk. We believe the front runners are a consortium of French and US producers and venture capitalists, and the war chest is supposed to be considerable. It will have to be to get any oil out of this region. But if it works, the returns will be huge.'

'Is the UK involved?'

'No. Our government wasn't invited and chose not to offer anything. The view was that in the current economic climate it doesn't seem a viable issue – at least, not yet. There was also the question of al-Shabaab's involvement. The best judgement was that it would end in tears one way or another because terrorists are terrorists; they're made up of disparate groups and clans and that makes them volatile. Hussein Abdullah was the original lead man – the only one, in fact, until he got hit by a drone strike, but he was at best untrustworthy. His deputy, Liban Daoud is almost as bad in our view, but he does have a lot more influence than did Abdullah.'

'That doesn't make him a good bet, though, does it?'

She shrugged. 'The French and Americans seem to think so; they're placing their trust in

139

him to make this thing happen. All we can do is watch and wait.'

A rush of conversation nearby washed over us as a group of men approached and stood close by, chatting. The accents were American, and Angela said, 'Can we do this outside? I don't have much time.'

'Sure. I figured Tom diverted you from somewhere else.'

She smiled. 'Well, it's not a city I'd choose for a vacation. I hear you've been across the border. Are you going back?'

I studied her eyes as she asked the question, and thought I saw a faint flicker deep down. After what she had gone through in Somalia with Tober, it would have been understandable if the idea of ever going back there had given her sleepless nights. But there was something in the tone of the question that made me wonder.

'Maybe. Probably. It depends on what you're about to tell me.' I led the way out to the front of the terminal, where we could stand in the shadow of the building out of earshot.

Angela took out a cell phone and showed me the screen. It held a photo of Lunnberg. He was in uniform but there was no mistaking him. 'Colonel Clay Lunnberg,' she recited. 'I believe Tom gave you a summary of his career?'

'A snapshot, sure.'

'Lunnberg's a sort of modern-day Oliver North, only smarter. He's managed to move out of the military and into a role with the Defense Clandestine Service where he gets to act as a go-between brokering deals with all the gloss of

140

the US government without necessarily involving anybody signing off his work. This oil business is one of them. He's very tough and smart, and willing to go where others won't. That makes him a valuable asset for this kind of assignment. So far we haven't been able to find anyone remotely close to the White House, the State Department or any other official body who will admit to knowing anything about him other than what's on his public résumé. That made us think this was one of those back-door operations that has more to do with big business than the administration. In fact we're certain of it.'

'He's a rogue operator, in other words.' Lt Colonel Oliver North had been working for the National Security Council and earned himself a lifetime reputation by selling arms to Iran to release US hostages in Lebanon, then funnelling the money through shell companies to support Contra rebels in Nicaragua. He'd broken several laws in the process but he'd survived, rogue or not.

'It looks like it. We've discovered four names linking Lunnberg to major power brokerage deals in the past couple of years, mostly names that came out of nowhere but with high net worth. I won't bore you with the details but these are extremely wealthy, mostly venture capitalists fronting groups of energy investors who like to stay in the shadows. These recent deals are unique in that they involve people and regimes you wouldn't want to get into bed with, all anxious to trade oil, gas or minerals and agreeing to cooperate in exchange for large down payments of cash to smooth the way.'

'So we're not talking Exxon or Chevron.'

'No.'

'What about the French side of the deal?'

'That was a surprise. On the surface it seems logical, if risky, given the region and circumstances, and it makes sense bringing in the French because they know the area better than anybody.' She gave a wry smile which implied there was a but.

'Go on.'

'We're not sure the French are completely aware of everything being discussed, or how much they will benefit from any arrangement. In fact we're certain it won't be as beneficial as they think.'

I waited, wondering what else there could be.

'Vale contacted some people in Washington, mainly US intelligence community watchers and internet geeks. The kind who dig up rumours and gossip about the CIA, DIA and NSA, and trade it between themselves for fun and kudos. They're like the UFO watchers who like to trade film of so-called landings, little green people and stories from Area 51.'

'So-called? You mean none of that's true?'

She smiled patiently. 'A lot of what they find is groundless. But a story that keeps coming up is that Lunnberg has a dedicated team working with him; former special ops people, intelligence pros and others. They jump when he calls and operate worldwide, apparently independently of the DCS but using their facilities when necessary.'

She was right; I'd met a few of them, led by Ratchman and Snake-Eyes.

'The latest rumour is that Lunnberg recently lost

142

one of his team. Nobody knows where or how, but a former sergeant named McBride dropped off the grid within the past few days. Until a few months ago he was an undercover army intelligence specialist. He resigned and was last reported heading for Djibouti. After that, nothing.'

'If he's undercover, there might be a good reason for that. He could be having a comms problem.' I was thinking about Mogadishu and the poor signal reception down there.

She shrugged. 'Possibly. The thing is, Lunnberg doesn't believe in transparency – it's the way he operates and why people use him. He also likes to stay one step ahead. With that in mind, it's not such a long hop from here to Mogadishu, and even if Lunnberg is working this thing in tandem with the French, it would be a natural move for him to run a side-operation without telling anybody.'

I nodded but I was thinking of something else. Since Masse had turned out not to be the dead man in the deserted building in Mogadishu, leaving aside the introduction of an unknown element into the equation, we were left with only one possibility. It had to be McBride.

'This hard drive you mentioned,' Angela continued, 'is supposed to carry details of the transactions and negotiations with Hussein Abdullah, right?'

'That's what I was told.' By the tone of her question, I got the feeling I'd been sold a pup. She confirmed it.

'We think that's a cover – a genuine one, because there would definitely be a lot of questions asked if and when such talks became known,

143

especially involving al-Shabaab. You don't get to keep a secret like that for long, especially in today's world of instant communications.'

'But?'

'We think there's a lot more to this hard drive than a bunch of people around a table talking oil.'

'Like what?'

'From data we obtained through other sources, we believe it also contains a list of planned terrorist targets around the Middle East, Africa and Europe – possibly even the United States.'

I let a few seconds drift by as I digested the implications of what Angela had just said. For one, it explained why Tom Vale had sent her here to tell me in person, rather than hoping to persuade me to help in a simple phone call. The mere existence of such information, if true, was too important to ignore, and he was clearly counting on persuading me to get out there and find it.

'Has Vale got anybody working on this?' I meant, had he sent out his own people, like Doug Tober and the Basement, to find the hard drive.

'No. He proposed a plan but it was vetoed without further discussion. He's hoping to raise the issue again.' She gave a dry smile. 'Some of our leaders are wary of getting involved when there are already two major players out here. I'm afraid it's down to you . . . if you're willing.'

'How does this terrorist aspect connect with oil deals?'

'Several months ago we picked up some internet chatter about a number of planned high-profile

144

attacks, mostly suicide bombers and truck bombs aimed at maximum impact. Some of the targets were in Somalia, especially in and around Mogadishu, others were across the border in Kenya aimed at the African Union forces. But they never happened. Instead there were attacks on a number of low-level targets that just seemed random, as if somebody was sticking pins in a map. It wasn't until one of our systems experts mashed the data through an analysis program that the two looked like being connected.'

'How?'

'Mostly by the movement of people and materials. Known extremists were suddenly not where we thought, but turning up in places nobody had considered. Mistakes made by a couple of small groups, offshoots of al-Qaeda or al-Shabaab, led to finds of arms and explosives that had clearly been assembled ready for an attack. Several arrests were made and that led to the discovery of documents pointing towards money movements to places where no known terrorists had been seen before. It all pointed to a build-up of activity, yet the locations where we knew there had been real and viable threats of attack suddenly went quiet. It was uncanny.'

'It sounds as if somebody was being persuaded to switch attacks from some targets and go for others instead.'

'That was the only explanation. And too many of the links in the documents and the personnel involved led us repeatedly to one man: Hussein Abdullah. It was too much to be a coincidence. At first we figured we were wrong. After all, would a leader like Abdullah have been so easily turned from his ready-made targets? He was known to be a planner and a forward thinker, laying down ideas months before they happened. In addition he'd always been a hardliner and hated the French as much as the Americans. His father was allegedly killed by Foreign Legion troops some years ago, and he lost other family members in a drone attack in Iraq. But the no-brainer we couldn't ignore was that if any switch in plans was made, it would have been on his say-so.'

'They must have had something on him.'

'Yes, and we think we know what it was. Several years ago three senior members of the Islamic Courts Union, which was the ruling group in the region and the forerunner to al-Shabaab, were killed in a rocket attack. Two more were shot a few days later at a secret mountain hideout by troops from the then Somali Transitional Federal Government, and several bases were raided and destroyed. It was seen as a decisive move by the government to rid itself of the ICU. The problem was, nobody could figure out how the TFG could have planned and executed the raids so quickly. They were already stretched and lacking suitably trained men or the planning capability, yet they accomplished the raids with what looked like insulting ease.'

'Somebody sold them the information?'

'Exactly. And we now know who that was. It was Hussein Abdullah. It was his way of getting rid of the Council and climbing towards the top of the tree.' She shrugged. 'If his betrayal had ever become known, he wouldn't have lasted five

146

minutes. In the end, its suppression became the price for his cooperation.'

'So why were the new targets hit? Did he change his mind?'

'Not really. It meant Abdullah and his followers could still be seen to be following their jihadist ideals and plans, while switching the focus away from "protected" targets. Don't hit target A because that's not part of the deal – hit B. Nobody cares about B.'

If it was true it would amount to a cold-hearted lottery. Far from preventing terrorist attacks, the arrangement meant actually suggesting other, less important targets instead. Capable of generating shock and fear, they were still targets and people were dying. And all in the name of commerce.

'And this list of potential new targets?'

'We think it's a different approach. We're not sure if they're connected, but any threat has to be taken seriously. The general consensus is that the European targets will be handled by al-Qaeda using recruits from among the North African communities in Morocco, Algeria and Tunisia. They each have extensive links in mainland Europe, so they'll find it easier to get operatives in place and equipped locally.'

'Clever.'

'Yes. It'll mean that no blame attaches to al-Shabaab and Daoud and his people will be able to show clean hands. By the time they take place, it's likely that any exchange of money will have happened, so it will be too late to claw it back.'

It was just the kind of twisted logic that

extremists would follow, playing both ends against the middle and shrugging their shoulders in innocence when the bombs began going off. If they were believed because it was expedient to do so, they would benefit; if they weren't, they would simply use the cash to set up new campaigns. Win-win for al-Shabaab.

She fixed me with a hard look. 'It's vital we get hold of that hard drive, Marc. Abdullah was very computer-savvy and rumoured to keep extensive records on everybody he dealt with, even his friends. I would say especially them. So the target list is just a small part of it. There's much, much more.'

'He sounds as if he was paranoid.'

'Exactly.'

'What will it accomplish? Abdullah's dead so it can't hurt him now.'

'He is, but his deputy, Daoud isn't. He'll keep the attack schedule and the discussions rolling because it's in his interests to do so. If Abdullah's earlier betrayal of the Islamic Courts Union and the switch away from prominent targets ever sees the light of day, Daoud knows he'll be under the spotlight, too. It's the way their minds work; if one part is infected, chop off the parts associated with it. We don't object to that happening, but we want to stop any further attacks and put a few maggots inside al-Shabaab at the same time. With luck it will sow suspicion and cause the movement to implode.'

'And blow this oil thing out of existence.'

She pulled a face. 'The way it's been described to me is, eggs and omelettes.'

148

It made a kind of sense. Almost. Laying bare the extraordinary agreements with Abdullah and Daoud would stop the deliberate random hitting of soft targets and cause havoc among their ranks while they tore apart the suspect leadership. I doubted it would eradicate al-Shabaab's aims altogether; they would simply regroup and reform. But it would take time, and time was critical.

'Is breaking this open entirely London's plan?'

'Not at all. I'm not authorised to tell you who else is involved, but this has been building for some time. Let's just say there's some heavy cooperation going on in the background.'

I understood. It sounded as if Washington was looking to see the clandestine oil deal go down in exchange for clean hands all round. *Non est mea culpa.* Don't look at me, pal.

'But no feet on the ground?'

'We can't use conventional forces to find the hard drive, which is why we're going to have to rely on you . . . if you're willing to continue. I don't wish to insult you, but I'm allowed to say we will pay you for your contribution.' She gave a twisted smile. 'The special relationship may look like crap to the outside world, but on the inside it's still holding.'

Amen to that. Recent reports of dismay in the White House about the UK government's commitments in the Middle East had caused some damage that would probably not outlast the terms of either current premiers, but it wouldn't stop the cooperation between intelligence agencies on both sides.

I walked away from Angela and stood in the

149

sun for a moment, wondering what – and who – to believe. This was elevating an already complex situation into something else altogether. And I was being asked to trust that I was doing the right thing purely on the say-so of one MI6 officer and others behind her.

I walked back to join her. 'What's the likely outcome if I don't find it?'

'The oil deal is probably on the skids, anyway, so that would be no great loss. There are signs that investors are jittery. The crucial loss would be that we miss a valuable opportunity to score a hit against Daoud's network in this region. That would be bad enough, but even worse, the soft targets on the list will continue along with ones we don't know about. If recent attacks are any guide, we know there must be more to follow but we don't know where.' She hesitated. 'Europe is almost certain to be on the list. After the recent attacks in France and Belgium, we know there must be demands within the organisation to keep up the pressure and make Europe hurt. With no exposure from the hard drive, Daoud's influence will spread and his group will grow with him. He'll be untouchable. In a matter of weeks or months he'll move back to hitting bigger targets because that's what he'll have to do if he wants to prove himself and survive.' She hesitated. 'There's something else you've probably already considered. Lunnberg knows the hard drive is out there. He must know what it means because his name will be on it along with a lot of others.'

'Like who?'

'Members of al-Shabaab and their affiliates on one side. If we can sweep them up it will put a serious dent in their operations. Other names of interest will be Lunnberg's contacts and the money people behind this deal. He'll do whatever he can to stop them becoming public knowledge because they won't go down without dragging him with them.'

'And he has the means to do that.' I was thinking of the men who'd taken me out of the hotel, proof that Lunnberg had brought along his little army of private contractors. I told Angela the two names I'd heard, Ratchman and Dom. 'If it helps, they're two of Lunnberg's back-up team; it would be useful to know their backgrounds.'

She nodded. 'Got it. I'll see what I can find. I'm not sure we can go that deep in his organisation without hitting firewalls and alarms, but I'll get the geeks to try.'

The geeks. The IT specialists, hackers and electronics experts now used by all intelligence agencies worldwide. The new frontline soldiers in an increasingly technological war.

'Good. Anything you can get.' Knowing one's enemy has always been a battlefield mantra. It began with knowing who had the best bow or the strongest armour; now it was down to knowing not only what weapons they were carrying but who they were.

'Just keep in mind, Lunnberg missed you once but we think you and André Masse will be top of his take-out list. The current betting is that number three will be Daoud himself, and somewhere in a remote hangar there's a drone with his name on it. Frankly, Marc, whether you find the hard drive or not, as far as Lunnberg's concerned you're all too dangerous for him to let go. He's going to come after you.'

All that left my next move in no doubt: I had to find that hard drive. And along the way maybe track down André Masse.

Sixteen

I took the same air taxi to Mogadishu as before, but if the pilot recognised me he gave no sign. I was travelling with four others, three men and a young woman who was made to sit in the back as far away from me as possible. I didn't mind and was relieved nobody wanted to talk. The less they knew about their fellow passenger, the less they could give away if questioned.

As for the pilot, a lean, spindly guy, if he was curious about why a westerner would wish to fly into a danger zone like Mogadishu, he didn't ask. All he needed was a reservation and payment by cash before departure, and the promise of a car at the other end, for which I had to pay a small deposit here and the rest on arrival.

I'd spent the night and most of the day in a small hotel not far from the airfield, working on the premise that says if in doubt in potentially hostile territory, stay on the move and when you find a place to stop, keep your head down. The less time you spend out in the open, the less likelihood there is that you'll be spotted.

On landing at the taxi airfield to the north-east of Mogadishu I was directed by the pilot to a tin shed on the far side of the field. I walked across and found a battered red Peugeot being watched over by an armed guard who looked at least in his seventies. When I pointed at the car he didn't ask for any ID but held out a piece of paper with a figure scrawled on it. I guess there weren't too many white men passing through here looking for a rental, so he was ready and waiting for the transaction. There were a lot of zeroes on the paper but it was cheaper and less noticeable than hiring a high-profile vehicle at the airport. When it came to profile, I was looking for zero-to-near invisibility.

I checked the tyres and fuel gauge, and satisfied it would run without going dry on me, handed him a bundle of notes. He gave me a set of keys and showed me how to operate the door locks, pointing at them in the 'locked' position and mimed that if I was driving I should never leave them open. He drove the point home by pointing his gun through the window on the driver's side, then placing a fingertip against the side of my head and making a *baf-baf* noise. It was good advice; intersections in Mogadishu are prime sites for car jackings and random robberies, usually with extreme violence, which is why few drivers stop if they can help it. It makes for interesting driving, and the warning might have carried more weight if the old man hadn't laughed at the end and slapped his thigh.

I nodded at his gun, an old AK47 with a highly-polished stock and butt that had probably been passed down through his family. 'Is that for sale?' I still had the SIG Pro but I had a feeling I might need some back-up firepower.

He shook his head and patted it to show it was a valued possession. Then he motioned at me to wait and walked to the back of the hangar. He put the AK down with care, before dragging out a couple of long metal boxes from beneath a workbench. When he stood up he was holding something wrapped in sacking. He threw this aside to reveal two curved magazines and another AK which he held up with a triumphant grin.

At first sight it didn't look good. The gun was old, it was dirty and looked as if it might have been used to dig over his vegetable patch. But Mikhail Kalashnikov had designed and built his weapons to take the worst possible battlefield treatment and still come up firing, so I checked the magazines, which were full, and operated the mechanism. It was a little sticky but I figured some oil would soon clear that up.

The old man must have read my mind. He cast around on the workbench and came up with a small plastic squeeze bottle of machine oil. I took it and waved at the gun, magazines and oil, and he held up the same piece of paper he'd showed me for the car. So far he hadn't uttered a word. Maybe he just liked the number.

I paid him and stowed everything inside the Peugeot while he stood and watched. He gave me what looked like a blessing as I left, which probably demonstrated how highly he rated my chances of survival. But I nodded thanks as I drove away, on the basis that I might need all the help I could get.

By the time I got close to the city it was getting dark. In many places in Africa this would not have been a great time to be driving around. Here in Mogadishu, it was insane. But driving in daylight would have been worse; there's no easy

155

way to hide a white face, and unless you have a paid team of armed guards watching your back, progress is likely to be very brief and final. I drove with the SIG under my thigh for easy access, resolved not to stop for anybody or anything short of an armoured vehicle with a big gun.

I drove towards the sea front, avoiding as much as I could of the main routes into the city, passing through one shanty district after another and praying I didn't stray into a dead end and become boxed in with nowhere to go. I was making my way towards what I hoped was the last place anybody would expect to find me: the six-storey building where I'd left the dead man.

My previous visit had showed the area to be pretty much deserted, and I figured I could use it to wait until later in the night before going in search of the hotel where Masse had left the hard drive. It meant making my way through the city, but there was no way of avoiding that. Look anywhere in Mogadishu and there are houses – lots of them.

Once I got the hard drive I was going to head out and find somewhere to lay low until daybreak, then take the air taxi back across the border. If I stumbled on Masse at the same time, all well and good, but I wasn't counting on it; he'd made himself scarce and unless Lunnberg's group had taken him out, he was deliberately keeping his head down for reasons best known to himself.

I drove into the area where the office block was situated and found the shell of a small warehouse just off the main street. The inside was empty and accessible, and I reversed in ready for a fast exit. Then I tried ringing Masse's number again. There was no signal, so I took the SIG and the AK and sat outside the car where I could give the guns a thorough clean with the oil, while keeping a weather eye through a hole in the wall on the approach road from the city, in case I got a repeat bunch of visitors like last time.

Seventeen

Finding the air taxi pilot had been a stroke of luck. But Ratchman had always believed that you had to get lucky sometimes. So far a sprinkling of good fortune had helped him through a chequered career with minimal damage, so he wasn't about to question it when it came along.

Pushed by Lunnberg to make progress on finding Masse, he'd been asking himself how the frog spook could have moved around so easily in a region where the roads were shit, facilities non-existent and everybody and their cousin carried a gun and knew how to use it. Masse worked for the French intel outfit, the DGSE, but according to Lunnberg he was pretty much on his own most of the time and left to work the region as he saw fit. So what was his secret?

The solution came in the form of a drunk, an Australian aid worker name Paul, who told him that the only way to cover any distance quickly in Africa was to use one of the small taxi flights operating across the continent. Of course, the aid worker stressed, staring wistfully into an empty glass, you had to take the rough with the smooth – and there wasn't a whole lot of smooth. In fact some of the planes were downright shaky.

In spite of having little time for drunks, Ratchman sensed this guy might be on to something. So he got him another beer and a bourbon chaser and told him to keep talking. He learned very quickly that most of the pilots were fine, but a lot of the locals seemed to possess a death wish. If you got a Russian, you had to hold onto your hat but they were pretty good; they just didn't much like following rules or flying totally sober.

'So where are they willing to fly?' Ratchman asked. Maybe the drunk was too far gone and talking rubbish, but maybe not. He'd soon find out. 'Mogadishu?'

'Sure, Mogadishu,' Paul said. 'It's a cool place if you're prepared to take a little risk along the way.' He grinned and put a finger in his mouth and pushed out his cheek in an obscene gesture. 'There are girls down there who really know how to give a guy a good time, if you know what I mean.'

Ratchman knew about Mogadishu; you'd have to be dead from the neck up not to, with all the news reports of bombings, shootings and pickup trucks full of gunmen roaming the streets. The place was like a snapshot of hell. He also knew that some men liked to flirt with danger, getting their rocks off in a kill zone adding some extra spice. He couldn't understand it himself; he was strictly a clean sheets and plush hotel kind of guy. But each to his own.

'So give me a name,' he said to Paul, ordering more drinks. 'Who would you recommend?'

Paul stumbled for a second, then took another drink and blurted the names of two private taxi firms, both small, reliable and discreet. In spite of his drunken state, he remembered their numbers, accompanied by laying a finger along his nose and giving a slow wink. 'But don't tell everyone; we don't want the whole world crowding us out, right?'

'Damn right,' Ratchman murmured, making a note of the numbers on his cell phone, and poured his whisky into the other man's glass. He hadn't touched it and Paul nodded his thanks. 'I have to go. But thanks for the chat.'

Outside, he'd sucked in a few deep breaths before calling up the two air taxi firms to get directions. One had replied that their only plane was in the workshop and hadn't flown for a week after hitting a herd of goats. The other had told him how to find the airstrip and he'd called up Domenic, his Latino right-hand man, and told him they were going hunting and to bring his gun just in case.

Domenic had picked him up five minutes later, and within fifteen minutes they arrived at a flat piece of land a few miles outside the city. It was dark but they could see a windsock hanging limply above a makeshift hangar made of sheets of corrugated steel, and further over an old shipping container with an open door and a light on inside.

The air trapped inside the container was like an oven, and hit both men in the lungs as soon as they entered. The man behind an ancient wooden desk didn't seem to notice and gave a welcoming smile that threatened to split his face in two. On the wall either side of him were two large faded photos, one of Queen Elizabeth and the other of Nelson Mandela. In the back were a camp bed and a gas stove, and an armchair that looked as if it had been rescued from the city dump. A small badge on his shirt gave his name as Marten.

'Where you wanna, go, guys?' He was pencil thin with tight, curly black hair, and his accent was flat and hard.

'Mogadishu,' said Ratchman. 'Can you do that?'

'Sure I can. Mog's easy. Just got back from there, in fact, when you called. Arrange a car that side, too, if you need it.' He smiled broadly. 'Just tell me what you want and I can fix it.'

'That's an interesting accent you have there,' said Domenic, flicking through a local map. 'You're not from around here, right?'

'No way, man. Zimbabwe, down south. I flew with the army down there. When it all went to shit and you had to be a favourite to get on, I decided to do my own thing up here.' He grinned and added, 'Plenty of your boys like to cross the lines and are happy to pay, know what I mean?'

'The borders, you mean?'

'Sure. Lots of hot spots if you know where to find them. And I do.'

'Is that a fact?' said Ratchman. 'How about hotels in Mogadishu. Know any good ones?'

Marten nodded and pulled a short list out of a rack. 'These are all good, in the centre of town.' Then he scribbled a name across the bottom. 'But if you're looking for a bit of quiet, this is just outside the centre. Say I sent you and you'll get a good rate. It's where I send most of my passengers. Just don't go wandering around on your own where you shouldn't, though, or some little bugger'll hand you your nuts in a tin cup. By the way, who recommended me?'

Ratchman hesitated for a second, then decided to take a chance. 'A guy named Masse. French. He said you wouldn't bust us up too much when you land and knew your way around.'

Marten smiled, but it wasn't as broad as it had been. 'Masse? You sure?'

'Yeah. André. Medium height, nice guy.'

'Yes, I know him. Only what you said, that doesn't sound like him. The guy's got a serious depression most of the time. Hates flying and doesn't talk much. What'd you do – get him drunk and promise him a ticket home?'

Ratchman exchanged a look with Domenic. Something was off. He figured he'd just made a mistake and showed he didn't actually know Masse at all. But if it was a bluff it was too late to go back.

'Say what?'

'What is it you boys really want, eh?' Marten got to his feet. He was well over six foot and looked rangy, and the smile had vanished altogether. When he brought his hand up he was holding a gun.

Domenic wasted no time; he stepped fast round the edge of the desk and pointed a semi-automatic at the pilot's head. He said, 'You already gave us what we wanted, you dumb fuck,' and pulled the trigger.

The shot was deafening, bouncing around the interior of the container, and Marten ducked as the bullet zipped past his head. He dropped his gun and turned to look at the hole that had been drilled in the picture of Mandela.

162

Ratchman clutched his ear and winced. 'For fuck's sake, Dom – you trying to blow my eardrums or what?'

'Sorry, Ratch,' Domenic replied calmly, and stared at the gun with a puzzled expression. 'Damn if it doesn't pull a little to one side. It must be your lucky day, Marten. Next one goes through your head. Want to pick up your shitty little gun and try for a replay?'

'No.' Marten shook his head. 'That ain't necessary, sir. I didn't mean no offence.'

Ratchman smiled and waved away a veil of gun-smoke. 'See, Dom? Now that's what I call service. You've been elevated to a sir already.' He leaned across the desk and plucked a colour photograph off a pinboard fixed to the wall. The photo showed Marten, a pretty young woman and a cute little girl with red ribbons in her hair. Ratchman waved it in the air and instantly saw the pilot's eyes widen. 'I've got another question for you, Marten. When you last went to Mogadishu, did you give a lift to an American named Portman? He might have been travelling with Masse, maybe alone. Medium height, dark hair, eyes like piss-holes in the snow. Or, should I say, sand. Maybe you've seen him.'

Marten swallowed and nodded. 'He's made a couple of trips, the last one earlier this evening. Quiet guy but tough underneath, you know what I mean? He hired a car the other end, too. Cash.'

Ratchman stared at him, for a second or two uncomprehending as the words went by. *This evening?* How the hell? Portman was supposed to be in a hole somewhere courtesy of three

163

former legionnaires. 'Wait, wait, wait . . . let me get this straight; you flew Portman to Mogadishu this evening? Are you sure about that?'

'Positive. He paid cash, no questions.'

'Did he say where he was going?'

'No, sir. He didn't look like he'd tell me anyway, so I didn't ask. Nothing to do with me.'

Ratchman grinned. 'Yeah, that sounds like our boy.' He took out his phone. 'You wait here with Dom and be good, you hear? I have to make a call.'

Outside he breathed easier in the cool night air and called Lunnberg. It didn't take long and he was relieved he was out here instead of anywhere near the colonel.

'He's *what*?' Lunnberg's voice came spitting out of the phone like acid. 'Are you certain?'

'Yes, sir. The pilot knows him from a previous flight. And I have a lead on where he might have gone in Mogadishu, too. What do you want us to do?'

'Find him. Find him and end this. You'd better get your men and vehicles ready to travel. I'll make the arrangements and call you back.'

Ratchman went back inside and waved the photo of Marten's wife and daughter. 'You've been a big help, Marten. But there's something you have to know: Domenic, here hates putting his gun away without using it. A bit like those little Gurkha fellas with their big-assed knives. You got lucky this time – he only plugged old Nelson. But you tell anyone about our little chat and he won't come straight back here, no, sir. He'll go find your pretty wife and daughter and deal with them. And believe me, he's ace at finding people. Then he'll come back and talk to you. So no blabbing to anybody about our little visit. Understand me?'

Marten nodded, his lip tight. 'Yes, sir. Understood.'

Ratchman leaned across and slid the photo in Domenic's top pocket, then nodded and walked out.

Eighteen

'Do you know what a fuck-up is, Victor? What the expression actually means?' Lunnberg was pacing around his room like a caged animal, his body language tight and his eyes centred on the French intelligence officer who had just entered after being summoned. It was just gone 1 a.m. and the sky outside was peppered with pinpricks of light. The area around the hotel was quiet, with a mournful ship's siren the only sound coming off the gulf a good distance away.

Dressed in a neat blue shirt and dark pants, Lunnberg was showered and clean-shaven, and smelled of soap, in spite of the late hour. The air-conditioning in the room was turned up full and the atmosphere was like an ice box, none of which helped make Petrus feel welcome.

'Of course,' Petrus replied cautiously. He was in pants and a shirt with no tie and looking ruffled by the phone call that had woken him. 'Why do you ask? What has happened?'

Lunnberg held up an imperious finger and said, 'Two good questions, Victor. Why do I ask? Well, that's easy. It's prompted by the certain knowledge that you and your compatriots – your colleagues – do not have a fucking clue about how to conduct a clean-up operation.' He stopped pacing and turned to face Petrus with his hands behind his back, head up and chest thrust out aggressively.

Like Adolf Hitler, Petrus thought, bristling at the man's body language. 'With respect, *Mister* Lunnberg, I resent your tone—'

'Fuck your resentment, *Monsieur* Petrus. And fuck your respect because I don't need it. Instead, you should be asking yourself why I'm talking to you like a piece of shit. Or do you not have the balls?'

Petrus turned towards the door, his face white with suppressed anger. The American was acting like a pig and he didn't need to stay for this. 'I am not interested in what you have to say. I consider this meeting over.'

'You might. I don't. As to what has happened, it's my duty to inform you that your three men are dead. Or did you know that already and had decided not to tell me?'

Petrus stopped and spun round. 'I don't understand. What are you saying, dead?'

'Your three top guns . . . the men you provided to work alongside mine to clean up the mess caused by Masse and this freak, Portman. Ex-Legionnaires, you told me; the pick of the crop, you said, who would go to any lengths to get the job done. Aren't they the words you used?'

'Yes, I said that. But something is wrong. They were leaving the country after dealing with Portman, as instructed. Your own men handed him over to them.'

Lunnberg nodded in an exaggerated fashion. 'You're right, Victor, my God, you're so right. That's what happened. But did you actually check to see that your men did leave?'

Petrus looked stricken. 'No. Not yet.'

'Right. So the fact that my men handed Portman to *your* men, which we agreed was the best way to handle this issue, if I recall, to keep it all compartmentalised, makes it all *my* fault. Is that what you're saying?'

'*Bordel de merde!*' Petrus hissed in a burst of anger. 'How did they die?'

'Portman, who else? They were discovered a few hours ago just off a mountain road beyond some shithole village called Arta. The lead boy – JoJo? – had dragged himself back on the road but he died minutes after being found. Busted ribs and a punctured lung, the medics reckoned. The other two were dead, one with a cranial depression, the other of a gunshot wound. As you can imagine, questions are now being asked and I'm being forced to fight a rear-guard action to explain it away.'

Petrus frowned. 'But how did you find out? Arta . . . that is Legion territory up there.'

Lunnberg smiled without a trace of humour. 'I like to keep an eye on as many facets of an operation as I can, that's how. And guess what popped up? Three bodies and no sign of an assailant. Good thing one of us has a finger on the pulse, don't you think?'

Petrus looked sick. 'What about Portman?'

'Not a trace. Gone like fairy dust. But I happen to know he flew out to Mogadishu yesterday evening. My guys even found the pilot who took him. How about that?'

Petrus didn't know what to say. 'I can't believe it.'

'Christ, Victor – and I'm sorry I laid into you just now, which was unforgivable of me *and* unprofessional – but that man is seriously beginning to piss me off. Did you know he'd been here before, by the way – with your own Foreign Legion?'

'What? Are you sure?'

'Yes. Whether he served with them or was on attachment is open to doubt, I don't know. But that's immaterial. The fact is, this bozo goes into a secure vehicle with three very tough legionnaires, and he gets out leaving them dead and dying. I'm guessing, of course, that he didn't know them from his time here, but if he did, it means he's one cold son of a bitch, wouldn't you say?' He snapped his fingers before Petrus could speak. 'Oh, and he took their car and drove away – probably right back here to Djibouti. Hell, who knows – he could have been sitting in this very hotel earlier, sipping a nice cold beer.' He did another turn and stared through the window. 'Jesus, can this really get any more fucked up than it is?'

'What about Masse?'

'I don't know. There's been no trace. All my boys got was the Brit, Doney. When they found out he didn't know squat about Masse or the hard drive, they dumped him out in the scrub. He's probably buzzard meat by now.'

'Dead?'

'Of course dead. In case you haven't heard, dead men don't blab. It's a proven fact.'

Petrus shook his head, as if that might make matters clearer. 'What do we do now? If Portman is out there, he will talk.'

'Not if we bring him down first.' Lunnberg's eyes glittered. 'I had my guys ask around, and it seems Masse was using a local air taxi company for getting into Somalia and back. It was one of many local initiatives set up by us, would you believe. Some non-government mission to help give a boost to small business start-ups in the area.' His tone was layered in sarcasm. 'Damned if these things don't always come back and bite us on the ass.'

'Us?'

'You, me, the UN, overseas aid, probably even *Médecins Sans Frontières* and the World Scout Movement. Fucked if I know, but that's where a lot of our dollars and euros went. Masse was in the habit of using the taxi company to slip across the border and Portman probably did the same.' He stared at the French man. 'You didn't know, did you?'

'I did not need to know. Masse had his methods and I didn't question them as long as it worked. You must know how it is; men working in deep cover have to make their own arrangements. We cannot dictate what they should do because the situation is fluid and changes day to day.' He stopped, as if aware that he was rambling. 'Have your men spoken to this taxi company?'

'That they have. It seems Portman and Masse travelled into Somalia separately. The pilot even knew a flea-bag hotel where my guys figured Masse might be staying. I'm sending a team in to check them out and see.' He considered the matter for a moment, then said, 'It would help if you could get some more men on your side to help out – preferably guys who know the region.'

'I'm not sure I can do that.'

'What does that mean, not sure?' Lunnberg looked ready to spit. 'We have to find this turkey and soon. This is a joint effort, don't forget; you're in this as much as we are. We need more bodies on the ground. The first three you supplied weren't up to the job so make sure the next team's better.'

Petrus looked defeated. 'I'll see what I can do.'

'Make sure it's good, my friend – and quick. The sooner they arrive here the sooner they can begin searching the city. If Portman isn't in Mogadishu there's only one other place he can be: right here under our noses. And frankly, with what I now know about this guy, I don't feel happy knowing he's in the same country.'

'I understand. But if he's in Mogadishu? That's a big place to search – and dangerous.'

Lunnberg checked his watch. 'Not for my guys. In fact they should be getting ready to leave about now, anyway. The plan is to arrive at a point twenty klicks outside Mogadishu and drive in. They should be in the city about 03.00 hours.'

Petrus raised his eyebrows. 'That soon? Impossible.'

In answer, Lunnberg cocked his head to one side and raised a finger towards the ceiling, where a clattering sound was making itself heard above the air-conditioning. It was a common enough sound over the city and the military base at Lemmonnier, with night missions a regular occurrence, and a sound Petrus had grown accustomed to ignoring. But Lunnberg seemed to find it particularly relevant. 'Chinooks make everything possible. It's over a thousand miles by road to Mogadishu, so I pulled a little weight over at the special forces camp and their tactical group agreed to get off their bunks and fly my boys in with their vehicles. Sounds like the ride just arrived.'

Petrus looked surprised. 'Won't the Somalis object?'

'They would have. But when their defence minister heard he'll be receiving an ex-gratia payment for the use of their air space he decided to overlook the intrusion and went back to bed.'

'What are their orders?'

'Simple: find Portman and the hard drive and dispose of them.'

'And Masse?'

'Him, too. Collateral damage, Victor. Shit happens.'

Victor Petrus walked back to his room in a daze, wondering at what point this assignment had begun to slide out of control. It was supposed to be a joint exercise between the two countries and their relevant agencies, but Lunnberg had virtually taken over on arrival, leaving Petrus in the dark, even to the extent of arranging an incursion into Somali territory to find Masse and Portman and dispose of them.

He felt a tiny worm of guilt about Masse, but he wasn't pretending feelings he didn't have. The man had always been left to do his own thing while paying lip service to procedure and orders, and the relationship between them had never been easy. But so far it had proved sufficiently effective and nobody had minded; Degouvier himself had said more than once that he should allow Masse the freedom to operate as he saw fit.

Petrus had often considered that Masse's main strengths – his intimate knowledge and experience in the region – could easily turn into a liability. He'd been out here on his own for too long, especially after his wife had left him, and had recently made little secret of his desire to return to France. Petrus suspected that he had dreams of re-uniting with his wife, and had said as much to Degouvier. But he'd been fobbed off and told to let Masse run for a while longer, as putting in a replacement at this juncture would take too long.

Now it had blown up in their faces. And all because they had lost the initiative to Lunnberg and his team of killers.

He returned to his room and thought hard about what to say to Degouvier. He already knew that there would be no more resources. The three sent in earlier had been the maximum allowed, and now that had ended in disaster the door would be slammed shut on any further commitment. God alone knew how he was going to explain the losses so far, but he would have to face that later.

Before calling Paris he dialled Portman's number. It was probably a waste of time like earlier attempts, but if he could speak to the American, he might at least rescue something from this *débâcle* and find out what had happened. Exactly how much trust he could place in him after the deaths of the three men was open to doubt. The call went to voice mail and he rang off. He checked his watch. Degouvier should be in the office waiting for news. With any luck what Petrus was about to tell him would make him wish he'd stayed at home.

Nineteen

I gave it forty-five minutes before moving, taking occasional sips of water from the supplies I'd brought with me. Nothing had stirred save for a couple of stray dogs, and I was pretty sure I wasn't being watched. I left the AK in the back of the car and held the SIG by my side and started walking.

The distance to the building was about three hundred yards, most of it past other tumbledown structures I could use for cover. It was a ghost town and I paused regularly on the way, checking my back-trail and listening to the night. I came to a stop before making the last hundred yards across open ground. Nothing moved and there were no sounds save for a few rustling noises of night creatures going about their business.

I reached the front of the building and stepped through the entrance, which was littered with broken glass and debris from the volley of gunfire that had made holes in the rotting fabric and exposed some of the core structure. I moved over to the crashed elevator and checked for the rope, but it had been taken down. It was bad news but only if somebody turned up like last time. Since I wasn't planning on staying around long, I decided to tough it out and get moving. The sooner I was up there the sooner I could get back down and be on my way.

Another reason I was here was to see if the dead man had been taken away. If he had I'd wasted my time; if he hadn't, I was going to run another check of the body to test a theory.

The stairs were covered in even more grit and debris than the last time, testimony to the damage done by the assault team gunning the inside and using fragmentation grenades. I didn't dare use a flashlight yet, so I was pretty much feeling my way. Six floors was a long way to climb under these conditions and the air was clammy here, making breathing difficult. I stopped each time I came to a window where I could look out towards the city. If anybody was going to turn up it would be from that direction, and if I saw lights coming, I'd have maybe two minutes to get back downstairs and out of here and duck into cover.

I got to the top floor and stepped through the doorway into the room where I'd found the body. The ambient light up here was better, with the soft glow of starlight coming through the window spaces, and I immediately saw the dark shape on the floor. I also smelled it. The soldiers who'd attacked the building had clearly decided not to move it, and my first instinct was that they'd left it in case anybody came back to claim it. But that made little sense, and I figured they had merely taken the easy option because to take it with them would involve explanations, paperwork . . . and nobody had given those orders to do so.

In the meantime the heat and insects had begun their work, and the body was in an advanced state of decay, the air filled with the stink of decaying flesh.

I checked the entire floor first, scanning the outside through the window openings for signs of movement. I had a good view of the surrounding streets from up here and, further over, a distant array of working lights from the port and a few in the city centre. Nothing and nobody moved close, which suited me just fine.

I went back to the body and put a couple of plastic bags on my hands for protection. This wasn't going to be pleasant, and I had no real reason to be doing it, but the theory I wanted to test was simple: some private military contractors, especially working alone under deep cover, were rumoured to carry some form of ID or currency concealed about them in case they got compromised or captured and needed to buy or bargain their way out; or if the worst happened, they could be identified and somebody notified of their death. It wasn't a universal rule and not something I'd ever done, since most of my assignments were short-term, in-and-out trips relying on staying on the move and out of trouble.

I crabbed over to the body with one ear cocked for visitors, and knelt down. As I got close a furious buzzing sound exploded around me as a swarm of flies rose in the air like a dense blanket, hundreds, maybe thousands of darting shapes flicking at the skin of my face and hands, desperate not to leave the feast and annoyed at being disturbed.

I took a flashlight and a knife out of my pocket. I shaded the light with my fingers to check the dead man's shoes. They were sturdy but worn down on the heels and scuffed, which I figured was intentional; nobody goes into this kind of war zone with shiny brogues and razor creases unless they're looking to get noticed. Good clothes equate to money and that means an easy target.

A couple of careful slashes with the knife took care of the laces, which were strained and biting into the leather because of the swollen condition of the feet and ankles. I checked the shoe heels first. They came away easily enough but there was nothing concealed there or under the feet. I scanned the rest of the body, rolling it to see if there was anything taped to the small of the back or beneath the arms. That left the belt, which was almost embedded in the dead man's waist. It was made of double-layered webbing and caked in dried blood from where he'd been stabbed. I cut it away and moved over to a blind corner of the room where I could risk using the flashlight for a closer look.

At first glance it looked ordinary, with nothing special about the buckle and no obvious hiding place . . . until I came to a halfway point approximating to the wearer's spine. The webbing showed a slight bulge at this point, and I sliced open the stitching. A slim wad of US dollars, the universal currency, was folded into the gap, and alongside it a sliver of plastic no thicker than a cigarette paper. It wasn't marked with any name or numbers, but there was a bar code on one side. I guessed if it was scanned with a reader it would reveal a name and possibly a contact number if anybody cared enough to check it out and make the call.

As I put the plastic in my pocket I heard a sound from down below. It wasn't much; maybe a street dog foraging for food. But when I heard the crunch of grit echoing up the stairs I knew I had bigger company.

My time was up.

I removed my shoes and tied the laces together and hung them round my neck. The next few minutes were going to be uncomfortable, but walking down the stairs in shoes would make too much noise. I stepped out onto the landing and listened. Two men whispering, maybe were egging each other on. That was a good sign if they were locals looking for something to steal; not so good if they were armed and ready to shoot.

I moved down the stairs towards them, keeping tight to the inside wall housing the elevator shaft. I passed the fifth floor landing, then arrived at the fourth, and heard a whisper just below. They must have sensed my presence and stopped.

I looked at the shaft doors which were partially open, and bent down, feeling for a piece of rubble. I fastened on a chunk of plaster about the size of a baseball, and tossed it through the opening. A couple of seconds silence, then a muffled clatter when it hit the crashed elevator at the bottom.

One of the men gave a yell, and I hit the stairs on the run. Instinct alone would have made them look down, expecting somebody to have entered the building behind them. I took advantage of that and came round the bend in the stairs and flicked on the flashlight.

It caught them with their mouths open and looking at each other in shock. Two young guys, no more than late teens, early twenties. Their clothes looked ragged and worn, and one was carrying a long machete with a rusty blade, the other was holding a hefty stick.

I pushed the SIG forward into the light so they could get a good look. As young as they were, they recognised the poor odds against a semi-automatic and froze.

Using the gun barrel I motioned for them to put down their weapons. They did it, and when I pointed down the stairs, they grabbed hold of each other and scurried down, trying not to break into a run. I didn't bother asking what they were doing here; they were probably homeless, oppor-tunists looking to find anything they could take and sell. Had they been serious they would have come in like the last group I'd seen here, armed with more than a machete and a stick.

We reached the ground floor in silence, and I whistled to get their attention. When they turned and looked at me, they probably thought that was it; they were dead. But I pointed to the front door and motioned for them to go.

Three in the morning in central Mogadishu is a place of shadows, of stray animals, of gutted buildings and vehicles and dangerous young men armed with automatic weapons and too much ammunition. It's not a place for the faint-hearted, the innocent or the over-imaginative. You have

180

to go there knowing the odds and the risks and not to treat it without the utmost caution.

The fabric of the city at first sight is by turn a mix of ancient buildings and ruins, elegant villas, commercial and government buildings . . . and dense, low-level housing and squalor. The colour scheme varies from glittering white to mostly drab grey, although right now I was staring at dark and darker, with occasional oases of light where the more obstinate or courageous among the inhabitants were carrying on life as if each day were their last and the dangers outside were simply to be tolerated. I'd already passed several burned-out buildings and wrecked cars, the presence of ambulances and emergency services showing signs of the most recent attacks. These locations of violence were often uncomfortably close to wide boulevards wearing the style and grace of Italy or France in their layout and design, and the contrast was vivid, but mostly sad.

Intersections posed a potential choke-point, with groups of young men standing around looking mean, many armed and prone to sudden bouts of excited aggression. There were also plenty of government troops, and trucks full of what looked like African Union soldiers, all heavily armed and watching out for the next potential spike of violence. The tension in the atmosphere was like a wave, and I drove with the SIG under my thigh and the AK on the passenger seat. If I had to bail out for any reason, I would need the firepower to fight off an attack and get clear. Although I was keeping my eyes at least three blocks ahead of my position, scoping for a diversion around a trouble spot if I needed one, I was counting on not stopping for anything or anyone.

I'd been driving for twenty minutes, and was close to the section of the city housing the hotel Masse had told me about, when the inside of the car was lit up from behind. Three lights, two of them vehicle headlights and the third a spotlight. Whoever was on the spot was dancing it around in my rear-view mirror to distract me. I hung a left and watched in the mirror as I was free of the light for a moment and the outline of the vehicle behind me became clear.

It was a pickup full of men, rifles waving in the air like the quills on a porcupine. I couldn't make out any uniforms and suspected they weren't wearing any. When they swung left after me and the driver began leaning on his horn, I knew I was in for a chase.

I put on speed. With no way of knowing who they were, I wasn't about to stop for a chat. Pickups full of gunmen didn't always mean insurgents, but the alternatives could be members of a local clan or gang. Whoever they were, I doubted I'd be able to come up with a convincing story as to why I was driving about the city at this time of the night. Or why I was carrying a handgun and an assault rifle.

I hit another turn and blasted along a narrow street full of litter and soft debris. It was probably a regular market area, but thankfully with no cars or carts to get in my way. Unfortunately, the same held true for the boys in the pickup, and they were soon on my tail.

When they began shooting, I decided enough was enough. The first shots were spaced out, aimed over the roof as a warning. When I failed to stop, somebody back there got excited and let loose a couple of volleys, most of which missed the Peugeot completely and hit houses and shops on either side of the street. But it was only a matter of time before one of the shooters got lucky and either hit me or burst a tyre.

I turned again, leaving it to the last second to slam on the brakes and haul the wheel round while hoping I wasn't about to end up in somebody's courtyard, nose buried in a solid stone wall.

Pickups full of men are inherently unstable, even if well-maintained, which I guess this one wasn't. I'd seen plenty of examples of vehicles hitting a corner too fast and flipping over, spilling their cargo like skittles. I wasn't about to outgun these guys but I could try and upset the driver, who was probably being urged on by his pals, slapping him on the back and daring him not to use the brakes but to keep his foot planted on the floor.

As we screamed along a narrow street towards an intersection with a wider boulevard, a couple of shots pinged into the back of the Peugeot, one taking out the rear window. This was getting serious. I had to find a way of ditching these guys.

Then I saw my chance. Up ahead a bunch of mostly young men were crowded around a car that had ploughed into one side of a large stone archway and spun round. One wheel was buckled beneath the bodywork, and the men were shouting and laughing, jabbing at the driver with their guns. It was easy to see they were up to no good. When they heard us coming, they forgot about their victim and went quiet, turning to see what was bearing down on them. The trouble was, most of them were right in my way and showing no signs of moving.

I grabbed the SIG and stuck my arm out of the window, letting off a couple of shots at the pickup behind me. I wasn't expecting to hit anything, but the response was immediate. Now I really was of interest and had to be stopped. A sustained burst of firing came back, again mostly missing me but striking the buildings around the group of men up ahead instead.

They reacted the way I wanted, mostly diving for cover and clearing the centre of the street, their startled faces lit up by the spotlight. But a couple stood their ground on the sidewalk and decided that if I was being fired on, I was being oppressed and in need of support.

Either way, they began shooting at the pickup, those without guns dancing around and encouraging the others to blast it off the road.

As I hit the boulevard and turned the corner, I glanced back and saw the pickup wobble under the onslaught. The spotlight blew out followed by one of the headlights, and suddenly the front wheels gave way as the driver tried to make a tight turn to escape the bullets. The last glimpse I had was of the pickup rolling over, spilling men and guns across the street before ploughing upside down into the front of a burned-out café.

* * *

I stopped only when I was sure I was no longer being followed. Holding the SIG I jumped out to check the tyres; being immobilised right now would be the worst kind of news. I was pretty close to the hotel Masse had mentioned, but with all the activity I'd created, I knew I had to get clear of the area before a bunch of troops and police began crawling the streets looking for somebody to shoot.

The car was fine. I wasn't bothered by the hole in the window because cars were random victims of stray bullets most days of the week, and a lot of drivers figured it wasn't worth getting repairs done when they could get the same damage the next day.

As I was about to get back in, two men appeared from a side street about three hundred yards away. They were both armed and stared hard at me for a second, before beginning to jog-trot down the center of the street towards me, waving their rifles in the air and shouting. If they were expecting me to put my hands up, they had another think coming.

I ducked into the car and pulled out the AK. A SIG was no good for this kind of distance. I hadn't had a chance to check the sights on the AK yet or see if the old weapon would stand a discharge, but now was a good time to find out. I aimed somewhere in between the two men and fired once, and saw the round kick up a puff of dust where it struck the road thirty feet behind them. Pulling slightly to the left and high. I fired again, kicking up the road right between them, and one of the men stopped in his tracks, then turned and ran off.

185

His buddy was either brave or high as a kite and kept coming, picking up speed and pushing his rifle out in front of his body and loosing off a couple of shots in my direction without even aiming. He was either supremely optimistic or unaware that a gun is only as effective as the person using it. Maybe he'd watched too many westerns, where shooting accurately from horseback on the run was the norm and looked easy. His friend was shouting at him, probably to back off, but it didn't seem to have any effect.

This was getting silly. If he continued firing off rounds, all it would take was for one to get lucky and I'd be down or I'd have a blown tyre. Either way would be disastrous. I took aim, breathed out calmly and squeezed off a shot. The gunman seemed to skip and stumble for a second, then dropped his rifle and rolled to one side and lay still.

The second man was nowhere to be seen, so I got back in the car and drove away. Five minutes later I was parked in a quiet back street bordered on both sides by high walls and trees. The hotel was called the Mamet and situated on the corner of the back street and a main thoroughfare, with a side door set in the wall. Even in the poor light I could see the building possessed an air of faded grace, with patches of plaster missing from the wall and a general air of sadness and neglect. I gave the side door a try but it was locked. There was nothing for it – I'd have to go in the front.

The entrance was a double glass door with an elegant but heavy wrought-iron grille behind it.

Both were locked, but in the dim light from inside I could see a concierge sitting behind a tall reception desk, his head just visible as he stared out at me with wide eyes. I used the flashlight to show my face and he looked startled. I guess seeing a white face at this time of night wasn't that common.

He opened the door a crack and peered out at me. 'Sir, it is very late,' he said softly. 'I am not permitted to allow you entry as I know you do not have a booking.' He spoke with careful precision and looked saddened at not letting me in, as if he had somehow failed in his main duty.

I took out a couple of notes and held them up for him to see. 'I don't need a room,' I said quietly. 'I just need to speak with you. I am willing to pay for your time as I can see you are a conscientious person.'

He blinked, although whether it was my polite approach or seeing the money or the fact that I didn't want a room, I couldn't tell. But he was clearly intrigued. Eventually, he opened the door enough to allow me in, then closed it again quickly after checking the street both ways.

The foyer was cool and smelled of lavender and mint, and contained a couple of soft chairs and a bookcase. The walls were covered in faded posters of times long gone, and the light I had seen came from a reading lamp behind the reception desk.

'Sir,' the concierge said, resuming his seat, 'how may I help you?'

I put the notes down in front of him. He looked at them but made no move to pick them up, waiting for me to speak my piece.

'A friend of mine stayed here recently,' I told him. 'A Frenchman named Masse. He was in room five.'

He nodded, eyes closing briefly. 'Yes, that is correct, sir. I remember.'

'He left something in the room and asked me to pick it up next time I was passing through.'

He looked at me without expression, as if passing through in the middle of the night in this violent and unstable city was perfectly normal. 'I have cleaned the room, sir. There is nothing there, I assure you.'

'Would it be possible to go to the room and look?' As I said it, I placed two more notes on the desk. 'This is for disturbing you so late.'

He thought it over, then nodded. If I wanted to waste my time and pay for the privilege, who was he to argue? The notes disappeared. 'Please, sir, follow me.'

We climbed the stairs and he led me to a door on the first floor. Taking a bunch of keys from his pocket he unlocked the door and let me in, switching on the light. The room was clean and cool and also smelled of lavender and mint. The window was open, letting in a breeze that carried a mix of smells from the city around us, some of them less than pleasant. It probably accounted for the need for fragrance in all the rooms. I stepped inside and looked towards the bed for the air vent Masse had mentioned.

It was down by the bedhead, just behind a small wooden cabinet. The concierge watched without comment as I bent and put a finger behind the grill to test it. It fell out of the cavity without a problem and I saw a layer of plaster dust on the beam below. I already knew what I was going to find, but I felt around inside, anyway. Nothing. No hard drive, just a thin layer of dust and dead insects.

'Has Mr Masse been back here in the last couple of days?' I asked.

'No, sir. I am sorry. He has not.' He was looking right at me when he spoke, and I guessed he owed some loyalty to Masse that over-rode any honesty to a stranger.

'Did he always use this room when he was here?'

He nodded. 'Yes, sir. Always this room, number five. He enjoyed the view of the street. Behind the hotel is a garden with many flowers, but he liked to hear the sounds of people.'

'Is anybody else staying here right now?'

He shook his head. 'It is very quiet just now, sir. Out of season, you see.' He said it with a perfectly straight face and I believed him. I also felt sorry for him; as far as I could see the season didn't look like coming back anytime soon.

Before I could ask another question, there was a rattle of gunfire in the distance, muffled by the surrounding buildings. The concierge seemed not to notice and stood away from the door, a signal for me to leave. Our transaction was done.

I nodded, and was about to turn and leave when my cell phone buzzed. I took it out and pressed the button, and a familiar voice said, 'You have to get out of there.' It was André Masse, sounding oddly calm for such an urgent message. 'Don't wait, leave now.'

As he finished speaking the sound of a powerful

engine drifted down the street and through the open window. This time the concierge looked concerned. I walked over to the window, which fronted on the main street, and took a look.

A pale coloured SUV, possibly a GMC or Ford model, was slowing to a stop fifty yards away, its headlights flaring off the walls of the buildings on either side. The lights snapped off but nobody got out. I couldn't tell how many passengers were inside but it had to be more than one for a vehicle that size. A flare of light came from the other direction and an identical vehicle stopped the same distance away and also killed its lights.

It was too much of a coincidence seeing two such vehicles arriving here right now. And it didn't take much to work out who might have had the muscle and means to get here in the middle of the night: it had to be Lunnberg. As I'd seen already, he had access to the men, weapons and vehicles. I couldn't see inside either car but I was willing to lay a large bet that they were the same squad that had taken me out of the hotel in Djibouti. The question was, how had they known where to come?

I went to say something to Masse but he'd already gone.

The concierge touched my arm and said, 'I will show you out, sir. You may wish to use the side door.' With that he turned and hurried down the stairs, beckoning me to follow.

I thanked him again and told him it might be better not to let the men in, or to stay well out of their way until they'd gone. He nodded gratefully, and I got the feeling he would stay at his post no matter what.

I got back in the Peugeot and drove well away before turning on my lights.

All I had to figure out now was what the hell I did next.

Twenty

Ratchman ordered two of his men into the hotel, while two from the other car circled the block to cut off any chance of Masse slipping away if he was inside. He'd got a feeling this place was the most likely bolthole for the Frenchman, and with luck they'd find him shacked up with some young Somali girl instead of attending to business. Maybe they'd get double lucky and stumble on Portman, too. He was still smarting at being told by Lunnberg how easily Portman had got away from the three ex-legionnaires, and with such deadly effect, and how he should have taken care of it himself. The main thought on his mind now was catching up with the man and putting him out of the game for good. Then they could deal with Masse.

So far it was going according to plan. The Chinook had dropped them ten miles outside the city, before lowering the ramp and allowing the two Ford Raptors to roll out. Minutes later it was taking off again and heading in a wide curve back towards Djibouti.

After checking the coordinates, Ratchman had ordered both vehicles to head for the building where Petrus had told Lunnberg the body of a white male had been found. What Petrus didn't know was that in all likelihood it was former US sergeant, Josh McBride. And neither could he ever know. Ratchman's instructions on the subject had been crystal clear: if the body was still there, it must not be identifiable by the Somalis or the French.

On arrival they had spread out and covered the area around the industrial site, checking for opposition. In the distance they could hear sporadic gunfire around the city, but nothing close by.

Ratchman had taken two men with him to check the building floor by floor while the others remained on lookout outside ready to repel any attack.

The all-too familiar smell had hit them while they were two floors away, and Ratchman had decided not to waste time searching for anything. If Portman had been here already, there would be nothing useful left to find. He nodded to Domenic, who placed a small thermite charge beneath the body and set it off. As they ran back down the stairs, there was a muffled explosion and a flash of bright light as the thermite and barium nitrate mix ate the body away with a fierce heat.

Moments later they had driven clear of the area and headed straight for the hotel Marten had named. Although it looked closed up tight at first, it was showing a dim light in the reception area. Ratchman gave the men a few minutes to check out the building before following them inside, leaving the driver at the wheel. He found an older man sitting on the floor in front of the reception desk. He was unhurt but had both hands behind his head and looked terrified, one of his legs shaking uncontrollably and his foot drumming on the tiles. A former marine named Carson was standing over him with a pistol pointed at his forehead. The sound of footsteps echoed from the floor upstairs, and the slamming of a door.

'What does he say?' Ratchman asked, and pressed his foot on the man's leg to stop the drumming.

Carson said, 'He's the night porter. Reckons Masse was here but not for a couple of days now. In fact he says the place is empty. Jesse's up there making sure he ain't lying.'

'Is that correct?' Ratchman toed the man in the side with his boot. It was a gentle nudge but hard enough to show he wasn't fooling, and the man nodded. 'Have there been any visitors looking for Masse?'

'No, sir.' The man said carefully, his voice almost a whisper. 'Trade is regrettably not good at the moment. This is a quiet season for us.'

'Quiet?' Ratchman snapped out a brief laugh. 'I bet the fuck it's quiet. You ask me, you should put that on TripAdvisor, my friend. Quiet season. Except for all the gunfire and car bombs every night. Am I right?'

'Very true, sir, yes. It is a sad time for us.'

'No shit. It's like Tombstone. But I guess you wouldn't know about that, would you – Tombstone, I mean.'

The man shook his head.

'So, Masse's been and gone and there's been nobody else asking after him.'

'That is correct, sir.'

Ratchman debated giving Carson the nod to sign him off, but just then his cell phone rang. It was Domenic outside in the other Raptor.

'We've got company: a bunch of guys in a pickup just pulled in a hundred yards behind us down the street. They're armed and looking ready for a fight.'

Ratchman switched his phone to broadcast so that Carson could hear everything. 'Are they government?'

'Not unless they're going to a fancy dress party. There's about six guys all told and they're waving a bunch of AKs and a couple of RPGs. Their shitty pickup looks low on the springs like it's about to do a crap.'

Probably bandits high on khat, Ratchman thought. That wasn't good news. Khat was the drug of choice in these parts, a plant which produces a sense of euphoria and excitement, making some users believe they were bullet-proof. It wouldn't take them long to make a move, as the Raptors would be too tempting to ignore. Once they kicked off it wouldn't take long for a bunch of others to join in, eager for a piece of the action.

'How long have we got?'

'Not long. They're trying to figure us out, probably – or waiting for backup. Who can tell?'

'Right. We're coming out. Are you boys all loaded up?'

'Yes. We didn't see anybody, although a car was heading away to the west as we arrived. It wasn't burning rubber so it could have been anybody.'

Ratchman made a rapid assessment of the situation. If Domenic and his men were facing away from the bandits, it would be easier for Ratchman and his team to tackle the men in the pickup head-on. One thing was certain: they weren't going to allow two prime muscle vehicles to drive off into the night. The moment they made a move, the bandits would follow very quickly and wait for a chance to hit them.

'Listen up. We'll come out of the hotel and back to our vehicle. Then we'll roll down the street like nothing's wrong. As soon as we pass you, move forward and make a sharp left down the side of the hotel and follow that car your guys saw. We'll take care of the pickup.'

'Take care of meaning what, exactly?' There was an edge of excitement in Domenic's voice and Ratchman knew the Latino was keen for some action and would be happy to deal with the pickup in a heartbeat.

'Put them out of business, what do you think? Don't worry, Dom – there's plenty more out there for you to deal with. Now, get ready. We'll track your cell and meet up in fifteen on the edge of the city.'

'Copy that,' Domenic acknowledged. 'See you then.'

Ratchman signalled to Carson. 'Get Jesse down here now. We go out to the car together, then drive along the street until we get close to the pickup. But wait for my call. We need to be up close and personal to take out these guys, especially the RPGs.' At such close quarters, even a poor shot with a rocket propelled grenade would cause havoc.

'Right.' Carson called his colleague, his voice echoing up the stairs. Moments later Jesse, a skinny young black guy with a shaved head, joined them. He was carrying an assault rifle, barrel up and the butt tucked into his hip.

'What's up?'

'We're leaving,' said Ratchman. 'Back to the car, no looking around and keep your weapon low but ready. This is going to get hot. You set?'

'I hear you. What about him?' Jesse nodded at the night porter.

'It's his lucky day. He lives.' Ratchman looked at the porter and pointed to the door. 'Go take a look. Are the men in the pickup al-Shabaab?' He didn't actually care who they were, except that there was a difference in fighting ability between a bunch of opportunist bandits and members of the terrorist movement. The latter would be more prepared for a confrontation and trained to deal with opposition.

The porter climbed to his feet and walked over to the front door. He peered out for several seconds, then came back and said, 'Sir, I think I know these kinds of men. They come to this district many times. They are criminals. I think they will not want you to leave.' He struggled for the words. 'There are many like them who do very bad things.'

'Is that a fact?' Ratchman pointed to the chair behind the desk. 'Well, we can do very bad things, too, so I suggest you go sit down and don't move. We're just leaving.'

The man nodded and sat down behind the desk, eyes lowered and murmuring softly to himself.

Thirty seconds later the men had gone, leaving the hotel empty and heavily silent, as if a storm had just passed by.

By the time they returned to the Raptor, Ellison, the driver, had the engine ticking over and ready to roll. Ratchman climbed in the front alongside him, and the other two jumped in the cargo area at the back and braced themselves.

Carson reached into a canvas bag at his feet and produced two rounded objects. 'Frags ready to go,' he said with a grin, referring to fragmentation grenades. 'Boom-boom time. This is gonna get noisy, folks.'

Ratchman said, 'You all got ear plugs, you better use them.' Then he tapped Ellison's shoulder. 'Nice and steady now, like we're on a Sunday afternoon ride. Go past Dom until you get close to the pickup. We're just cruising, so no rush. We don't want to spook them.' He got an affirmative and turned to the other two in the back and called, 'We wait until we're alongside and take out anybody holding an RPG. Then dump a couple of frags among 'em and a burst of fire. Jesse, you work on the guys in the front; we don't want anybody chasing us. After that we go fast and far. Got it?'

It was rhetorical, but they grunted affirmatively, taking deep breaths to steady their nerves and each inserting soft earplugs against the coming gunfire.

Ellison pulled away from the kerb and drifted along the street, passing the junction alongside the hotel. All the lights in the building had now been extinguished. There was no other traffic and no pedestrians in sight. As they reached the other Raptor they saw Domenic give them a thumbs up and a large grin. Then they were past and approaching the pickup, sitting a hundred yards back, its lights out. Outlined against a dim pool of light further down the street they could see the shapes of armed men standing in the open back to watch them come, and a flare of instrument lights on the faces of the driver and passenger.

'What if they open fire before we get there?' said Ellison.

'They won't,' Ratchman said. 'They want this vehicle way too much to spoil it. They'll wave their guns and expect us to stop like good boys and hand it over.'

As they drew level with the hood of the pickup, Ratchman lifted an assault rifle off the floor and told Ellison to slow further. Just as they drew level with the men in the back, they heard a shout from one of the bandits, who had clearly seen something he didn't like. Ratchman fired a burst of automatic fire into the group of men at point blank range, aiming at two figures swinging RPGs over their shoulders. Meanwhile, in the back, Jesse was sitting ready with his feet braced against the bodywork. He opened fire into the front of the pickup, blowing out the windows and ripping apart the thin metal of the cab structure, seeing both men go down.

The noise was deafening, echoing off the walls of the buildings on either side of the street and accompanied by screams from the men in the pickup as they were struck by the blast of withering gunfire.

Carson lobbed his two grenades in among the men and shouted, *'Go, go!'*

At that, Ellison stamped on the gas and took them down the street while Carson picked up a semi-automatic pistol and turned in his seat, calmly blowing out the pickup's rear tyres and causing the vehicle to squat at the back like a downed buffalo.

Seconds later, as they were turning the corner, twin explosions echoed down the street and the pickup was engulfed in flames.

As Ellison took them fast down a narrow street heading west, Ratchman turned to his cell phone and watched as the tracking device picked up Domenic's vehicle ahead of them and approximately two blocks north.

His phone rang. It was Domenic, sounding buzzed with excitement. 'You all clear?'

'Clear and rolling,' Ratchman replied, amid a chorus of shouts from the other three men. 'They didn't know what hit them.'

'You lucky bastards. Are we calling in the Chinook?'

'Not yet. I got a feeling about that vehicle you saw driving away. There's nobody else moving around here, so why was there a car near that particular hotel? I want to take a closer look.'

'Got that. We'll see if we can find it. It's dark where we are so it should be easy enough to catch the headlights if he's still moving. Too risky to drive far otherwise, in case he hits something.'

'I hear you. We'll follow your signal on a parallel track.'

He switched off and sat back. It was Masse or Portman, he could feel it in his bones. Either one would do just as long as it led to the recovery of the hard drive. Settling things with Portman would be a bonus. Then they could dump the bodies before heading for home.

Twenty-One

I heard a crackle of gunfire some distance behind me as I headed away from the hotel. I couldn't tell if it was connected with the two SUVs or was one of the many random acts of violence that takes place in this city most nights of the week. Put any mixed bunch of bandits, terrorists and trigger-happy regular army on the prowl in a lawless place like Mogadishu, and it's like setting off a string of firecrackers and hoping the flames don't spread.

As for the SUVs, however they had arrived here, whether on my trail or Masse's, it was likely that they'd done so through a combination of chance, good instincts and information. Whichever way it was, our situation didn't look great.

I kept going and tried Masse's number. It rang twice before the signal dropped out. I placed the phone on the passenger seat and thought about my next move. I couldn't go back to Djibouti until I found out what had happened to him. It was obvious that he'd already recovered the hard drive in spite of the porter's denials, and had even been close enough to see what was happening and warn me. What I couldn't figure out was why . . . unless he needed me to help him get out of the country.

I was about to try his number again when I

caught a flicker of light in the rear-view mirror. It was momentary, then gone, but with no other vehicles in sight it could only mean that the SUVs had latched onto me. It was tough to judge but I reckoned the light had been maybe half a mile behind me, and very bright with a bluish tinge. That discounted most other vehicles I'd seen so far, which were old, their headlights yellow and dull, if working at all. Whoever was behind me was driving something much newer and faster.

I put on speed and dowsed my lights, hoping nobody would step out in front of me. But that soon proved too dangerous when I saw a cow loom up by the side of the road for a second and stand looking at me as if daring me to hit it. I swerved just in time and felt the front wheel touch the kerb, then corrected and turned the lights back on. If I crashed now, the men in the SUV would find me easy pickings.

Part of my plan for getting back out once I recovered the hard drive or Masse, whichever was the most useful, was to drive back to the airfield and find some cover until the air taxi could come and get me. But with these guys so hot on my tail, that would be courting disaster. I was going to have to be inventive.

My phone buzzed, taking me by surprise. It was Masse.

'Where are you?' he asked. His voice was tinny and trembling with vibration, and I guessed he was on the move in a vehicle over rough ground, probably the same kind of street as me.

'No idea,' I told him truthfully. 'I'm heading west and must be close to the outskirts of the city. But this is new territory for me. Where are you?'

'I'm heading the same way. We're probably in the same quarter. Can you see the minaret of a mosque to the north of your route?'

I looked round, trying not to slam into the side of one of the many buildings on the side of the road. 'I can see two.' It wasn't too hard, even in the dark; they were taller than any other buildings and stood out against the sky.

'How close?'

'One is about two hundred metres away, the other much further over. That one's got a faint light in the top.'

'That's good. You're heading the right way. What are you driving?'

I told him and he said, 'You need something less obvious if you want to get out of this. We must meet up and dump your car. That is the only way.'

'Fine by me. But where?'

His voice dropped out for a few seconds, before coming back halfway through a sentence. '. . . and drive inside.'

'Say again – I didn't get that.'

'There is an abandoned grain store on an intersection maybe three kilometres ahead of you, to your right. Drive behind it where you will find the doors have been taken off. Put the car inside and wait for me. I will join you shortly.'

I put on speed, one eye counting down the distance. Three kilometres wasn't far at this speed, and I'd have to be ready to slow down enough to turn without using my brake lights. A clutch of shanty buildings came up, with the reflected glow of my lights from the eyes of several animals tethered behind a rough stick fence. Goats, mostly, maybe a couple of cows. I changed down and allowed the engine to take the strain, and saw a larger shape in the distance, among a collection of mud or brick buildings.

This had to be it.

I swung in behind the larger building and immediately saw what Masse had described. It had once been a fairly substantial structure of metal and stone, most likely a government project to help local farmers, but a lot of the material used to build the rear wall and doors had been plundered and taken away, probably used by locals to build or repair their houses and make stock pens for their animals.

I aimed for the inside and drove in, slamming on the brakes. Then I jumped out and grabbed the AK and the SIG. If Masse had made a misjudgement I was about to make a glorious last stand here. It wouldn't be of Alamo proportions but just as fatal.

The lights behind me were approaching fast. They were making no attempt at subtlety but aiming at speed and a quick finish. Something must have alerted them that I was in danger of getting away and they'd had orders to end the chase.

Then another glow of lights appeared from the north, moving on an intersecting line towards the road I'd just left. I couldn't see the vehicle but it was obviously going at a lick. If it continued on its present course it would eventually meet up with the oncoming SUV.

I checked the AK. If they were together I was in trouble. I hadn't got enough ammunition for an all-out fight, especially if the men in the SUVs had modern assault rifles as I suspected. But I didn't have to make it easy for them. Besides, a gut feeling told me they had no intention of taking me alive, but of simply wiping me out, problem solved. In which case all they had to do was pour a bunch of rounds into the building and sooner or later I'd be down and dead.

The vehicle approaching from the north disappeared for a moment behind some buildings before reappearing, this time on a collision course with the approaching SUV. There was a blare of a horn and a flare of lights, then a crunch as the incoming vehicle hit the SUV at an angle, driving it off the road into a patch of waste land. The SUV driver had probably been distracted sufficiently by the horn to have failed to react to the collision in time, and had momentarily lost his hold on the wheel.

The second vehicle broke contact and continued towards me, the driver flashing his remaining headlight. I grabbed my bag and headed for the outside. When it pulled up alongside I dropped to one knee with the SIG pointed at the door and waited. The vehicle was a pickup with a long bed, of the kind used by small construction professionals. The bodywork was battered and dusty, and the front fender caved in from the collision. But the engine sounded good to go.

Masse stuck out his arm and banged the side of the door. 'Are you coming or not?'

* * *

206

'I'm guessing they were Lunnberg's men back there,' I said as Masse tore across an intersection. The pickup bounced twice, bottoming out as we hit a drainage gulley and making my teeth ache, and scattering a wall of litter in the air behind us. I really had to write to the city authorities and ask them to set up a road improvement program.

'Correct. Driving Ford Raptors, too. Good vehicles for this terrain. I probably know the dealer who supplied them. He brings them in for the Special Forces guys who like serious off-roading.' As he shifted in his seat a wave of sour body odour came off him. I wondered where he'd been hiding up for the past few days and whether he even noticed the state he was in. His hair was a mess and he hadn't shaved in a while, and his eyes were flicking wildly back and forth between the road in front and the rear-view mirror like a man high on narcotics.

'You recognised them?'

'Yes. I saw them with Lunnberg in Djibouti. They are mercenaries . . . but they prefer to call themselves private military contractors.' He made a vile noise in his throat and spat through the open window. 'Lunnberg has the most to gain from seeing that we do not reach Djibouti in one piece. I think he also sent his little army to deal with the body of the man he sent looking for me.'

The man in the office block. McBride. I wondered if Masse had worked out who the man had worked for or whether he had some inside information he wasn't sharing.

'You think?'

'It's the only explanation. It's the sort of thing Lunnberg would do: he is not a man to put all his trust in one person or action, but always has a back-up plan.' He tapped the wheel in a nervous tattoo with the palm of his hand. 'I read about him. Petrus sent me a briefing paper when we learned who would be running this deal for the Americans. He is well known in certain circles.'

It sounded to me as though the French had the same information on Lunnberg as Angela Pryce, and probably just as full of holes. Known or not, Lunnberg had turned out not to be the kind of team player the French had expected. To a man like him information is power, and if he could gain the upper hand in what was supposed to be a two-sided arrangement, while suppressing any information about his own involvement if things went badly wrong, he would come out with clean hands.

That reminded me. 'You have the hard drive, right?'

He looked at me and shook his head. 'It wasn't there.'

He couldn't help himself and it showed. 'I don't believe you.' Just to demonstrate how much I didn't believe him I took out the SIG and held it against his thigh. 'This won't kill you immediately I pull the trigger, but it'll put paid to any hopes you have of doing the French tango when you get back home. If you make it that far.'

He tried to laugh it off but failed, flinching away from the gun. 'Hey – Portman, come on! You want to get out of this godforsaken hellhole or what? You need me, remember? You won't get anywhere in this country if you kill me!'

'You want to bet your life on that? I've been in worse situations. If I dump you out on the road for Ratchman and his men to find, we'll see how much *they* need you. Now, the hard drive. Where is it?'

He held out for about ten seconds before caving in. 'Yes, OK, I got it. I got it.' He, took a silver biscuit from his pocket. It was identical to the one I'd found on the body. 'But it is mine to return, Portman. I have worked very hard for this for a long time. They will owe me for getting it back!' His eyes looked wild and he stuffed the hard drive back in his pocket.

'Owe you what?'

'A return ticket. I want to get out of here. My best way of doing so is to take this back with me. Not you, not Lunnberg, not even that *salaud*, Petrus.' He jabbed a thumb at his chest. 'I have gone through too much for this.' He closed his mouth with a snap when he nearly hit a large pile of something by the side of the road. 'Sorry,' he muttered, and focussed instead on not getting us killed.

I figured there must be a whole lot of bitterness and stress built up inside Masse that had been seeping out for a long time, and his superiors had failed to spot it. But whatever his complaints, he wasn't behaving professionally, more like the only kid on the block who owned a football. If he wasn't careful he was going to find his boss very unsympathetic if he got in the way of

Petrus's own ambitious plans to see this thing through and head on back to Paris with the hard drive.

It made me wonder what Lunnberg would think about that, and I glanced behind me and saw another glimmer of light in the darkness. It didn't seem a lot closer than before, but it didn't need to be; all they had to do was stay on our tail in the hope that sooner or later we would make a mistake or simply run out of road. Once that happened they would be all over us like a rash.

I put the gun away and heard him breathe a sigh of relief. He glanced at me. 'You're a scary son of a bitch, Portman, you know that? Is it me those men are after . . . or you?'

'If we get caught you can ask them.' I jerked a thumb behind us. 'They're right there in our smoke. Any suggestions?'

'Of course. We keep going on our present route and meet up with Marten at first light and go home.'

'Who's Marten?'

'The crazy Zimbabwean who flew you here.' The way he said it sounded so simple, but I knew it would be anything but. Right now we were heading out into open country with only one road to go on, and we couldn't keep running for ever.

'How do we do that? Even if we stay clear of the SUVs, the plane won't be able to land in the dark. That gives us several hours to play hide-and-seek until dawn. Do you have any spare fuel?'

He nodded. 'I have a couple of containers in

the back but not enough to get us to the border – even if I thought it would be possible. It's very bad terrain and very dangerous. If we don't run into insurgents we will hit Somali forces, and they don't stop to ask questions in the dark – they will shoot first and drive away afterwards.'

'Can we reach the airfield where the pilot dropped us?'

'No good.' He thumbed the air behind us. 'There's no direct route and I'm sure these men will have thought of that. The moment we change direction they'll head us off. The only way is to hide up and get Marten to come to us.'

I didn't like leaving the decision to Masse, but I didn't have a lot of choice. This was his turf and he knew it inside out. And if we were to get out of this immediate mess, we needed each other to cooperate in dealing with the opposition. Two against at least six was not the best odds in any kind of fight, and I didn't know how proficient Masse was when it came to combat. Wisdom says you always allow for any opposition to be at least competent, but in a running fight it would be numbers that counted most.

'Then what? Are you going to head for the airport in Djibouti and fly out with the hard drive like a tourist?'

'No. Lunnberg and Petrus will have somebody monitoring all arrivals and departures. I might get into the airport but I do not think I would be allowed to leave.' He took out his phone and dropped it in my lap. 'Speed dial number one. It is to Marten. Tell him we need a pickup at first light.'

211

'Will he do it?'

He gave a tight grin and steered around a couple of goats squatting by the side of the road. 'Only one way for finding out, right? If you promise him many dollars he will land over the roof of Mogadishu police station itself.'

I noticed Masse's English was getting a little ragged and figured he was stressed and tired. It was a worry because I needed him to be on top of his game if we were to get out of this. I looked behind us and saw there were now two sets of lights.

They weren't giving up.

After a dozen rings Marten came on sounding throaty, as if he'd just rolled out of bed. 'Jesus, Masse, what do you want? You any idea how late it is?' He'd clearly been expecting to hear Masse's voice, so I held the phone out towards the Frenchman, who understood what I wanted right away.

'Marten, *mon pote*!' he shouted over the noise of the engine. 'Talk to my friend Marc, will you? We need your help. Only I'm a little busy right now.'

He nodded and I took the phone away and turned on the hands free so Masse could hear him.

'You brought me in last night,' I reminded Marten, 'and arranged a car.'

'Oh, yeah, I remember. The Yank. I didn't know you and Masse was buddies. What the hell have you two got yourselves into down there? That Masse's normally ready for a long chat, so I figure you must be in a spot of bother.'

'You could say that.'

'Well, no surprise. Would it be anything to do with a couple of guys came by to see me late yesterday? Nice fellas, named Ratch and Dom. They put a bullet through my picture of Mandela and threatened to do nasty stuff to my wife and kid if I didn't tell them where Masse had gone.'

'Think yourself lucky – they usually aim for the head.'

'That's what the skinny greaser said. Sorry . . . that's not politically correct but who gives a shit, right? A Latino with a squinty look about him, anyway.'

'I know him. We met.' Snake-Eyes. Otherwise known as Dom or Domenic. He and Ratchman obviously liked travelling as a pair.

'So what can I do for you?'

When I told him he went quiet for a few seconds. I let him think it over; it probably wasn't every day he got asked to risk life and living for a couple of people he didn't know that well.

'Where are you?'

'About forty minutes north-west out of Mogadishu.' I checked the screen to make sure that Masse had GPS and said, 'Just a second.' I clicked on the GPS finder and read out the coordinates.

Another long pause, then he came back. 'Holy shit, man, that's not good. You're a long way from a decent landing site. Can you make it back to the airstrip where I dropped you?'

'No. Turning back from here is not an option.'

'Right, don't ask. I get it. OK, there's a place I know about a hundred-and-forty Ks, maybe a little more, from your location. It's by the Shebelle

213

River up by Dinlaabe. Masse'll know it well enough. It's used by hunters and a few others I've taken in there from time to time. The road up there is shit but that's Somalia for you. But I got to tell you, man, there's a problem with my plane.'

'What sort of problem?'

'When I got back after dropping you off I nearly went in nose first. The tail assembly's already stripped down and the mechanic found a problem with the rudder cables. He should have the spares tomorrow morning and should only take a few hours tomorrow to fix. But it means you'll have to lie low until first light the day after. Can you do that?'

It was a setback but I couldn't see a way round it. I looked at Masse to see if he had an opinion or whether he thought Marten was spinning a tale to get more money out of us. But he merely looked back and said, 'We can do that.'

I'd have had more confidence in him if he'd tried a little harder to look like he believed it.

I relayed the answer to Marten.

'Great. There's something else. Before I say yes, I need a couple of guarantees from you or Masse. Solid ones, right? Nothing that's going to fade the moment you run into serious shit.'

'Go on.' As if the shit we were in wasn't serious enough already.

'This is like, bad territory where you're headed. Apart from the various clans who hate each other's guts, there's al-fucking-Shabaab and bandits all over the place. Throw in the Somali Government forces and African Union, all chasing the others around every rock and tree like dogs on heat, and I have to say you got yourselves in a bad situation. I usually fly over that shit, not land right in the middle of it.'

'Can you do it or not? If you can't, say so.'

'Hey, man, of course I can do it, no worries. Just sayin' that's all. Sure, they'll see me coming for miles, and if we get stuck on the ground longer than five minutes we're all dead, know what I mean? But yeah . . . it's do-able.'

Do-able. It's a nice word full of maybes. But it was as good as we were going to get. 'Good. What sort of guarantees do you want?'

'If I lose the plane, I'm done. Like, for good. I owe a bundle on it. So that's one thing – the easiest. But I've got a family to look after, too. If I get chopped I want them taken care of. Can you promise me that?'

I thought it over. There was nothing else for it and it was no use bluffing. 'I can't but I know a man who can. I'll have to call you back. But first give me the co-ordinates for this airstrip; we'll make for it anyway and figure something out later.' One thing was certain: we couldn't just hang around where we were.

He gave me the numbers and I signed off and looked across at Masse. He'd heard pretty much all of it and wasn't looking happy, but resigned.

'*Nous sommes foutus,*' he muttered, in that peculiarly Gallic way when a Frenchman thinks he's out of options. 'We are screwed. I cannot promise Marten any of that stuff – my superiors will never go for it.'

'Not even for possession of the hard drive?'

215

'You are joking.' He made a hoarse noise in his throat. He seemed to have trouble getting his thoughts out, but when he did it was in a rush. 'You think Petrus is going to take this back to Paris? Not immediately. He will talk to Lunnberg first, I guarantee it. And the moment the colonel has our location he will send over a drone and *baff* – all his problems will disappear in one hit. You, me and the hard drive, *vaporisé*.'

I didn't like to admit it but he was right. The moment Lunnberg got a fix on our location we'd be sitting ducks for an air strike. And if he could get his hands on a drone – and I wasn't betting against it – neither we nor anybody else would see or hear it coming. For Lunnberg it would be a clean kill with nothing sticking to his hands. If anybody did find the evidence, it would be palmed off as an accident, or a missile gone astray.

'How about this airfield Marten mentioned?' I wanted to focus on the positive rather than what might happen; allowing Masse to wallow wouldn't help us get out of this situation.

'Yes. I think I know it. I've been there once . . . but it's a long way from here.'

'It's our only choice, then.' I got out my phone and dialled Tom Vale. He wasn't going to be pleased because I guessed he'd be in bed, but we were running out of options. I got patched through a duty officer in London, who asked a couple of questions to verify that I wasn't a bored teenager with a spy complex, and heard him rattling a computer keyboard in the background before suggesting I wait. Thirty long seconds later Vale came on, his voice crystal clear.

'Marc. You keep strange hours. I take it this is related to what you told Angela Pryce?' Considering the time of night he sounded surprisingly chipper.

'It is.' I told him where we were and what we were carrying, and how we were hoping to get out of the country. I talked fast because there was a danger we'd lose the signal and I needed his cooperation. Thankfully he was accustomed to urgent messages and didn't waste time asking pointless questions.

'Leave it with me. I'll have my chaps look up this Marten character and make sure he's covered all ways. Tell him he'll be receiving a call. As for your . . . current situation, I can't promise boots on the ground or any of that useful stuff, but I'll have somebody at the Djibouti end casting a watchful eye on Marten's family. Is this hard drive worth it?'

'I haven't seen it, but there are people on the dark side who think so.'

'Then I think that's good enough. Good luck.'

I thanked him and used Masse's phone again. Marten answered immediately and I said, 'You've got your guarantees. You'll be getting a call with the details.'

'A call. Where from?' He sounded sceptical, which was no surprise. He'd probably had enough stress in the last forty-eight hours to last him a lifetime.

'The source is London. A man named Tom Vale. You might like to let him know where your wife and daughter live so they can provide cover, just in case.'

'Christ, man – Marc, is it? You're not spinning a line, are you?'

'No.'

'Sweet. That's a lot of juice you got there. Call me impressed.'

'Just keep it to yourself. Are we on?'

'Damn right, my friend.' He laughed. 'See you at first light day after tomorrow. Only don't be late because this is gonna be a fast pickup with no stops for coffee or a *braai*, you understand me?'

I told him I understood and switched off, and signalled Masse to put his foot down. I checked behind us. The lights were still there and making no attempt to hide. It led to a question that had been bothering me. 'How did they get here from Djibouti?'

Masse shrugged. 'Chinook, probably. I thought I heard one in the distance before I got to the hotel. They had to bring their own transport and a Chinook would have swallowed them easily.'

If that was correct it was an indication of the amount of pull Lunnberg possessed. He'd been able to call up one of the US military's heavy-lift beasts, and they didn't come from a rental company by the hour. I wondered how high he'd had to go to get it signed off. It reinforced Masse's earlier opinion that if Lunnberg wanted to call up a Reaper and drop a missile on our heads, he'd be able to do that, too.

An hour later we made a fast stop-and-change-over. Masse soon fell asleep and began snoring. I noticed his cell phone on the seat beside him and picked it up. Call me nosy but it helped while away the time. I flicked through the numbers dialled list. It wasn't easy to do, given the road we were following, but it was too good a chance to miss. When in doubt, find out. And right now all sorts of doubts were crowding my mind demanding to be settled.

Most of the numbers listed included a name or abbreviated indicator, such as 'cab, 'hair', 'teeth', along with four restaurants and a couple of Paris numbers without names which I figured were either family or other private callers. But among them was a number that had been called several times over the past couple of days. It had no identifier, so I figured it was either a security issue and Masse hadn't wanted to use it, or he knew the number so well he didn't need reminding.

Either way, it was a detail worth checking out.

Masse stirred in his seat and looked out through the windscreen. I dropped the phone by my side to conceal the light and waited. He stared without comment for a minute, then his eyes closed again and his head lolled back against the window. I gave it a count of ten to see if he'd stir again, then checked the screen and memorised the number before switching it off and dropping the phone on the floor by the side of his seat.

Another hour on and the lights behind us had disappeared. They'd either dropped back to give themselves room to plan an attack or were in a fold in the terrain. What I was pretty certain of was that they hadn't given up and gone home.

I shook Masse awake and suggested he get ready to take the wheel again. My eyes were scratchy with tiredness and the layer of dust being stirred up inside the car by the air-con system. I needed some sleep, even if only for a few minutes. Work in this business for long and you soon get in the habit of taking sleep when you can get it.

We made another lightning-fast stop without showing our brake lights, and Masse got quickly back up to speed again. After a couple of minutes he got fidgety and began checking his pockets, slapping his sides and chest with his hand and muttering to himself.

'You got a problem?' I asked.

'My phone,' he confirmed, digging his hand into the back of the passenger seat behind me, then feeling down the side by the transmission bulge, each move threatening to wreck our chances of going any further every time he took his eyes off the road. 'I had it here . . . you know I did. I'll have to stop.' To prove it, he began to slow down.

'Forget it. We don't have time. Keep going and I'll look for it.' I made a show of checking all around my seat and running my hands across the floor, then found his phone and held it up. He snatched it off me and put it away like it was his favourite rabbit's foot, and I wondered why he'd got so worked up.

'Sorry. My mistake.' He threw me a sharp look and I guessed my play-acting had sounded convincing enough to show him I had no idea where his phone had been.

For good measure I leaned across and tapped the fuel display. I had no way of knowing whether me checking through his calls list might have activated an indicator that it had been used since I'd spoken to Marten, but the less he thought about it the better. 'We're down to half a tank. Did you say you've got some spare?'

'Yes. In the back.' He peered at the gauge. 'I'm sure we're good for another thirty minutes on this tank, maybe longer.' He turned and looked back at the darkness behind us. 'We seem to have lost our followers. We can stop soon and refill.'

Refill. It sounded so mundane, so ordinary. Stop, get out, stretch and fill the tank. Like being on a freeway and seeing a BJ bar and grill coming up. Only out here there was nothing like that and the guys we had somewhere on our tail out in the dark would be waiting for the tell-tale flash of our brake lights to know they were in with a chance.

Even as I processed the thought, I heard a bang and the glass by my head shattered and dissolved into a million pieces.

Twenty-Two

I kicked back instinctively in my seat and reached for the SIG while Masse swore loudly and stamped on the gas, making the engine whine in protest. I checked to the rear, but couldn't see any lights. I couldn't see how the two vehicles could have caught up so quickly without us spotting them. Then I noticed a neat hole in the window on Masse's side, which gave me a possible trajectory. The shot must have come from somewhere off to our right flank.

'Are there any other roads out there?' I asked, pointing that way.

He shook his head. 'Roads, no. Nothing but scrub and dead ground . . . maybe the odd track used by herders and traders.' He looked in the mirror and came to the same conclusion as me. 'It can't be the Americans . . . probably bandits or the military.'

Given the choice I was happy to settle for bandits. They would be less disciplined and less heavily armed, and easier to deal with. Government or African Union forces, on the other hand, would opt for bringing a lot of firepower down on us if they thought we were up to no good. But since whoever it was out there had already opened fire, it didn't look as if they were going to stop us first and ask questions anyway.

I brushed the broken glass off my clothes and

used the SIG to knock out the remains of the window, then tried to figure out where the shot had come from. It was difficult getting my bearings because the road here was particularly rough and the pickup was bouncing around on its mushy springs like a half-filled water bed. And although there were a million stars in the sky and no cloud cover, what light there was threw up too many dense patches of shadow to make out anything with clarity. It would have been clearer sticking my head under water in a pool.

Then I heard another shot, and saw a flash out in the dark, followed by twin car lights flicking on a couple of hundred yards away. They were too low to the ground and too small to be a military truck, so I figured I'd got my wish. Bandits.

Moments later the lights were coming in our direction on a converging course. Whoever they were must have been camped by the side of a track and had seen us coming from a long way off. All they'd had to do was wait to make sure we weren't a heavily-armed army truck that could pound them into dust if they tried stopping it, before deciding to send us a warning shot to stop us and see what we were carrying. That hadn't worked so now they were coming in to take a closer look.

I was proved right moments later when we flashed by a narrow turning with the oncoming vehicle lighting us up from barely a hundred yards away. A couple of wild shots came our way but nothing touched us, and I guessed the track they were on was too rough for accurate shooting. But it would only be a matter of time before they got behind us on better ground and got lucky. If they did that, we were done for. If they didn't finish us off, Ratchman and his men certainly would.

We had a couple of options, neither of them great. We could both keep on running and hope the bandits didn't catch us, which seemed unlikely if they knew the roads well; or we could stop and fight. But the second option meant taking on an unknown force, all the time knowing that the SUVs were going to catch up anytime soon to join in the fun. It would be too good to hope that the two sides would leave us alone and take each other on, but there are times when even the most hopeless scenario seems worth consideration.

Masse was coaxing as much speed from the pickup as he could get, and for the moment it seemed to have taken his mind off his phone. I picked up the AK and checked the magazine, which was full, and put some thought into how I was going to do this. I would only get one chance to get this right, otherwise we were both going to be put through the mincer.

Surprisingly, the lights of the new arrival had started to fall behind, and I figured they must be driving a sub-standard vehicle and had relied too heavily on surprise or fear to make us stop. That gave us a slight edge and I told Masse to keep going as fast as he dared.

'Until when?' he demanded, his eyes wide in the muted glow from the dashboard lights. 'We cannot outrun them for ever – not in this terrain.'

'Maybe not,' I agreed. 'If we're lucky they'll get overrun by the two SUVs and blown off the road. Hopefully that will slow the SUVs down until we can find somewhere to hide.'

'And if not?'

'Then we stop and fight. What weapons do you have?'

'A Beretta nine mil. But two magazines only.'

It wasn't anywhere near enough, but it would have to do. Pistols were only ever useful for close-up work; beyond about thirty feet it was just punching holes in the scenery and scaring the birds.

I was staring through the windscreen, evaluating our chances, when I saw what appeared to be a rise in the road up ahead. It was difficult to tell but there was just enough starlight to see the road level against the sky. It wasn't much but it might be the best bit of luck we were going to get.

I pointed ahead. 'Get past the top if this rise and stop the other side.'

'What are you going to do?' His voice rose a notch and I hoped he wasn't going to bug out as soon as I was out of the car. If he tried it, I'd shoot him.

I lifted the AK. 'If we stop to take them on along a flat section of road we won't stand a chance. Behind that hill, I'll have the element of surprise.'

'God, Portman, you're crazy. It will never work.'

'Have you got a better idea? If the men in that pickup are anything like the ones I encountered in Mogadishu, they'll be high on khat and eager to kill. They won't be expecting anybody on foot to jump out at them.' I wasn't entirely sure about the khat aspect of my argument, but the odds were in my favour. 'Get ready to stop when I tell you but don't use the footbrake. We don't want to give them advance notice that we're springing a surprise.'

He still looked at me as if I was nuts, but didn't argue as we hit the first stage of the slope. I checked behind and saw the pickup's lights, yellow and feeble in the distance, bouncing about on the road. Then our engine note began to fall as the momentum dropped, and Masse gave it more gas to take us over the crest and down.

The moment the hood dipped again I unlatched the door and said, 'This will do. Wait for me a couple of hundred metres along and keep the motor running.'

He nodded and switched off all the lights, then hauled on the handbrake lever. I stepped out before the pickup had stopped and watched him drive away. As soon as I was sure he was going to stop, I turned and hoofed it to the crest of the rise and hunkered down to wait. Peering over the top I saw the lights bobbing about in the distance. The noise of the engine was a hum over the night air, but with it came a ragged sound as if struggling to breathe. It might explain why they had taken off after us: they needed a change of transport and we looked like a good target. I figured if they didn't blow up first they'd be here inside a couple of minutes.

I checked the AK and settled myself. And waited.

Twenty-Three

Two miles to the rear, Ratchman was wrestling with tiredness and the wheel, having taken over from Ellison who had promptly fallen asleep against the door in spite of the bumpy ride. The other two men were also getting what rest they could in the rear, occasionally stirring to cast an eye out the back and sides for signs of pursuit.

They were all feeling the effects of their trip from Djibouti and the drive out of Mogadishu. The hot contact near the hotel, in spite of having gone to plan, had put them all on edge. Every time they turned a corner or squeezed down a narrow street lined with darkened buildings, they had expected to find themselves facing an ambush or a blockade. Twice they had spotted other vehicles packed with armed men, and it seemed evident that word had gone out about the gunfight, and groups of bandits or insurgents were now combing the city for the two SUVs.

Although disposing of the gunmen in the pickup had given them a welcome burst of adrenalin and triumph, the downside had soon caught up with them as they drove out of the city and into the dark of the open countryside. Out here there was no guarantee that they were safe because they were still in bandit territory, as open to attack for no other reason than being an interesting target for whoever wanted to take the

SUVs, or a military patrol wanting to check their credentials.

Getting free of the city had brought welcome relief and a chance of relaxation. Catching up with Dom and the other men hadn't taken long, and the two SUVs were now a quarter of a mile apart, with at least one set of eyes in each vehicle alert for signs of trouble.

Dom's car had suffered minor damage earlier after being side-swiped by a pickup driven by a single man, and for a few minutes he had lost sight of it as he'd struggled to regain the wheel and get back on solid ground. But then brake lights had flared ahead of them as the other vehicle had skidded to stop and another man had appeared from a deserted building and jumped aboard before it had taken off again. It had to have been Portman, but Dom had been forced to jump out and kick part of the ripped fender out from the front wheel before continuing. By then, the other vehicle had disappeared.

Ratchman, at the time nearly half a mile behind, had received the news in silence. If they'd been travelling in closer formation they might have been able to do something about it. But they had lost that initiative and would have to catch the other vehicle as soon as they could. He'd told Dom to fall back and then leap-frogged him, telling him to keep up as best he could.

Now he was focussed on getting some more speed out of the SUV. He'd already caught a glimpse of tail lights up ahead, and figured maybe ten minutes until contact, maybe fifteen at most if the pickup noticed they were coming and put on speed, too.

He checked his watch. It would soon be time for him to report in. Lunnberg was getting more demanding the longer this went on, but since he was the one paying their wages, it was his call. The sooner they got what they had come for, the sooner they could head for home and be out of this shithole of a wasteland.

Before he could reach for his phone, it rang. He picked it up and checked the screen. No caller ID. 'Yeah?'

'What have you got? Something good, I hope.' Damned if it wasn't Lunnberg, jumping the gun. He sounded alert and ready and, as always, impatient for news.

'We're on Portman's tail and we think he's got Masse with him.' Ratchman explained what they had found at the office building.

'Was it McBride?'

'No idea. I never met the guy. The body was too far gone to tell. He was white, though; that's all I can say.'

'Then it must have been him. Pity.' In spite of the word, Lunnberg sounded unmoved by the revelation, as if the man's death was no more than a figure to be written off and forgotten, dropped casually into the 'lost' column of whatever ledger men like him liked to keep. 'You destroyed the evidence?'

'Done and gone.'

'And the hotel?'

'We drew a blank; if Masse or Portman had

been there, they'd skipped town. We had a little trouble from some local bozos, but the boys dusted them down good. We're currently following Portman north-west into open country.'

'North-west? There's nothing out that way but rocks and bushes.'

Ratchman didn't waste time asking Lunnberg how he knew that; the colonel would have checked the terrain for himself already. 'I'm not sure what he's doing. Could be he knows of another landing strip like the one he came in on, or maybe he figures he can continue running until we lose interest and go home.'

'That's not going to happen.' Lunnberg's voice was flat, leaving no room for argument.

'I figured. Either way they won't get far. They're driving a crappy little pickup on a lousy road, so we can take them whenever we want.'

'Not yet. Follow them, keep them on your radar but don't hit them until I say so.'

Ratchman was surprised by the change of tactic. 'Is there a problem? I thought you wanted these two dead and buried first chance we got.'

'I do. But I've been thinking, this man Portman could present us with a problem. He's known in Langley and I have to find out whether he's been in contact with them recently. If he has and he's being tracked, his disappearance will bring down a lot of heat on our heads. When you do it, you might have to be creative, so it looks like a third-party hot contact.'

'Bandits, you mean? That shouldn't be too difficult; there are plenty around here. We can dress it up to look like Portman and the Frog strayed into the wrong kind of people, no question.'

'That would be ideal. Don't worry – you'll get your chance. I'll be in touch.'

Ratchman signed off and dropped the phone in his pocket with a feeling of irritation. He figured maybe Lunnberg had been too long out of the field and had forgotten how unpredictable these situations could be. Like they could just hang back until he decided what to do, then sail up unseen alongside Portman and Masse and blast them off the road. Yeah, just like in the movies.

Lunnberg's call had woken the other three men, and they were sitting up and checking their weapons. Nobody was speaking because there was nothing to say. It was Ellison who eventually spotted something and broke the silence. 'Boss, is that them up ahead?'

'Who else?' said Carson from the rear seat. 'Ain't nobody but us fools out here.'

Ellison grabbed a pair of binoculars from the glove box and struggled to get a fix while bouncing around in his seat. Then he said, 'I'm not so sure. It's a different light array.'

Ratchman looked at him. 'Are you kidding?'

'No, I'm not. My uncle Ned had an auto dealership and I got to recognise them when I was a kid, especially on pickups and small trucks. Never lost the habit, either. That one's too far off to tell what it is for sure but it's not the one we've been following from the city.'

Ratchman leaned forward and peered into the dark at the tiny specks of red light up ahead. Damned if he could tell what they were, but if

Ellison said they were different it was good enough for him.

'It must have joined this road somewhere. Whoever they are, they're in our way but they might be useful.' He turned to Ellison and said, 'Call Dom and tell him to close up on us and have his guys awake and ready. We'll use the vehicle up ahead for cover until we get word from Lunnberg, then we take them both out.'

Ellison nodded and got on the phone, and got an affirmative that the men in the other car were primed and ready to go.

Ratchman said, 'Carson, you got that rifle ready?' Carson was their nominated sharpshooter, and came equipped with an M4A1 carbine and the eye of a professional hunter.

'Sure have, boss. What's the plan?'

'When we get the word, I'll get up close to the vehicle in front, then stop long enough for you to hit them with a few rounds. If that doesn't work we'll hit them hard and fast and take them off the road. Then we go straight on through and hit Portman. I'll slow down now so you can get in the back. Jesse, you go too.'

'Sounds good to me.' Carson grinned in the back and opened his window ready to climb out. The rear cargo area would be an ideal gun platform for shooting when the time came, and not the first time he'd used one like it. The moment the speed dropped and Ratchman gave him the nod, he passed his rifle to Jesse and slid out, swinging himself with ease into the back. Then he took the rifle from his colleague, who followed him out and got ready to back him up.

As the cold night air flooded the vehicle, the mood among all four men lifted at the thought of impending action.

Twenty-Four

Back in Djibouti, Colonel Lunnberg's mood wasn't quite so upbeat. He dropped his phone on the bed and stared out across the dark waters of the gulf with a growing sense of frustration. He was wondering how long this was going to take. They should have had this mess wrapped up a couple of days ago, instead of which here they were chasing shadows around Somalia and still no closer to retrieving the hard drive and disposing of the evidence that could see them all locked up for many years if it went public.

He swore mildly at the nagging thought and eyed the navigation lights of a frigate sitting offshore. It was here on escort duties for a French aircraft carrier and helped monitor air movements over the region, and he almost envied its air of detachment and serenity. Almost but not quite. Lunnberg had never been one for sitting still for long, and he wasn't going to sit and wait for this business to play out without taking action. Doing nothing wasn't an option in his book, even if it meant going against the wishes of those above him when the opportunity presented itself.

He dialled a number in Virginia and got through to a contact named Henry Seibling, a senior analyst in the sprawling intelligence community housed in several high-security buildings among the tree-studded landscape.

Seibling owed Lunnberg for a favour the colonel had performed for him two years before. It wasn't much in Lunnberg's view, just a nod and a wink towards some developing markets that had enabled the man to make a quick buck and plan for an early retirement. But Lunnberg never did favours for nothing, and he figured now was the time to collect. He needed information about Portman, and Seibling, who worked in the bowels of a section dealing with highly sensitive human records, was the source who could get it.

'Clay?' Even in a single word Seibling's voice became instantly guarded, and Lunnberg figured the analyst had been hoping this was a call that he would never have to take. 'This is a surprise.'

I bet it is, thought Lunnberg savagely. And right now you're sitting in your nice BarcaLounger at home, wondering why I'm calling and trying not to mess your pants as you figure it out. 'Henry, I must apologise for this late call,' he said smoothly, 'but I have a little favour to ask.'

'What kind of favour?'

'I need some information on an individual.'

'Well now,' said Seibling carefully, a nervous tone entering his voice. 'I don't know about that, Clay. You know I can't access personnel files . . .'

'I'm not asking you to do that. This person is not a government employee, so I'm not expecting you to break any rules. I just need to know if he's currently – how do I say this – *attached* to any of the agencies in any way. That's all.'

'I see. What's this about? I mean, I'm very grateful to you for your past help, as you know, but—' his voice dropped a notch to a whisper, which meant he was hoping his wife couldn't hear him – 'there's a lot of risk involved here. I can't simply enter the name in a search engine and give you what you want. It's not like using Google – there are audit trails and internal firewalls that stop me going above a certain level.'

'Marc Portman, Henry,' Lunnberg continued heavily, ignoring the excuses. 'He's a private contractor and gun for hire who has worked for the agency on at least one occasion that I know. All I need you to tell me is, does he still have a connection to them?'

'Connection?' Seibling's voice became a squeak at the word, revealing his fears. To him, the only connections worth worrying about were the people in power on the upper floors of the building; the men and women who could make a career, but also end it by rooting out at will and send to jail anyone caught doing anything not in accordance to the rules of the job. 'What do you mean?'

'Does he have a current contract?'

'Well, like I just told you—'

Lunnberg brushed his words aside with an impatient snap. 'I'll call back in one hour, Henry. That should give you plenty of time. I know you can get to your office inside twenty minutes from where you live, and I know you keep unconventional hours like so many of your colleagues, so please don't disappoint. I'm sure you would hate Catherine to find out that her retirement is likely to be very lonely with you gone. And visiting hours in our correction facilities are so inconvenient.'

'*What*?'

Lunnberg disconnected and set his phone timer.

Not that he needed it but he liked the idea of precision when it came to applying pressure on individuals. It let them know that he wasn't fooling around.

Next he rang James Warren. He hadn't heard from the power broker for a while, which always made him nervous. Non-military types lived by different rules to those in or out of uniform, and while they enjoyed playing by the slow rules of commerce, Lunnberg needed to know what was happening at the top end of the operation.

'Mr Warren's office.' A soft female voice answered and Lunnberg hesitated, feeling a tingle of alarm. He'd dialled Warren's private cell phone as always – the one Warren used for strictly off-the-books discussions – and had expected to hear the man's voice. Nobody, but nobody else had ever answered before.

'I'd like to speak to James, please,' he said. 'It's urgent.'

'I'm sorry, but he's not available right now. May I ask who's calling?'

'That isn't necessary, ma'am. As I said, this is an urgent matter and I need to talk with him.' He found he was gripping the phone like a vice and forced himself to relax. 'When will he be . . . available?'

'I'm not sure, sir. Can I take a message? I'm certain he won't be long. If you would like to give me your number, I'll—'

Lunnberg ended the call and resisted hurling the phone across the room. Something was wrong; he could feel it in every fibre of his being. Over the years he had developed the hunter's instinct for knowing when the suits in and around Washington were stalling or making a change of plan. But for a man like Warren to allow somebody else to use his private phone, this wasn't just a stall; it had to be bad news.

He left his room and hurried down to the ground floor, where he found the night porter signing in a late arrival.

'Yes, sir?' the man said, when the guest had gone.

'I need a drink.' Lunnberg figured the bars were closed, but he didn't care. Right now he needed something to occupy his mind. He pulled out some folded notes and pushed them into the porter's hand. 'Whisky. Neat. A large one.'

The porter nodded gracefully and pocketed the money. 'Of course, sir. Should I bring it on the terrace?'

Lunnberg nodded. The terrace would be fine. It would be cool and swept by the night breeze coming off the Gulf, and seated among the carefully tended palms would be the ideal place to calm his nerves and think.

Two stiff whiskies and three tours of the terrace later, his phone alarm buzzed. He called Seibling. A woman's voice answered, and he guessed it was the analyst's wife; she sounded distraught.

'Henry's been detained,' she muttered tearfully, when he asked to speak to her husband. 'He went to the office to get something and there was some kind of alert.' Her voice rose to a shrill note as if voicing the words had just made her realise the enormity of what this meant for her husband. 'He's being questioned by internal security officers!'

Lunnberg swore silently and ended the call without identifying himself. Seibling had messed up somehow and got himself caught. But he felt no sympathy for the man. He had been quick enough to accept the chance of making some fast money when it arose, and now things had gone bad. He thought back about the phone he'd used to call the man and the possibility that Seibling might rat him out. The phone was untraceable and he'd been very careful to leave no trace of ever having been in contact with the man before. He might face a few questions if Seibling did try to implicate him, but as far as he was concerned it would be a dead end.

He immediately dialled Ratchman's number. It was time to close this down. Whether Portman was connected or not no longer mattered. He had to disappear and fast.

'You have a go,' he said, when Ratchman answered, his voice faint against the noise of the car engine. 'Take them out and lose them.'

'You got it,' Ratchman replied. 'Going in now.'

Twenty-Five

I waited for the incoming vehicle to get closer. It was taking its time, and I wondered if they were stalling to wait for reinforcements from the north. If they did that we were in danger of being trapped on a narrow road with nowhere to run but left or right. I wasn't sure what kind of terrain lay out there, but I was betting the pickup Masse had acquired wasn't built for it and would probably fall apart before we'd gone very far.

I turned and checked the road behind me to see if anybody was approaching from that direction, and cocked an ear to the night air. Apart from a faint rumble from the pickup Masse was driving, nothing else stirred and no lights showed anywhere along the road.

I turned back and found the buzz of the oncoming engine gradually changing as it got closer, from the tinny hum with that ragged sound in the background we'd heard earlier, to a heavier rattle and the throb of a loose exhaust system that sounded terminal.

When I estimated it to be about four hundred yards away I knelt on the crest of the rise and lifted the AK to my shoulder. The vehicle was outlined now against a cloud of dust billowing up in its wake like a shroud, and even in the poor light I could see it was an open pickup with a group of men in the back holding onto the frame, their weapons raised in readiness.

I counted it down to three hundred yards, then placed two rounds in the radiator grill just above the centre line. The idea was to cause maximum system damage and not simply to hit the engine block, which might easily deflect the shots. I needed them to stop and stop dead, rather than keep on rolling. I didn't wait to see the result but crabbed across to the other side of the road and took up another position in case any of the men had noted my muzzle flash.

For a second nothing happened. Then the pickup swerved violently. I guessed the driver must have realised belatedly that his crappy engine wasn't entirely to blame for the double bang and that he was actually taking incoming fire. He seemed about to lose control, but instinct must have told him there was nowhere to go without risking hitting soft earth off the road and rolling over, and he evidently managed to grab the wheel back in time and keep it level. From the way the engine continued running I realised that whatever I'd hit wasn't going to be enough.

They were close enough now for me to hear a lot of yelling, and a second later the men in the back began spraying the top of the slope with gunfire. I heard the zip of rounds going high over my head and rolled away to take up another position. As I did so I saw dust kicked up by some lucky shots right where I'd been lying.

This was getting serious. None of the men on board was in any position to take careful aim, so it could only have been random shots that had come my way. But if you spray off sufficient fire-power you'll eventually get lucky and hit something, proving that random can kill, too. I rolled again and took aim, this time dead centre at the windshield on the driver's side, and squeezed the trigger.

By now the pickup was still on flat ground but close to the beginning of the rise. If it didn't stop now, in about ten or fifteen seconds I was going to have them right alongside me. But I needn't have worried. Suddenly the engine died and the wheels went crazy. A couple of figures flipped out of the back as the pickup tipped over and skidded sideways across the road, the screech of rending metal echoing all the way to me in the night air.

It was time to go.

I was turning to run down the slope to join Masse when some of the dust cloud that had followed the pickup cleared to reveal a set of powerful lights about a quarter of a mile behind. And just behind them, another set.

It had to be the SUVs. And they were coming up fast.

I stood up to give myself some elevation and aimed over the wreck of the pickup at the first car and fired twice. It probably wouldn't do any damage at this distance, but if it made them think twice it might give us a few vital minutes while they cleared the pickup and got back on the road.

Even as I thought it, I saw the flash of muzzle fire from the first SUV and figured he was shooting at the pickup and hadn't yet realised what had happened or that I was here. All he wanted to do was get them out of the way.

When somebody by the pickup began to return fire I thought good luck with that and turned and jogged down the slope to where Masse was waiting with the engine ticking over.

Twenty-Six

'What the hell!' Ratchman swore loudly as a shot came out of nowhere and slammed into the bodywork, taking out one of the front lights and blowing a ragged hole in the wing. 'Carson, hit them now!' He slowed down to give Carson a steady platform for firing, all the time wondering what they were running into. Whoever or whatever lay behind the cloud of dust up ahead, it was opposition they had to deal with – and do it fast. Then the dust began to thin out and revealed that the tail lights had disappeared. Had they gone off-road or what?

'Where are they?' he shouted.

'Something's happened,' said Ellison, his head out of the window for a better view. 'I think they crashed but I can't see shit in this dust.'

Moments later Carson ducked his head inside the vehicle and confirmed it. 'Dunno what the hell's going on up there, boss, but it looks like they flipped over and are side-on across the road.'

'Did you do that?' Ratchman shouted back.

'I hit 'em, sure, but not that good. Maybe it spooked the driver and he panicked – I can't tell.' He swore as a round cracked by overhead. Bringing up his rifle he began firing again with a steady thump-thump of rounds reaching out to the crashed vehicle and the figures around it.

Ratchman said to Ellison, 'Get Dom to come

alongside. When we get closer, we split up and go off the road, one on each side to catch them in a pincer movement. But tell him to take it easy – we don't want any busted axles. And keep the line open for further instructions.'

'Got it.' Ellison got on the phone and relayed the message to Dom in the car behind. Moments later Dom was alongside them with one of his men firing from the back of the vehicle ready to accompany Carson. For a while they held that formation, then Ratchman saw clear space at the side of the road.

'Hold on tight!' he warned, and turned off, bumping over the rougher terrain and ploughing through clumps of tangled brushwood and coarse grass while Dom took his cue and did the same.

It worked. The men in the crashed vehicle stopped shooting and began to run as they saw that the two approaching attackers were going to outflank them on both sides. One of them turned and fired twice in haste, but a lucky shot from Carson knocked him off his feet.

'OK, back on the road!' Ratchman shouted, and both SUVs began to make for the hard surface again. Moments later they were less than a hundred yards from the pickup and slowing down, using their lights on full beam to illuminate the scene.

'Yeah!' Carson shouted, and banged his fist on the roof. 'Get closer and I'll nail them!'

Just as he spoke, a figure rose up from behind the pickup and opened fire with a handgun, emptying the magazine and retreating up the slope, before being hit by a volley of shots from Dom's vehicle.

'Carson's been hit!' Jesse yelled. He grabbed his colleague as he crumpled slowly onto the floor, his carbine clattering down the windscreen and across the hood. Carson's feet were drumming frantically against the back of the cab and he was threshing around in a panic. *'He's coughing blood!'*

Ratchman hit the brakes. 'Ellison, go help the others clear that fucking heap of shit out of the way. I'll see to Carson.' He jumped out and ran round to the back just as Carson's head rolled to the side, his eyes open and sightless. Even in the poor light he could see the black shadow of a bullet hole in his throat oozing a thick layer of blood running down into his shirt.

He stood up and looked around as a single gunshot sounded off to the left, then another further away. Then silence. He had a churning feeling deep in his gut as he turned back to a man he'd known and worked with for several years. It was too late for Carson but they still had to clear the road and get through. There would be time for regrets later.

Dom arrived on the run, an assault rifle across his chest, and stared down at the body. 'Jeez, how did that happen? They were nothing but fucking rag-head bandits!'

'Doesn't matter who they were or how it happened – it just did. Let's get on with the job.'

Twenty-Seven

'What happened back there?' Masse demanded, working the gears to take us out of there at maximum speed. It wasn't as fast as I'd have liked but we were moving and unscathed; you live for small victories like these and hope they keep coming.

'Bandits down, one,' I said briefly, 'but the SUVs are still coming and not far behind.'

He didn't say anything to that, but focussed on the road ahead. I knew what he was doing: he was winding through the route inside his head and checking the cut-offs and holes in the ground we could head for and wait for the trouble to go on by.

I checked the AK to see if it was holding up. I had no idea when it had been used last, but it seemed to be living up to the brand reputation for durability. I just hoped we didn't have to make a stand in a drag-out fight, because we simply didn't have the weaponry or ammunition between us to last for more than a few minutes.

Our main problem other than getting caught was finding somewhere to hold up for a full day, then a night. In open countryside with few roads and too many bad people, it was going to be a tough one. But since we didn't have anybody to call on other than Marten, there was no point getting defeatist. If there was one skill I had, it was keeping my head down.

'How long will it take to get to Dinlaabe?' I asked.

He waved a hand. 'Three hours if we're lucky. Who can tell in this country?'

Three hours. It was too long; it would be sunrise in a couple of hours max and we'd be caught out in the open if we didn't manage to find cover before then. I checked the rear again but saw nothing. The SUVs had either been held up by the crashed pickup or they were playing it cute and driving without lights. It was a risky strategy, but they were playing for keeps.

After a while we caught up with a heavy truck being followed closely by an open 4WD containing four men in camouflage uniforms. The truck was holding the centre of the road and didn't look like wanting to move over. The men in the 4WD turned to stare at us, shielding their eyes against our lights and looking edgy.

'Armed escort,' Masse explained. 'The truck drivers pay them so they can travel by night and earn double wages, but not many drivers want to risk it. We have to get past them or they will slow us down.'

'Can we push past?' We had to get past them without getting shot or the SUVs would be sitting right on our tail. The way the men in the back were eyeing us and brandishing their weapons, and the position of the truck in the centre of the road, it didn't look likely, but we had no choice.

'Sure. You'd better cover your head.'

I did so and Masse hit the horn and pulled up close behind the 4WD, then turned on the interior light and cut the headlights.

248

When the men saw that we weren't a bunch of thugs packing guns or RPGs, they waved us to go by and flashed their lights to warn the truck driver we were coming. It might have given me more confidence if they hadn't all been grinning and crowding over to see if we got mashed under the truck's wheels and spat off to the side of the road in a mangled heap.

Masse put the headlights back on and hit the gas, taking us up level then past the 4WD, the men in the back slapping their hands against the side of the vehicle in encouragement. It was a tense moment. All it would take was one man to get nervous and we could find ourselves coming under fire. But that wasn't the worst of it; the truck driver wasn't playing the game and held his position, leaving less than half a car's width to get by. It wasn't going to be enough; I could see soft sand and rocks at the edge of the road, neither of which would do our vehicle any favours if we went off the hard top.

I'd reckoned without Masse's expertise in this part of the world. He leaned on the horn until he got the truck driver's attention, then began to ease up to within touching distance of the rear wheels and began flashing his lights. For a while nothing happened. I could see the driver watching us in his side mirror but he didn't seem to care. When he began opening and closing his mouth in an obvious shout, I figured he was finally getting the message; if we came off the road he probably wouldn't escape unscathed – and he was trying to get a delivery made.

The moment he eased over, Masse hit the gas

pedal and took us through, a volley of stones and coarse sand clattering against the bodywork from the truck's tyres, accompanied by a heavy blast of exhaust fumes and dark smoke.

It was a close call. The pickup was shaking in the displacement effect caused by the large truck body, but we made it and got a long blast on the horn from the driver. Fortunately, we didn't meet anybody coming the other way.

Masse eased off the pedal once we had left the truck behind and looked across at me. 'Reminds me of the *Périphérique*,' he said, referring to the boulevard around Paris which to most foreigners had all the atmosphere and appeal of a deadly chariot race. He gave a short laugh. It was the happiest I'd seen him so far.

An hour later a faint glow began to show over our right shoulder. It would soon be dawn and our chances of finding cover were narrowing fast. We also had to feed the fuel tank and we couldn't do that by stopping at the side of the road.

'I have it,' Masse said suddenly, and began to slow down. 'There's a village about ten kilometres ahead. It's big enough to hide in if we find the right spot. I don't think they will risk attacking us there.'

'It's your turf,' I said. 'Let's do it.' I had a feeling that whatever lead we might have gained on the SUVs would be narrowed down very quickly once they got past the crash site. If we weren't concealed by then, it would be too late to do anything.

We passed a few isolated huts made of a variety of materials, their shapes resembling upturned bowls, but nothing large enough to offer any kind of shelter for the pickup. The road dipped and began to run through a shallow depression, giving us shadowy glimpses of straggly *dhirindhir* bushes and acacia trees caught in the headlights on either side. It felt good to sink below the skyline behind us; whatever time we gained out of sight would give us a slight edge to find somewhere to disappear for the rest of tonight and the next day.

'It's just up ahead,' said Masse, and began to slow down.

Just then my phone buzzed. I checked the screen. No caller I.D. I tried to think who, among the very small group of people with this number, might be calling at this time of night. Whatever the guess, I would have been wrong.

'Watchman, come in.'

I had one of those incredulous moments, when logic tells you it can't be so; that whatever you're going through has only a set number of possibilities, and anything outside that simply doesn't compute. It's a temporary thing, like picking up your phone on vacation in a foreign country and finding somebody from way back in your past wanting to play catch-up.

Then I remembered who the person speaking worked for. 'Now that's a welcome voice. Hi, Lindsay.' I know, not exactly smooth, but it was late and I was tired. Sue me.

Lindsay Citera, a young comms specialist with the CIA, works deep in the heart of their Langley HQ surrounded by computers and screens and breathing the sterile atmosphere of all such

251

environments, where clean is essential if only to give a feeling of stark efficiency. Unlike most comms specialists I'd worked with, most of them top rate, Lindsay was on another plane; she had helped me out of a number of hot spots in the past by her skills with maps, satellite systems, signals know-how and calm resourcefulness in moments of extreme tension.

'We figured you could use some help,' she replied. 'And before you ask, the comms are secure.'

I wasn't going to, but it was good to know. Modern end-to-end encryption technology means communication between users can now be made secure very easily, especially for short-term periods, after which a hack might be possible. But I figured if anyone had the highest grade military systems available to make that unlikely, it would be the CIA.

'We?'

'Mr Vale alerted us to your situation and Brian Callahan assigned me to assist. Can you confirm if this is your location?' She spoke calmly and read out a series of numbers, and I checked on my cell phone for the GPS position. The numbers were correct.

'You're tracking my phone?'

There was a smile in her voice. 'I am now. Smart, huh? You're a long way from home. In fact, out in the boonies.' Her self-control in moments of stress was impeccable, and one of her strengths. It went a long way to helping see through the problems of a situation, and giving guidance to get an operative out of a sticky spot with the minimum of chatter. 'Are you currently with Mr Masse?'

Tom Vale had been busy. He must have had the report from Angela Pryce and given Callahan and his bosses a full briefing on where I was and what I was doing. I told her yes. 'I thought this was a non-recognised situation.' I meant there was no official involvement for the CIA because whatever was happening here was strictly a French affair along with a little-publicised partnership with Colonel Lunnberg and his bunch of DCS pirates.

Turns out I was wrong.

'I'm authorised to tell you that there has been no sanction by the US government for what is happening right now. Colonel Lunnberg is being recalled to Washington for discussions regarding his activities in the region and the French have been notified that any American involvement is withdrawn with immediate effect.'

That sounded like a painful situation on both counts. Somebody in the administration had to have taken an executive decision to pull out of the deal and sever all ties with the French, risking a government-level row in the process. Otherwise known as a hand-cleansing operation, it would no doubt be touchy for a while on the back-channel diplomatic scene, but that was better than having all the dirty laundry aired in the media. As for Lunnberg himself, he was probably wondering what lay in store for him back in Washington. 'That's good to hear. What about his men? They're on our tail and anxious to do nasty things to us.'

'Unfortunately, his men are beyond our reach. Lunnberg claims they are out of comms contact and can't be recalled.'

'Are they official?'

'Absolutely not. They're contractors hired by Lunnberg against official policy. I'm authorised to tell you that at least two of them are currently the subject of investigation for alleged war crimes, and will be arrested the moment they return to a point at which they can be intercepted.'

Great. Official language for saying they would be arrested as long as somebody saw them. The reality was that they would probably vanish like smoke before that could happen. Out of sight, out of the news.

'Who are they?' It didn't really make much difference at this stage, but any information gave me an insight to what we were facing.

'The group leader is Vincent Ratchman, known as "Ratch" – a former paratrooper with the 82nd Airborne. His 2 i/c is Domenic Morales, an ex-marine. They are the two under investigation. The others have no records other than having each done tours in Afghanistan and Iraq both as serving military and as private contractors. They haven't been judged to have broken any laws as far as we can see.'

'That reminds me, there's something you might care to check out for me.' I explained about the body I'd found in the office block in Mogadishu, and the barcode sewn into the belt. 'I'll send you a snapshot and maybe your tech section could decode it.'

'Of course. You think he was American?'

'Masse seems to think so. I think it might be McBride.'

'I see. Anything else I can do?'

'An armed drone or two would be nice – maybe a fighter plane if you could rustle one up.' She had once arranged for a Russian fighter to intervene on my behalf on an operation in Ukraine, but I couldn't see that happening here.

'Sorry. No fighters. If I had a drone for surveillance, you'd get it. But don't lose hope; I'm working on sourcing a spare out of Djibouti so we can see what's happening on the ground down there. What's your situation right now?'

I gave her a brief run-down of events since leaving Mogadishu, and what we were up against if we didn't manage to avoid the two SUVs and make our way to the extraction point to meet Marten. For now we were going to have to find a hole and wait out the following day and night before proceeding to the rendezvous. If we got there too early, it would increase the risk of the opposition finding us and making any extraction impossible.

She listened without interrupting, and when I ran dry said, 'I understand. I hope to have eyes over you at first light. Do you have any materials?'

I smiled. She meant weapons. Whether we were armed or not, there was nothing she could do about it other than keeping her fingers crossed. But she wanted to know for herself and I appreciated it. Like many operatives in the field, I'd worked with some comms people in the past who were strictly business and never asked questions they could not affect in any way. That was fine and a product of sound training. But it sometimes left the person at the sharp end feeling a little vulnerable and uncared-for.

'We're good,' I confirmed.

Just then Masse waved a hand in front of my face and pointed through the windshield. A cluster of small buildings had showed up in the lights, and it looked like we were approaching the outskirts of the village he'd mentioned earlier.

'Time to go,' I told Lindsay.

'Copy that. Be safe. I'll be in touch.'

As I switched off, Masse looked at me. 'Who was that?'

'A friend in high places. Unfortunately, not high enough to help our situation right now, so we're on our own.'

'Did you mention drones?'

'Yes. Wishful thinking on my part. It won't happen unless we get really lucky. But you should be prepared to hear that there is no further mission to engage with al-Shabaab or anybody else in oil negotiations. That activity is now dead in the water.'

'Seriously?' He sounded shocked.

'Seriously. And to make double sure, the men following us have been disowned and two of them are awaiting arrest on charges of war crimes. Looks like everybody is retrenching fast and covering their asses.'

He shook his head but didn't say anything. I figured he was thinking about what would happen to him now the deal looked sunk. With nothing more to work on, he was more or less out of an assignment.

'So Lunnberg might call them off?'

This time it was wishful thinking on his part. 'Not a chance. I think they've been given orders to finish it and eliminate any loose talk. By that I mean us.'

Twenty-Eight

We entered the village through a section of closely-packed, single-storey houses – a sort of outer ring of dwellings. Some were of rough sandstone bricks, many were made up of sheet metal and other fabrics. There were no signs of the inhabitants, only clusters of goats, a few donkeys and emaciated cows and even a camel or two. If anybody was in, they had heard us coming some way off and were keeping their heads down.

When we hit the village proper, which was dense, untidy and spread across a couple of low-lying slopes like a rash, Masse slowed down, looking for something off to his left. We passed a couple of more substantial buildings, which I guessed were – or had been – local administration offices of some kind, then a compound with a high wall and double gates.

'Police barracks,' he said briefly. 'But nobody is there now. They kept being attacked so they gave up and moved into a military camp thirty kilometres to the west.'

I considered it briefly as we drove by. In most circumstances it would have been a useful place to hide; high walls and plenty of cover. But it would be way too obvious for Ratchman and his men to pass up without taking a closer look. Once they got inside they would be on a man hunt and we'd be trapped behind the

258

same high walls that were supposed to be our protection.

'Ah, I remember,' Masse breathed, and turned down a zigzag street closely bordered by houses, the engine noise pounding off the walls. If we'd hoped to enter the village unnoticed, forget that; everybody and his uncle must have been listening to us go by.

More twists and turns and the road began to rise, then dipped again down a slope to emerge in an open expanse of broken ground littered with refuse. The light seemed better here and signalled that dawn was coming up fast. We hadn't got long to find some cover and disappear.

I caught a glimpse of a junkyard full of wrecked vehicles, some of them in camouflage green with the remnants of regimental colours on the sides. They looked as if they had been in a war and I figured they'd been abandoned by whoever had once owned them.

Masse read my mind. 'Somali and African Union army vehicles,' he said. 'They get attacked and damaged and the army leaves them behind. It's cheaper and easier to get foreign aid to supply new ones than to retrieve and repair these. The locals sell what they can and cannibalise the rest. It's part of the circular economy.'

He swung the wheel and took us behind a row of wrecked trucks and stopped the pickup between a broken low-loader and a large tractor unit without wheels or an engine.

'We must hide the vehicle,' he said, and jumped out and scouted around until he found two old tarpaulins stretched over an engine block perched on a stand to offer protection against the sun. He pulled out a knife and slashed through the ropes holding them, and slung one of the tarps across the cab of the pickup weighed down by a couple of truck wheels. Then he grabbed a cloth bag from the back and beckoned me to follow him.

I picked up my stuff and trekked after him. He'd done well and done it quick; looking back, the pickup now looked like any old wreck, with the truck wheels on top of the tarp adding to the picture of a vehicle at the end of its life. Masse led the way through another gap in the fence to the side of the compound, and across an open space to the warehouse I'd spotted earlier.

'This is deserted,' Masse said. 'Nobody uses it. We'll be safe here.' Up close it was less impressive than it had first appeared, and looked as if it had been thrown together using spare materials, although I was guessing it had been originally government built. It had no windows but two large double doors, and looked like a grain or foodstuff storage area, maybe erected many years ago at a time of drought. Either way, it looked like being our refuge until it was safe to move on.

As Masse went to step through a gap in the doors, I heard a faint hum coming across the rooftops.

'Wait,' I said. This had the same makings of a trap as the abandoned police barracks. From what little I'd seen, this village had only two large buildings, and we were now standing outside one of them. Ratchman would take one look at them and send in his men like rat catchers. He might miss the pickup hidden among the wrecked trucks, but he'd scour this place from top to bottom to find us.

'Why? It's perfect.'

'No. It's not. Hang on – I have a better idea.' I ran back to the junkyard and pulled the second tarp down from over the engine block, then hunted around until I found a piece of a truck fender. I hurried to the back of the yard where it merged into scrappy bushes and rocks leading to another section of scattered housing. I selected a patch of ground close behind a *dhirindhir* bush and scooped out a shallow depression from the sandy soil. I threw the tarp down over the top and weighed it in place with dirt and a few rocks, then for good measure tossed a handful of twigs on top. As foxholes go it wasn't great but it would have to do.

Next I checked the ground as far back as the first houses huddled together behind a line of stick fencing. I could smell animals on the far side and heard them shifting about nervously as I approached. Cows or goats, I figured, but I didn't want to get too close and spook them. What I needed to do was check out the area to see if there was an exit point in case we had to bust out and run.

I followed the fence until I found a section where the sticks had been pulled away. Beyond it lay a narrow alley between two houses. There was already a faint glow in the sky to the east, and although I couldn't see what lay beyond the alley, it was something we would have to take as we found it, good or bad.

Masse was following and giving me his hard-time stare. 'Portman, what are you doing?' he hissed, and looked around nervously.

'Looking for an escape route in case we're blown. This is it.' I indicated the alley. 'Remember this spot. If we have to, we go down the alley and hide out as best we can. The first chance we get, we make for the front of the junkyard and the pickup and get out of here.'

I turned and started walking back to the foxhole. Time was getting tight and we had maybe five minutes left. Masse followed close behind, tripping over the occasional rock or clump of coarse grass and muttering to himself. He may have lived out here for years, but I got the feeling he hadn't been much of an explorer in all that time and preferred the city life.

'I understand what you are saying,' he continued, 'but the . . . the hole you dug; it's out in the open. They will see us immediately! We need to be inside four walls where we can protect ourselves and form a – what is it – a defensive position.'

'Have you never heard of hiding in plain sight?' I said, and held the tarp up so he could slide underneath without disturbing too much of the dirt and stones. Then I slid in alongside him and made sure the AK was ready to hand in case I needed it. 'This is the best position, I promise. The first place Ratchman and his buddies will look is inside the building. They might take a quick look out here but they will see what they want to – what they expect to see.'

He grunted but said nothing, and checked his pistol. Maybe he was finally getting the message.

I lifted the edge of the tarp by my side and checked the light outside. Daylight wasn't far off and would come up quickly, flooding the area and pushing back the shadows. By the time the men in the SUVs got here and looked our way, they would have the sun in their eyes and we wouldn't even be a shadow on the ground.

I heard the sound of an engine. It was growing, the hum drifting over the buildings and across the open space in front of the junkyard. They were taking it steady, probably nervous about finding themselves in the tight network of back alleys and twisting streets, with the real risk of facing an ambush at any moment.

'This is crazy,' Masse said, and spat on the ground.

'Better this than dead,' I said, and placed a stick under the front edge of the tarp, giving me just enough of a view beneath the bush to spot anybody approaching . . . and a field of fire if I needed it.

Waiting for action you know is likely to take place is probably the hardest thing to do. You can follow the old saying of preparing for the worst while hoping for the best, but nothing is more stressful than waiting for that first moment of a contact, trying to ignore the what-ifs and the maybes. For one, you probably have only a vague idea of what the opposition forces consist of or what weapons they can bring to bear on you. All you can do is make sure you're in the best position you can find and are ready to respond to whatever gets thrown your way.

263

We had each brought bottles of water, and sipped economically as we waited. Dehydration can be an additional problem in tight spots, leading to dulled senses and slow reactions, and we were going to have to be fully alert in case our position got blown. In between, I kept my eye on the front of the building and the village beyond.

The first thing I saw was the spread of headlights. They were faint against the coming dawn, flickering over the store and touching the area to the front and sides of the junkyard, but focussed enough to show that they were heading this way. I could hear only one engine, and I figured the other vehicle was tackling the police barracks to cut down the amount of time they had to spend in the village. Ratchman and his crew were pretty much in the same situation as Masse and me, unless you discounted them being better armed and equipped and able to call up a Chinook to pull them out of the country if things got a little hot. But they were still in hostile territory and getting a Chinook here would take a while; it didn't mean they could be leisurely about finding us.

The engine died abruptly, and I waited for the sound of voices or footsteps. They would make their approach spread out to minimise risk, and moving fast to reduce being targeted. I figured they would check the outside yard first, but since a bunch of wrecked trucks wouldn't provide much of a hiding place, they'd quickly move on towards the building.

I heard a whistle. It was short and sharp, an

attention-grabber. The lead man directing his men. Then came an exchange of voices and a clatter as somebody kicked aside a section of thin metal. They wouldn't be taking chances, covering each other in turn and moving forward in a leap-frog manoeuvre. It's a particularly stressful kind of work, expecting at any moment to find somebody popping up out of hiding with a gun in their hand. I could almost taste the sense of nervousness they would be feeling, the adrenaline running high as they tried to anticipate whatever might happen next.

Masse moved his free hand towards the edge of the tarp for a better view and I motioned at him to stop. I'd just spotted movement at the front corner of the building. It wasn't much but there was now enough light for me to see the figure of a man standing there. He was holding an assault rifle to his shoulder and staring along the barrel, and looked primed and ready to open fire.

'Don't move,' I said softly. 'We have one armed man on foot close to the store and he's looking edgy.' I moved the AK a fraction and centred on the man's chest. If he gave even a hint that he'd seen us, I was going to have to put him down.

'What's he doing?' Masse whispered. He was breathing in short bursts and I could feel a tremor going through him as he tried to control his fears. He sounded as if he was on the point of breaking, so I increased the pressure on his arm until he began to calm down.

'Nothing. He's just standing there. He can't see us but he doesn't want to come down here because it's open ground and instinct tells him he'll be vulnerable if he does.'

Masse hissed and checked his pistol again. 'How can you know that? He might be about to open fire.'

'I know what he's thinking because I've been there. He's on high alert and if he'd seen anything suspicious he'd have called up his buddies by now to cover the area.'

'How do you know they won't kill us on sight?'

'They won't risk it. They have orders to get the hard drive and they won't kill you until they're sure you've got it.'

He absorbed that in silence, and I think he realised that once they had him, his life would last no longer than mine. 'I don't know . . . this is madness. We are going to get caught!'

I turned my head and looked at him. 'André. Take it easy. We'll only get caught if they see us. And they'll only do that if you make a wrong move.'

He blinked as he realised I was talking to him in French, and shook his head, making a bead of sweat break loose and roll down his cheek. It left a line in the layer of dust on his face. He took a deep breath and closed his eyes for a second. 'OK. You're right. I'm good. Don't worry.'

I focussed once more on the man by the building. He hadn't moved but had turned away, his head dipping as he checked the rest of the area. Whatever he saw must have looked safe, because he lowered his weapon and stepped back out of sight.

I breathed easier, and lowered the AK, glad the

man hadn't come any closer or stood there any longer. One thing Mr Kalashnikov hadn't been able to do was to make his weapons out of modern lightweight materials. It's an uncomfortable position, holding a heavy assault rifle to the shoulder for too long; even with all the training in the world, it's a strain on the neck and arms, producing the dreaded shakes and barrel wobble. Not good in a potential fire-fight.

The sound of breaking wood echoed from inside the warehouse, and I guessed the men had gone in to search the interior. I could hear snatches of conversation but not what they were saying. Depending on what was inside, they wouldn't take long to figure out that the building was a bust.

Another whistle, this one a double and sounding urgent, followed by a muffled shout. Then the sound of running footsteps and car doors slamming, and an engine bursting into life. There was a screech of dust and stones being kicked up and the engine faded as the vehicle drove away.

Something was up.

I waited a full five minutes in case they were playing smart and waiting for us to pop out. If they'd left a couple of men behind, we could find ourselves walking right into a gun. If that happened, we were done for and there would be no way out.

Masse didn't like it, I could tell by his manner. He wanted to get up and leave, but he also understood the risks if any of Ratchman's men were still around.

Just as I was about to stand up my phone buzzed. It was Lindsay. 'Watchman come in. You have a convoy approaching your location from the north-east, approximately two miles out. Three trucks, look like military with armed men in the back, possibly African Union or TFG forces. I have no up-to-date information on local troop movements, so I can't verify who they are. ETA your position eight minutes.'

'Copy that. You got the drone, then?'

'It's a short-term loaner,' she confirmed, 'on a diverted overflight, so it can't stay long. What's your location?'

'Look for a large structure and some truck wrecks. If your drone has thermal imaging, we're the hot spot behind the building.'

'Hold on. Just circling and . . . I have your location but the imagery is unclear. It looks like a warehouse . . . and is that a breaker's yard? Are you inside?'

'No. Close by but out in the open.'

'Copy that. I see a vehicle leaving . . . and another one waiting just down the street. Both SUVs. Wait . . . it's turning away and the other is following. Now heading out to the east from the village at speed and away from the approaching convoy. Sorry – I'm losing the picture feed . . . the controller has called urgent priority.'

At least it explained why the bad guys were leaving in such a hurry. The last people they'd want to tangle with would be the military. At the very least they would ask some pointed questions about what a group of armed white men was doing in the region. Or maybe they wouldn't take any chances and would simply blow them away as possible bandits or terror suspects.

'What's your plan?' Lindsay asked. Her voice was calm but she could clearly appreciate the threat facing us if the convoy came into the village for a closer look.

I said, 'We don't have time to get clear, so we'll sit tight.' Even if we got back to the pickup without being spotted and drove out of the village, we stood a high risk of being sandwiched between the SUVs and the incoming trucks. Neither was a good option.

'Got that. Good luck.'

I switched off and looked at Masse, who was looking even more concerned. 'The SUVs have gone but there are military trucks on the way in.'

'Trucks? Why – what are they doing here?'

'I have no idea. Probably chasing insurgents. It could be a coincidence. But we can't stay out here. It's going to get very hot under this tarp and if they're doing a close search the trucks might come right into this compound and drive over us.'

I got to my knees and crawled out from under the tarp, and that was when I heard the grind of heavy engines echoing faintly over the houses. They were still some distance away, but close enough to be a real threat.

Masse heard them, too. 'We should leave now and put distance between us.'

'That's no longer an option. We'd be spotted as soon as we drove out. The best we can do is hunker down and wait for them to go by.'

Masse stood beside me. 'Where are you going?'

I nodded at the warehouse. 'I want to check inside.'

'But what if it's no good?'

'We'll go to plan B.' I didn't bother telling him what that was; I didn't even like it myself.

Twenty-Nine

Colonel Lunnberg stared at his phone in disbelief before placing it with elaborate care on the table in front of him. Victor Petrus was on the other side, nursing a fresh coffee and staring through the windows of the restaurant at the approaching dawn while waiting for Lunnberg to finish his call. Other early birds were gradually filling up the tables and calling for coffee.

'Bad news?' the Frenchman said, turning to watch the American's eyes.

'No.' Lunnberg kept his face a mask and sipped his own coffee. 'Not bad. A little irritating, is all.' It was a lie. It had been far too early to take such a call, but as he had learned long ago, those in positions of power in Washington rarely kept regular hours when it came to dishing out unpalatable truths. And after what he'd just heard, he'd sensed a certain relish behind James Warren's words which effectively threatened to dismantle his very world.

'I also had an unwelcome message a few minutes ago,' said Petrus, unaware of his tension. 'My superiors want to know why we have not yet secured the data.' He shrugged. 'Of course I could not hide the fact that your men are – how do you say it – on the case, but they are not happy. Have you had any word from them?'

'No, Victor. I haven't. Not in the last five minutes.'

271

Lunnberg's eyes were like flint as he said the words, and he was only able to control his tone of voice with enormous effort. Having Petrus and his controllers getting antsy was merely adding to his feeling of irritation, and he was looking forward to being able to distance himself from the superior Frenchman when this was all over.

'Ah, so you know where they are, then?'

'Of course. They're on Portman's tail and have just entered a village where they think he's hiding. They should have him and Masse very shortly. But don't worry, Victor,' he added icily, 'out where they are, there will be no witnesses. Caesar's hands will remain clean.' He snatched up his phone and got to his feet, narrowly missing upsetting the table as he did so.

'I'm sure Caesar would be very pleased,' Petrus replied, displaying an unusual touch of sarcasm. 'But he's not here. We are.'

Lunnberg hesitated. 'What the hell does that mean?'

'My superiors are unhappy about the delay in retrieving this data. In fact, they have become increasingly nervous about any discussions with the Somali Government and . . . certain other parties.' He looked around to make sure nobody was within earshot. 'You know who I mean.'

Lunnberg understood only too well. It could only mean Liban Daoud, the al-Shabaab leader. 'What the fuck is going on?' he spat out, causing a number of heads to turn. He dropped back into his seat, his face pale with anger fuelled by what Warren had also said. 'They've known about him all along, Victor,' he hissed. 'They can't pretend otherwise. Now suddenly they're getting choosy about who they talk to? What else did they say?'

'They have heard rumours of disquiet in Washington also about Daoud. The general view is that he is too . . . toxic.' Petrus lifted his hands. 'I'm sorry. There's nothing I can do. It is over.'

Lunnberg stood up again. 'Like hell it is. I'm going to call my men again now just to make sure. I'll call you later.'

With that he turned and marched out of the restaurant and returned to his room, where he paced up and down for a while, forcing himself to calm down and not rip the place apart in the furious rage which was threatening to burst forth at any moment.

He took several deep breaths, replaying the words he'd been forced to listen to downstairs with a rigid half-smile glued to his face for Petrus's benefit. The same words that were actually condemning him for having taken actions that he had been persuaded, even forced, to take, by certain faces in Washington, chief among them James Warren.

'The shit has hit the fan, colonel,' Warren had announced without preamble. His voice carried a faint tremble and his words came out in a rush. 'They're closing down the deal.'

'What do you mean closing it down?'

'What it says. A couple of the major investors got nervous and dropped the ball late last night. Then three more pulled out when rumours began circulating. And that's just the start.'

'What rumours?'

'Stories that we've been doing commercial

deals with terrorists for oil rights. Are you absolutely certain that the data hasn't gone public through some other means?'

'Yes, of course. It's speculation, that's all. One of the investors must have talked to the wrong person about developing oil resources in the region and somebody put two and two together and come up with Daoud. It's the Somalis controlling this, not terrorists.'

Warren's voice dripped treacle. 'Well, colonel, you and I both know that's not quite accurate, don't we? The Somalis hardly know which way is up; all they want is for their fee to be paid into offshore accounts and for the rest of us to go get our hands dirty. Well, that's not going to happen.'

'But nobody knows what's on the hard drive. My team are closing in on it right now. We just need more time.'

'Time is what we don't have. I hate to tell you this but there's been talk of an investigation and even a senate hearing.' He paused then came back with a smile in his voice. 'Look on the bright side, colonel: you could end up with your own page on Wikipedia – just like Ollie North.'

'Why? It was never going to go entirely smoothly, you knew that as well as I did. And there was always a danger that Daoud's name would come out. But it wouldn't last long and who the hell would care as long as the public continued getting cheap oil and gas for their cars?'

'A year ago, colonel, maybe. But not now. Situations change. The game has got nastier across Europe and the rest of the world. The truth is we're being isolated every way I look and it

274

isn't going to improve. People I could count on for support even a couple of days ago are fading into the woodwork; others are unavailable or refusing to take any of my calls. And in this town that's like a death sentence. Do you know an analyst named Henry Seibling?'

'What – no, I don't think so.' Lunnberg was caught off-guard by the switch in topic and felt his throat constrict at hearing the familiar name. Christ, not this already. What had the fool gone and done?

'Really? Well, Seibling seems to know you pretty well. Have you ever done business with him?'

'No. Why – what's he saying?'

'He's currently being grilled by the Office of Internal Security in Langley. According to my inside source Seibling got busted with his fingers up to the knuckles in restricted personnel files. He's saying you pressured him to get hold of some personnel data. Is that correct?'

In spite of his shock, Lunnberg was processing his thoughts at lightning speed. He had to give an answer; a non-response would be worse than useless. When in doubt, fight back. He decided to go on the offensive. 'I-yes, I did – but there was no pressure. I asked him to find out whatever he could on the man Portman, but only because Portman is doing his level best to wreck this whole operation and putting American lives at risk. But forget about Seibling – with what I have on the little worm he'll retract his accusations pretty damned quick—'

'Frankly, colonel, I don't give a rat's ass about any of that,' Warren snapped. 'It was your arrangement with him, not mine. The truth is, you brought him into the equation and now he's singing to anybody who'll listen just to save his ass. And that means everybody from the FBI, CIA, NSA – probably the Daughters of the American Revolution for all I fucking know. This is a disaster and it's going to get a lot worse before the day's out. It's time to end it and get back here, colonel. And I suggest you start thinking about how to explain everything when they come knocking on your door.'

'But this isn't just me! You're involved, too – and the others.'

'You think so? Well, if you can find proof of that it'll be a minor miracle, I promise. Personally I don't recall signing or recording anything. Think about it.'

'What? But that's . . .' Words failed him as he realised the implications of what Warren was saying. Dammit, he couldn't do this! 'I've got men out there!'

'You said it, colonel. Your men. Your operation. My advice to you is, clean it up and close it down. Now.'

The line went dead.

Thirty

The air inside the warehouse was musty and cool, with a thin veil of white hanging in the air where Ratchman's men had searched the place and disturbed the dust. It was a large space with a high ceiling and a hard-baked floor, and must have once held supplies rather than machinery. There were no oil deposits to denote that it had been a garage, nor electricity or signs that there had ever been a power supply. And the size of the large double doors indicated that it had been used for trucks to back in and unload their contents.

I checked we weren't leaving tracks and walked to the back of the building. The first place anybody would look would be the far recesses of the structure. They were in deepest shadow, although that was changing quickly as the sunlight outside grew in intensity and flooded through the doors and the gaps in the structure's walls. All I found was a line of cheap benches and some sheets of rotting plywood leaning against the walls, some which I figured had been broken up by Ratchman's men in their search for us.

As a hiding place it was a no-go.

'Outside,' I said, and hurried back to the doors. It was pointless thinking about hiding among the houses, as the inhabitants couldn't be guaranteed to stay silent. That left only one place. Or more accurately, two.

'Pick a truck,' I told Masse. 'Preferably one with a hood but no engine.'

'What?' He threw me that look again, the one that asked if I was nuts.

'I hid in a breaker's yard once when I was a kid,' I explained quickly, listening to the truck noises coming closer. 'A local gang was looking to beat our heads in. They searched the buildings and cars, especially the trunks. But the only place they didn't look was under the truck hoods because everybody knows they're full of huge engine blocks. These aren't, but the guys coming here don't know that. Pick one, climb in and stay quiet.'

I waited for him to get the message and watched him clamber beneath the empty hood of a large Berliet and pull it closed it behind him. I selected another truck nearby and did the same.

Some lessons you learn as a kid never leave you. I just hoped the men in the trucks were dumber than some of the kids in the gang I'd run into.

The air under the hood was heavy with the smell of oil and grease, and every surface sticky to the touch. I had no idea how long it had been here but the sun and wind had done nothing to blast it clean of the muck coating the inside. I pulled the hood closed and lay back on the support struts where the truck engine had been seated and tried to get comfortable. I checked the SIG out of reflex although I knew it was good. If I had to take defensive action from inside here the AK would be cumbersome in the confined space, while the SIG would let me move faster and respond to threats from either side.

Minutes later I heard the roar of heavy engines coming through the village and the hiss and squeak of air brakes as the drivers negotiated the narrow streets. The utter silence predominant before was now blasted aside, and I could hear penned animals protesting at the intrusion and the frantic clatter of birds taking to the skies. Eventually one engine dominated the others as it came closer, hissing to a stop about a hundred yards away followed by men shouting and the crunch of running feet. The engine died leaving two others rumbling some way off. Three trucks, just as Lindsay had said. Then those engines were cut, too, and silence took over save for an occasional voice drifting over the air.

I peered through the air vents down the side of the hood to see what was happening. The first thing I saw was a man's back. He'd approached without me hearing him and was standing no more than fifteen feet away. Dressed in mismatched camouflage shirt and pants and a cotton *keffiyeh*, the checkered scarf worn around the head for protection against the sun and dust, he carried a carbine with a wooden stock over his shoulder. As he moved away I saw he was wearing sandals on his feet. So, not military after all.

He made a circle of the area peering into corners and behind the wrecks. I hoped Masse had seen him and wasn't about to make any noise. The man turned and came back towards the truck, swinging his carbine off his shoulder and holding it by his side. He hawked loudly and spat the contents of his throat on the ground, then took a corner of his scarf and wiped his face and eyes.

279

He was gaunt and bony, and could have been anywhere between twenty and forty. It made me wonder what the retirement age was for al-Shabaab fighters.

A shout floated up from down in the village followed by a shot. Then a scream rose, loud and shrill, and was cut off brutally by an extended burst of automatic fire. Another shout from nearby drew an answering call from the man nearest to me, and I heard his footsteps pounding away into the distance. Another rattle of gunfire, this time far off, with more screams followed by spaced out single shots, somehow more shocking and deliberate than the long bursts. I felt nauseous and not just because of the smell under the hood; whatever the men out there were doing, people were getting hurt and killed and I was unable to do a thing about it.

I sat tight, wondering how Masse was holding up. In spite of his long time working this region under cover, he really wasn't built for this kind of scene. Whatever training he'd had with DGSE probably hadn't included full-on combat or hiding from men who would surely kill him if they found him.

I sniffed the air, which had developed a newer, more pungent smell of burning rubber or plastic to overlay the aroma of oil and grease. It was being wafted through the vents from the direction of the village centre, and I knew instantly what it was. I'd experienced it too many times before; they were burning houses. Whatever these men were doing, it probably wasn't the first time they'd raided the village and wouldn't be the last, especially with the police barracks abandoned and no longer a threat. It was most likely a regular shopping visit for food or money and to throw in a little local terror to keep the villagers in line.

I checked through the vents on both sides. I couldn't see anybody but I heard voices in the distance, and laughter. Then I made a mistake; as I moved for a better look, the butt of the SIG glanced off a piece of metal with a distinctive clang.

Seconds later I heard the crunch of footsteps close by and a shadow shifted against the sunlight. I froze and looked down past the wheel arch. A man's foot appeared. He was standing up close to the truck with his face against the hood, and I could hear him breathing with a hoarse, asthmatic sound deep in his throat.

He banged on the hood and said something in a croaky voice. I couldn't understand a word but it sounded a lot like 'who's there?' Then his fingers appeared under the rim of the hood and threw it open, flooding the engine compartment with bright sunlight.

He was small and skinny, built like a kid but a good twenty years older. He had an AK slung on a strap across his chest and a bandolier of shells going crossways the other way, both of which made him look even smaller. He looked stunned to see me, his jaw dropping open, and I reacted instinctively. There was no time to see if he had any colleagues nearby, no point worrying about what might happen from here on in. I had to get him subdued and out of sight fast or we were done for. Before he could shout a warning I reached out and grabbed him by the shirt, pulling him towards me as hard as I could. It was like handling a bag of straw. He weighed almost nothing and flew off his feet with a soft yelp, joining me in the engine compartment. I slammed his head against one of the sold metal support struts, then reached up and pulled the hood back down, grabbing his AK and clamping my hand over the trigger.

I counted to ten. There was no sound outside, no indication that anyone had noticed anything. I looked down at the new arrival. He was out cold, with a bruise blossoming on his forehead. I checked his AK, which looked in an even worse state than the one I had, and unclipped the curved magazine. The shells inside were shiny and new, and gave me about another fifty rounds if I counted those in the bandolier.

I took off his *keffiyeh* and tore it in strips, using it to gag him and lash his wrists to the struts and using his carbine sling to do the same with his feet, and sat back to regain my breath.

I felt as if I'd run a marathon. Short bursts of intense activity coupled with a sense of alarm will do that, making the adrenalin race through the system. But the down side can leave you feeling tired and drained. The secret in the initial stages is to use it and control it, and not allow it to make you run off at half-cock when you should be staying still.

I counted to fifty, using my breathing to lower my heart rate. It was counter-intuitive, as every instinct was telling me to get out of here and find somewhere more secure to make a stand. My problem was, there was nowhere to go. These men wouldn't stay here all day and risk a confrontation with troops, and sooner or later they'd be gone. Until then I had to stay put. Only then could Masse and I make a move.

Eventually the trucks started up again and moved away, sounding their horns as they left the village. I looked down at my prisoner, who was now coming round and looking at me bug-eyed with fear. He must have heard the commotion even in his concussed state, and figured out that none of his buddies had bothered making a head count. He began to struggle and kick at me until I put the AK barrel against his forehead and told him to shush. I don't think he understood the word but he got the message and went still.

My phone buzzed. It was Lindsay. I switched it on and held it tight to my ear just in case the guys in the trucks had played cute and left somebody behind.

'Watchman, are you OK?'

'I'm fine,' I said softly. 'We just had company.'

'Copy that. I have camera coverage again and can see the three trucks leaving the village. What happened? There's a lot of smoke down there.'

'It was a raid for supplies. How far out are they?'

'Currently about a mile and moving at speed to the south.'

'Can you get a close-up of the scrapyard?'

'Sure can. Wait one.' A few seconds ticked by while my prisoner and I exchanged looks. Then Lindsay came back. 'Got it. Still can't get any hot spots, though. Where are you?'

283

'Unless you know what a Berliet is, it's a little hard to describe.'

'Did you say Berliet? Isn't that a French truck manufacturer?'

I grinned in spite of the circumstances. 'As my mother would have said, any sharper and you'll cut yourself. I'm inside one of their products waiting to get out of here.'

'Of course. Why didn't I think of that? Listen, I got the tech section to check that barcode you sent me. You were right: it was an identifier. His name was Joshua B. McBride, a former sergeant with the 66th Military Intelligence Brigade.' She went on to confirm what Angela Pryce had told me. 'McBride was born in Alabama but he was a career soldier and spent more time out of the US than in it. His specialty was Afghanistan and, more recently, Africa. I ran his personnel file and it says he left the military eight months ago and dropped off the map.'

'Was he a contractor?'

'Not at first, but he followed the pattern of others who went down that route. There are gaps, but he was last recorded as working in Afghanistan with a company called Pressway Logistics. It doesn't mention security contracting but it's a pretty obvious front.'

'I think I've heard of them.'

'I'm sure. It started out as a shell company before announcing its business as a logistics specialist. The founder and CEO is not a million miles away from you right now.'

'Lunnberg?'

'Correct. He tried to keep it quiet when he moved in with the people next door, but it got out.'

Next door to the CIA was the Defence Clandestine Service – the DCS.

'What happened?'

'They didn't want such an open connection with that particular industry because it was bad for publicity, so he allegedly cut all ties with them and sold out to his co-directors. But the general buzz here is that he's still running the place and they get a lot of work from the DCS and other agencies.'

'Good work. Thanks. Can you pass on the information about McBride? Somebody out there probably needs to know what happened to him.'

'Copy that. I had word from Tom Vale. He wants to know if you plan on leaving the way you discussed.'

'Tell him yes. We're hoping to make for a pre-arranged pickup point as soon as we get away from here.'

'Well, take it easy. I might not be able to get a loaner of this drone again, but if I do I'll let you know.'

'Copy that. Thanks for your help.'

'Anytime, Watchman. Out.'

I squinted through the vents either side of the truck to check the area was clear, then looked at my prisoner. 'I'm getting out of here, Ahmed,' I told him. I accompanied the speech with a bit of finger pointing. 'I doubt you understand a word I'm saying but I'm taking you with us. If I'm not mistaken, your pals made a mess of the village and left a few bodies behind. If the locals find you, they might decide to cut you into little pieces.'

He stared at me and shook his head. I was right: he hadn't understood. But as soon as I picked up the AK and reached up to lift the hood, I think he figured most of it out pretty quickly and didn't like it. He thought I was leaving him behind or about to dump him out in the centre of the village. He hummed like a buzz saw through the gag, so I put a finger to my lips until he quietened down. If he couldn't work the dangers out for himself if he kicked off, he was dumber than I thought.

I lifted the hood and dragged him out into the warm sunlight, and made him sit against the wheel arch. I hunkered down alongside him and waited, listening for the sound of voices. Not a peep. Not even the animals around the houses were making a squeak, as if they'd all reached an accord to stay silent for the rest of the day. I stood up and stepped out into the open. Thick smoke was hanging over the village in more than one location, and the crackle of flames reached me from down by the police barracks. The men had vented their displeasure on the place by setting it alight, along with a few houses for good measure.

When I was satisfied it was safe to move I picked up Ahmed and carried him across to the pickup and dumped him in the back with a signal to stay quiet. He nodded this time and lay back, eyes wide and throat working as he began to realise the position he was in. I padded across to the truck Masse had chosen and gave a soft whistle while I was a few steps away. I didn't want to risk getting shot by tapping on the hood and having him pull the trigger.

He emerged slowly and stood brushing his clothing and looking around. 'They are gone?' His voice was hoarse and he looked pale with stress, even through his tan. Like me he had oil and grease stains on his clothes and hands, but at least we were alive and standing.

'So far. But they might come back.'

'What do we do?' he asked.

'We leave. But first we load up with fuel and add a few props. You do the fuel and I'll do the rest.'

He walked to the back of the pickup. When he saw Ahmed he went goggle-eyed and turned on me.

'Don't ask.' I told him before he could say anything. 'He might come in useful later.'

He wasn't happy but he clammed up and took two containers out of the pickup, while I selected some sections of cut-away truck parts from the piles scattered around the junkyard. They were mostly large jagged pieces of metal, but lightweight, and I tossed them in the back of the pickup alongside Ahmed.

When I had a decent pile of scrap level with the cab roof I covered it and Ahmed with the tarps we'd used to disguise the pickup and the foxhole and threw on the truck wheels to hold everything in place.

For once Masse looked impressed. We now looked like a local shifting scrap metal. If Ratchman and his men were watching from the east, we would hopefully look genuine enough to fool them.

I drove slowly towards the centre of the village and the road north, keeping the engine noise down as much as possible. It was like moving through a ghost town where you know there are people but they're staying out of sight. The police barracks had been set on fire but had been only partially destroyed, marked by a thick pall of black smoke hanging across the street and shutting out the sun. I caught a glimpse of a few men down a narrow side street, staring at the damage, before they heard the engine and disappeared like wraiths.

At one point a little girl appeared at the corner of a small house and stared at us with bug eyes, until a woman ran out and snatched her up before rushing back inside, pulling her scarf around her face.

I counted five houses on fire or smouldering and saw three bodies, all men, covered in blood where they had been shot multiple times against a wall. It was plain that the deaths were both a warning and a punishment, maybe for some past transgression or a refusal to give up food or money. I had no way of knowing how many had died inside the buildings.

I stopped the pickup. It made Masse sit up with a start. 'What are you doing?' he demanded, looking around frantically.

'Calm down. Keep your eyes and ears open for engines. I want to see if I can help.'

'Are you mad? They don't want your help, Portman, they would rather see us both dead

– like that animal in the back!' He reached for my arm to stop me but I shook it off. He was right – I probably was mad and they wouldn't thank me. But there was no way I could simply drive away without doing something, even if it was checking the buildings for survivors.

Thirty-One

I tucked the SIG under my shirt and walked over to the first house, which was showing a lot of smoke and a small flicker of flames. An elderly man in a shawl and pill-box hat appeared from a narrow alleyway and shouted at me, so I pointed at the house and made a sign for a small child then lifted my hands in query.

He understood and shook his head, but pointed to a house across the way, where a man's body lay in the doorway in a pool of blood. The roof was smouldering and shedding thick grey smoke, and I could hear the faint crackle of fire eating through the structure of sticks and grass. The old man raised two fingers, so I nodded and signalled for him to stay where he was and ducked through the door.

Smoke hung thick in the first tiny room, which was a mess of destruction where the men from the trucks had stormed through, ripping and smashing everything they could find, even digging holes in the walls with the butts of their rifles. I ducked below the smoke and crabbed across to a gap in the wall with a curtain hanging down as a divider. I pushed it aside and saw a smaller room with rough cushions and blankets scattered across the floor. A girl was sitting in one corner staring at me with eyes glazed in terror. She had a shawl pulled across her face and a bundle in her lap and, as young as she looked, I figured she was the mother.

I beckoned to her to come with me and bring the baby. She either didn't understand or the urgency of her situation wasn't getting through. I didn't blame her, not after what she had just experienced. Then I felt a blast of heat on the back of my neck as the smouldering embers finally caught and flames roared through the dried sticks and grass which made up the roof and crept down the wall either side of the doorway.

There was no going back that way, so I checked the wall close to where the girl was sitting. It was made of thin plaster and sticks covered in a sheet of plastic. I kicked twice before the sticks gave way, then shouldered my way through to the outside in a cloud of dust and fabric, turning to encourage the girl to follow me. She blinked a few times, as if the noise of me breaking down the wall had finally got through to her, and nodded before gathering up her baby and slipping through the gap into fresh air.

I found the old man standing by the side of the house. When he saw me he ran forward to hug the girl to him, nodding at me and trying to smile. Three younger men had appeared along the street and were shouting between themselves and looking at me with obvious anger. Two of them carried heavy sticks and were moving towards me in a threatening manner, but the old man stepped between us and shouted at them. He evidently carried enough authority to make them hesitate for a moment, but it wouldn't last long. He grabbed my sleeve and dragged me towards the pickup with a shooing motion, pointing to the north. He was saying it was time to go and he was right. Emotions were running high and if I stayed any longer, no matter what I did to help, it would only take a couple of these hotheads to push the envelope and the situation would get out of control.

As we got close to the pickup, the old man stopped me and tugged a red *keffiyeh* from around his shoulders. It was dirty and torn, and he placed it around my head and made a motion of covering his eyes with his hands. The message was clear: anybody seeing me would see immediately that I wasn't a local, but the *keffiyeh* might help. He was right; the disguise wouldn't fool anybody up close, but it would do for now. I thanked him and climbed in the pickup and drove away.

As we cleared the outskirts of the village I could see the road to the north was clear for a good two miles. I resisted the temptation to slam my foot to the floor and get some distance away from here as quickly as possible. To anybody watching we had to look unassuming, a normal part of the landscape – at least as normal as it could get given what had just happened. But a pickup moving at high speed out of here would look odd. Hopefully, if Ratchman was watching us, he'd put the pieces together wrong, connecting our slow-moving loaded pickup to the junkyard and direct his attention elsewhere.

'Are you happy?' Masse muttered softly, his voice almost bitter. 'Now you have done your good deed for the day like a good boy scout – isn't that what they say?'

'If you have a problem,' I replied, 'spit it out.'

'You endangered us back there by stopping to play the hero. *That* is my problem. We should have left them to get on with it. Did they thank you for it? I doubt it.'

I looked at him. His face was puffed with anger and he was breathing fast, as if he'd run up a hill. 'You don't like these people much, do you?'

'I'm not paid to like them. I loathe them and their stinking lives. Any one of them, given the chance, would kill us as soon as look at us.'

There was no answer to that one, so I let it go. It was an extraordinary and passionate outburst by any standards, but sounded as if it came from the heart. Instead I said, 'We're clear for now, but you might like to keep your eyes open for dust clouds. Ratchman and his crew won't have gone far and they'll be eyeballing anything that moves.'

He nodded but said nothing. Whatever was eating him, he'd have to get over it soon. We were now exposed in broad daylight and still a long way off the location of the landing site, and staying out on the road could only last for so long before our luck ran out.

Masse eventually fell asleep, in spite of the jolting ride, and I wondered if this mission had all been too much for him. The fact that he'd made no attempt to help back in the village made me wonder if it was a lack of sympathy for the plight of the villagers or if he was suffering some kind of deep-seated trauma.

Thirty-Two

On a low bluff a mile to the east of the village, Vince Ratchman watched a loaded pickup bouncing slowly along the route to the north, dark grey smoke puffing from the exhaust. A pale flash of red showed the driver's headdress. Elsewhere nothing moved, save for drifting palls of smoke from the village and one or two figures running around trying to put out the fires. He and his men had been lucky, he figured, and had got out of there just in time. It made him wonder if news of their presence had filtered out to the authorities. He'd watched the trucks leaving along the road to the south and figured they were insurgents rather than local forces, and less of a threat. Even so, running into that many armed men would be a serious problem.

He focussed his binoculars on the village in the hopes of seeing something that might point to Portman still being in the area. It was possible he and the Frenchman had driven straight on through the night before and headed for open country, but he didn't believe it. He was certain they hadn't been equipped to go very far in this terrain, and Portman's training allied with Masse's reported local knowledge would have had them stop and rest up before continuing.

Behind him the men were talking in soft tones about Carson's death, and he sensed a rising atmosphere of tension among them. Carson had been popular, and his skill as a sniper had been invaluable to the unit, making his loss all the more keenly felt. He turned and clicked his fingers to get their attention.

'Bury Carson,' he said. 'Ain't no use us taking him any further.' There was also, he realised, the question of the smell, which was already becoming a factor and would only get worse as the heat increased.

For a second none of them moved, exchanging glances. Then Dom stood up and said, 'You heard the man. Find a soft spot and gather a bunch of rocks to cover him.'

Ratchman turned back to studying the landscape. Something was bothering him about the scene down in the village, but he couldn't put his finger on it. He ran the drive into the village through his mind, replaying the tight streets and ratty little houses, and stopping to check out a big old building that looked like a fort. It had been empty, with nowhere to hide a rabbit, let alone two men. Then they had moved up a rise to a junkyard with a line of wrecked trucks and stuff, and what Ellison had said was probably an old grain store. They'd seen nothing and heard no movement save for some goats and other animals behind stick fences. If there were people there, they had stayed out of sight. When they had picked up the sound of trucks approaching, they had left immediately and headed for this bluff.

Now something had changed and he wasn't sure—

Wait. He focussed on the junkyard.

'Ellison, c'mon here,' he called, and when the man arrived, passed him the binoculars. 'Tell me what you see down there.'

Ellison sat down and scanned the area. 'Well, some smoke, burning houses, a few rag-heads and the places we searched earlier. What am I looking for?'

'What's changed? Look at the scrapyard next to the place you said was a grain store.'

Ellison looked again and began to shake his head, then stiffened. 'Hey – there's a vehicle missing.'

'Yeah,' Ratchman agreed. 'But not just any vehicle; a crappy little pickup that shouldn't have been going anywhere.' He stabbed a finger towards the north. 'Like the one heading that way right now.' He could no longer see the pickup, which had dipped below the horizon but he was certain he was right. Ellison had just confirmed it.

'Hurry up with that,' he called out to his men, and got to his feet. It was time to head north and finish this.

Thirty-Three

We drove for an hour without seeing another soul. Miles of open countryside, of rocks, trees and bushes, of birds in the sky and on the ground. A few goats nibbling at tufts of coarse grass and spiky bushes, or huddled in the shade of a tree, but that was all. It was a little creepy and I wondered how any place could be so empty of human life when I knew there must be settlements and people out there, like the old man and his reluctant goat-herders with their AKs at the site where Colin Doney had died. I asked Masse what he thought but he'd sunk into some kind of dissociative state and didn't even acknowledge the question. Then a couple of big trucks loomed up ahead and went by in a blast of wind and trailing a long cloud of dust in their wake, leaning on air horns to clear us out of the way. I didn't argue and got off the road until they were gone.

We began to pull up a long slope to some higher ground, so I stopped near the top and studied the road behind us. Save for the dust cloud kicked up by the trucks hanging in the air I couldn't see a thing. But common sense told me Ratchman would be out there somewhere. He wouldn't have given up just because he couldn't find us; he knew the options for our direction of travel were extremely limited, and my guess was he'd already worked out that we were heading for some kind of RV. All he had to do was follow and hope to catch us.

I took a bottle of water and walked round to the back of the pickup. Ahmed must be getting thirsty and I didn't want him to croak on us. I pulled back the tarp I'd covered him with and stopped, the water forgotten.

Ahmed was staring up at me with open eyes. His throat and chest were covered in blood from an open wound just below his chin. If he hadn't died instantly, it wouldn't have taken long; the floor of the pickup was swamped with his blood and already attracting swarms of flies.

I checked the scraps of metal I'd piled in the back, but they were still firmly in place. No way could a sharp piece have toppled and killed him. That took me back to the village. Could one of the young men there have seen him in the back and stabbed him in retaliation? It was unlikely without him making a big deal out of it and alerting Masse.

Masse. He had a knife; he'd used it to cut the tarps free back at the junkyard. And he hadn't liked me bringing Ahmed along.

I looked round just then and found Masse watching me in the wing mirror. His expression was blank but the fact that he was seeing me at all meant he wasn't as out of it as I'd thought.

I flicked the tarp back over the body and got back behind the wheel.

'You killed him, didn't you?' I said. 'Want to tell me why?'

He shrugged, a gesture that was seriously beginning to get to me. 'He was a passenger we do not need. What were you going to do with him – give him our food and water and cut him loose? Portman, you're wasting your time. Rats like him exist only to kill us.' He turned away. 'Better that we don't have him to worry about.'

In a way it was hard to argue with him. Carrying an extra load when it wasn't called for was only adding to our problem. And Ahmed wouldn't have wasted a millisecond in putting a bullet in me if I hadn't silenced him first. Add to that the way his friends had burned and smashed their way through the village, killing innocent people, and he really wasn't worth a second thought. But the way Masse had done it without hesitation seemed senseless, and with no more qualms than squashing a bug.

I started driving again, trying to push the death out of my mind and focussing instead on what to do next. We couldn't keep the body with us, that was certain; the heat was already building up, wrapping itself around us like a heavy blanket, and the effects on the body would soon make it unpleasant.

The road began to take a gentle curve around a rocky outcrop rising by some fifty feet, and I had an idea. I slowed down, eyeing the side of the road, until I saw a gap in the shale and rocks. I kept going for another couple of hundred yards, then stopped and jumped out.

'What are you doing?' Masse asked, turning to study the road behind us, although there was nothing to see now we'd rounded the curve.

'Help me move this,' I told him, and tucked the tarp around Ahmed's body so I didn't get any blood on me. Masse took the other end and I moved sideways until we were standing at the side of the road. I nodded and lowered my end of the body and Masse did the same. Then I pulled off the tarp and threw it into the back of the truck.

I pointed at the outcrop. 'We're going behind that hill to wait out the day. I need you to move ahead of me and find a way.'

He looked doubtful. 'What if they check it out?'

'They won't. First they'll be suspicious as hell and expecting an ambush or an IED. It's what they've been trained to do. They'll eventually check the body because they'll have to drive past it, but then they'll be in a hurry to get out of here and back on our tail before anybody else shows up.'

Masse looked at me. 'You talk as if you have done this before.'

'I haven't – but I've been on the other end a few times. The rule is to get by and move away from the danger zone as fast as you can. Hanging around too long makes you a target.'

I walked to the pickup and got back in, and reversed back down the road to where I'd seen the gap in the rocks and shale. Masse saw what I was going to do and ran ahead of me, checking the terrain and pointing out where to avoid rocks, deep potholes and layers of soft soil. It was a hard grind and had to be taken slowly, even though I was tempted to put my foot down;

wrecking the steering or blowing a tyre would leave us stranded out in the open.

The ground was making the whole vehicle tremble and the scrap metal in the back bounce and tip dangerously close to falling over. It didn't help our manoeuvring on this kind of terrain, but I didn't want to throw it overboard just yet until I was sure it was of no further use. I was pretty sure Ratchman would have worked out by now how we'd fooled him, but he and his men weren't the only threat we had to contend with.

Eventually we reached an area behind the outcrop and a couple of hundred yards back in the shelter of what looked like the dry walls of an old riverbed. I climbed out and scouted around until I saw a couple of sturdy bushes and said to Masse, 'Have you got that knife?'

He nodded and took it out of his pocket. As he opened it the sunlight flashed off the blade, which was about eight inches long and looked razor sharp. There was also a brownish residue close to the handle. Dried blood.

I pointed to the bottom of the bushes and told him to cut them down. When he'd done it I took the bushes and jogged back to the road, and began sweeping at the soil to hide any traces of our passage, moving backwards as I went. It took a while, and was hot work, but an absolute necessity if we wanted to live. When it was done I grabbed the AK and the remaining tarp and led the way along the dried river bed to a point where we had a view of the pickup but couldn't be overlooked from the outcrop.

'Now what?' Masse asked. He was puffing like a twenty-a-day smoker and looked grey around the eyes and ready to drop.

'We wait. They'll be along soon enough.'

Thirty-Four

'Whoa – what the hell?' Ellison, who was driving, slammed on the brakes and swerved across the road, making the three other men in the SUV sit up and reach for their weapons. 'Possible IED ahead!'

'Bale out!' Ratchman shouted, and kicked his door open. 'Eyes open and take up defensive positions.' IEDs were often accompanied by ambushes, which made them an event of maximum threat. He jumped out and checked the area to either side of the vehicle but saw nothing. Not that he was reassured much; insurgents could hide like lizards under a small rock all day without moving and pick their targets off at will.

Dom's vehicle had stopped a hundred yards back, and the three men inside followed their lead and dismounted fast, making for the sides of the road, weapons at the ready and watching for ground disturbance to indicate IEDs having been planted in the soft shale. Experience told them that if this was an ambush, the opposition might also have an RPG as back-up. Disabling the team members would be any attackers' first priority, but the SUVs would follow if that couldn't be achieved quickly, to make escape impossible. Even if they tried to drive out of the danger area, the chances of them outrunning a rocket on this road were nil.

Ratchman signalled for Ellison to move forward and check out the shape lying a hundred yards away, while he and another man moved up either side of the road in support, stopping every few yards to look and listen. It was a move they had practised many times before and came instinctively. But experience didn't stop the feeling of vulnerability that crept across the back of each man's neck.

It was almost peaceful here, save for the distant call of a buzzard, the tick-tick of rocks heated by the sun, and the sound of sand crunching beneath the men's boots. Ratchman had no time or desire to appreciate it and made an urgent signal to move forward until they had closed to within thirty paces of the body.

'What do you see?' he called, watching Ellison crab closer, keeping as low as possible to the ground. They all knew it wouldn't help one bit if the shape was a disguised IED; depending on the amount of explosive the blast would sweep along the ground blowing rocks, grit and shale particles in front of it like pieces of shrapnel. Even lying flat didn't guarantee survival. But only the inexperienced or suicidal ever approached a suspect device as if they were out for a Sunday walk.

A shrieking sound among some low bushes off the road made them all whirl round, weapons at the ready. But it was a pair of guinea fowl lifting off in panic as one of Dom's companions moved around to cover the ground further out.

Ellison stood up and whistled. 'It's a body,' he called out. 'No device, nothing. Looks like he's been knifed and dumped.'

Ratchman swore, but with a feeling of relief. He'd been too close to too many IEDs to ever take them for granted. Those who did rarely survived for long. He stood up and joined Ellison, and they stood looking down at the body. Poorly dressed in faded combat gear and sandals, the dead man looked like a hundred other Somalis they had seen in the past few days. But it was obvious by his clothes that this man had been a fighter.

'I thought it was a kid at first, he's so small,' Ellison murmured as if to himself. 'But I reckon he's – what, thirty something?'

'Who cares?' said Ratchman. 'He's one more we don't have to worry about.'

'You reckon Portman did this?' Dom said, stepping up to join them and examining the stab wound to the man's throat. It looked like a straight in-out thrust, and death must have been fairly quick.

'No doubts whatsoever,' Ratchman replied firmly. 'He did it to slow us down and gain time.'

'What makes you say that?'

Ratchman pointed at the ground beneath the body. 'Where's the blood? If he'd done him right here, he'd have bled out. There's nothing. I tell you he planned this.'

The others looked at him, then began checking out the surrounding countryside. It was clear what was going through their minds: if this had been Portman's work as a delaying tactic, who was to say he wasn't out there right now with them in his sights?

'Don't waste time looking – he ain't there,'

Ratchman told them impatiently. In spite of himself he couldn't deny feeling a prickle of unease between his shoulders. In Portman's place he would have done precisely this to cut down the odds. 'If he wanted us dead, he'd be shooting by now. Let's move. I want to nail this clever bastard and go home.'

'What about this?' said Ellison, nodding at the body. 'Shouldn't we move it off the road?'

'Why?' Ratchman turned away. 'He wouldn't do the same for you.'

Thirty-Five

I heard the SUVs stop and cut their engines. Terse commands, distant but recognisable in tone, told the story, and we waited for somebody to appear on the outcrop, maybe even come round to check for tracks. But nobody did. Maybe they hadn't seen the point. Bad decision for them but lucky for us.

Several minutes later we heard the sounds of engines starting up and the SUVs heading away at speed.

'Is that it?' Masse looked shaken, as if this was the first time he'd ever come close to being caught, and went to stand up. 'They've gone?'

I grabbed his arm and held him down. 'Maybe. Wait here.' I got to my feet and moved forward towards the edge of the riverbed where we'd left the pickup, stopped to grab the binoculars, then climbed the slope forming the rear of the outcrop. It was hard going. The top layer of shale and sand was loose, making it difficult to climb without causing a constant rattle as the larger pieces tumbled and slid down the slope in my wake. But eventually I had an overview of the road running north–south, with a dust cloud to the north showing where the two SUVs had gone. I studied the terrain for a couple of minutes, but if they'd left anybody behind, he was well hidden. But frankly, I couldn't see it happening; they were in just as much of a hurry as we were and as much danger of being seen.

I skidded back down the slope, signalling Masse to join me, and got in the pickup. As long as we didn't break anything, we were now on their tail instead of the other way round. And providing we didn't get careless and move too close, we might be able to exert some control over events for a change.

'How far off are we from the RV?' I queried, and sipped some water.

Masse shook himself and checked the GPS on his cell phone. He seemed to be having trouble finding it, but eventually he said, 'Fifty kilometres. Why aren't we moving?' He was still showing signs of fatigue, even listlessness, and beyond answering a direct question had offered no ideas about how we should proceed from here on. That was fine by me as long as he didn't abandon hope altogether and become a dead weight on my hands. Dead weights were hard work.

'We'll wait here for a while and let them get ahead. You get some sleep and I'll keep watch from up there.' I nodded towards the outcrop.

He seemed happy with that and sat back with his eyes closed. By the time I got out of the pickup he was asleep, snoring gently. I climbed the outcrop again, dragging the tarp and some sticks with me, and made a rough bivouac to shelter from the sun. I wasn't going to be up here too long, but I would need the protection unless I wanted to bake my brains. The tarp would also help break up my outline if any vehicles came by.

I was lucky; none did. In fact, as roads went this one was strangely empty. It set me thinking about illegal roadblocks, and military checkpoints in the hunt for bandits and insurgents. Either one would slow traffic to a standstill as soon as news got out.

My original idea was to find somewhere to dig in until nightfall, then move closer to the RV ready for morning. It was as close as I had come to a definitive plan, preferring to play things as they came and prepare for the unexpected.

Which was a good thing. As I chewed over the merits of moving now or leaving it a while, I heard a number of faint cracks way off in the distance. I checked the road to the north through the binoculars, but there was dead ground out there and I couldn't see anything to explain the noises. But there was no mistaking what I'd heard.

Gunfire.

I gave it an hour before deciding to risk moving again. Whatever lay ahead would have to be faced sooner or later; geographically there was no way round it. The terrain off the road was impossible, with deep gullies and fissures running in every direction. Where there weren't rocks there was sand and shale. A military-grade dune buggy might have made it, but not this pickup, which would shake to pieces around us in minutes. Added to that was the need to keep going. It was already too hot and unlikely to cool down for a few hours, and at least on the move there would be some movement in the air. We might also find a better spot to lay up than this stretch of sun-blasted scrubland. I packed up my makeshift bivouac and hoofed it back to the pickup.

Masse woke up and stared at me groggily. 'What is it – are they back?'

'No. I think they might have been hanging around waiting for us to show up and ran into trouble.' I started the engine while describing what I'd heard. Three or four single shots, then a brief volley and a couple more singles. Then silence. I figured Ratchman's crew must have driven off a little way, then stopped to see if we popped out of hiding. It probably didn't matter to them if they were wrong and we'd gone on ahead, because they were in good vehicles and could catch us up anytime they wanted. But instead they'd found trouble waiting for them along the road – most likely in the shape of an illegal roadblock. If so they had answered in the only way that they knew how – by blasting their way through.

I bumped back onto the road and checked the rear-view mirror for anything coming up behind us. A large 10-wheeler charging along with its pedal-to-the-metal right now would have been useful, as we could have let it go by to act as a battering ram against any illegal stoppages. But the road from the south was clear. I moved forward at a steady rate, ready to drive off the road and grab the AK if we saw a threat up ahead.

Sure enough, as we topped a rise I spotted a line of old car tyres across the road. Lying nearby were three bodies dressed in combat uniforms.

When we got closer it was clear that in spite of the uniforms they were not government troops; the clothes were filthy and ragged and they wore sandals on their feet, and the weapons were strictly hand-me-downs bought cheaply on the open market.

I drove round the end of the tyres, which were linked together by ropes, following a double set of tyre tracks in the softer ground and a scattering of shell casings where the two SUVs had fought back. The dead men had each been hit by several shots, their weapons dropped where they had fallen. An ancient Mitsubishi pickup with a broken axle stood just off the road, which had probably been the reason for staging the road-block. Of all the vehicles they could have stopped to make forced take-overs, they had tangled with the wrong ones.

'Bandits,' said Masse unnecessarily, eyeing the bodies with cold indifference. 'Like vultures. They stop traffic and demand money. Most people pay because they have no choice. Sometimes they kill, anyway.' He didn't need to say the rest: that some didn't pay because they didn't want to and had the means to resist.

I continued driving. Twenty minutes later we saw a line of large trucks approaching from around a long bend in the road ahead. They were heavy 10-wheelers, riding on skirt-like clouds of dark exhaust smoke and holding the centre line. They were loaded high and covered with roped tarpaulins, each truck with a couple of armed men sitting on top of the cab.

I slowed and found a safe spot to ease off the

road. Masse was dark enough in the interior of the pickup to pass without comment as long as the drivers didn't stop for a chat. If they dropped their speed too much, however, they would spot my paler skin immediately, so I pulled the *keffiyeh* around my face as a precaution.

They didn't even take their foot off the gas, but blew past like thunder, causing the load on the back of the pickup to shake and peppering the bodywork with grit, stones and choking diesel fumes. The men on top of the trucks had their faces shielded from the dust and wind by shawls or *keffiyehs*, but none of them waved or acknowledged our presence. For all the lack of reaction we could have been invisible. Even so, I knew they were watching us carefully and it was soon clear why: each truck carried an International Red Cross flag and sticker. Carrying food supplies and aid equipment, all saleable on the black market, they would rate as a prime target for bandits driving around in pickups just like ours.

The last of the big vehicles went by and was closely followed by a line of smaller trucks, pickups and a couple of old cars. I figured these had tagged along for the protection, as limited as it was, in the hopes of getting through to their destination. I waited for a lull in the flow, then pulled back on the road and moved round the long bend ahead. It seemed to mark a point where the landscape finally began to change. Instead of rocks, shale, scrappy trees and endless scrubland, the colours now began to assume a subtle shade of something almost approaching green. In the distance I saw a darker area divided into ordered squares, with vegetation around the edges, and I looked at Masse and asked what it was.

'The Shebelle river,' he explained. 'It comes from Ethiopia through Somalia. This is one of the good agricultural areas in the country. The river brings life to many . . . and death also. The floods are very bad when they come. Many people live too close to the water. Sometimes they are swept away.'

The idea of so much casual death and destruction seemed not to bother him, and he soon put his head back and closed his eyes. I let him be; maybe he really had been out here too long and had become immune to the ease with which lives were lost, either by natural or man-made events. He wasn't much good as a lookout right now, anyway, and I preferred to rely on my own eyes and instincts.

Several times I was forced to slow down and pull off the road, spotting vehicles by the side of the road ahead. A couple were pale SUVs, but they turned out to be harmless government vehicles belonging to the local administrative regional offices. It made for a fractured drive, but it was better to be safe than sorry.

We stopped briefly at a roadside stall, where Masse bought fruit and a litre bottle of juice and made enquiries about whether some aid colleagues in a couple of pale SUVs had passed this way.

'Thirty minutes ago,' he told me, climbing back in. 'Seven men. The stallholder said they looked more like soldiers than aid workers. They bought supplies, too, then drove off very fast.' He opened the bottle of juice and took a deep swig, then dropped it on the floor by his side. When he belched I caught the sickly smell of sugar overlaid with something else.

'What is that, *alaq*?' I asked. Alcohol is illegal in Somalia. But I'd heard that the locals make an illicit substance with pure alcohol smuggled across the border from Ethiopia and mixed with fruit juice to disguise it from police.

He shrugged, reading my mind. 'It's not as bad as people say. It has a kick, that's all. You want some?'

I shook my head. If I wanted to poison myself I could think of quicker substances to pour down my throat. But having Masse using it was a worry, and I wondered at his mental state.

We ate as we moved, Masse sipping from his bottle and refusing any water. I tried to warn him off the juice a couple of times, but he ignored me, claiming it had no effect on him. In the end I gave up and focussed instead on thinking about Ratchman's crew. If they were only thirty minutes ahead of us, it meant they'd been in no hurry before encountering the roadblock. Since then they must have figured we were in front and would catch up with us in their faster vehicles. Just as long as they didn't have doubts and decided to wait for us to pop up in their rear-view mirrors.

It was time to get off the road. The closer we got to the RV, the more likely Ratchman would become suspicious about not catching up with us and to begin asking questions about pickups of people along this road. If he did that, it wouldn't take long for him to come to the conclusion that there hadn't been any, and that we must be behind him.

I looked across at Masse to see if he was helping with looking for a place, but he was almost out of it and struggling to keep his eyes open, his head lolling from side to side as we moved along the undulating road surface.

I decided to talk, to keep him connected. 'I got the names of two of the men up ahead,' I said. He didn't respond, but turned his head my way and stared at me as if I was speaking a foreign language. 'Ratchman is the leader, and his number two is a guy named Morales. They have history in business with Lunnberg. I don't know the others, though.'

He mumbled something I didn't catch, so I said, 'Say again?'

'McBride. His name was McBride.' It took me a second or two to realise that he was speaking in French, and I wondered if I'd heard him correctly. He spoke once more before going back to sleep, and giggled as if enjoying a joke. It was enough to make my skin crawl. 'He didn't see it coming. I pricked him and he went pop.'

I've spent many nights in bivouacs with companions or colleagues I didn't particularly like, but never with one whom, drunk or not, had just confessed to murder. That kind of admission doesn't make for an easy sleep. The only thing in my favour was that the level in the bottle of juice Masse had bought had gone down a long way and he was soon out of it and snoring like a hog.

Finding somewhere to hide in an apparently empty landscape is not as simple as it might seem. The pickup wasn't small enough to conceal behind the occasional tree, which made us visible to anybody driving along the road unless we took off into the back-country and risked coming to grief with a burst tyre or worse. I also wanted to be close enough to the RV to make a quick run to the airstrip before dawn ready for Marten to fly in and pick us up and get back out again as fast as possible.

The solution came by chance about ten miles short of the airstrip. It was a dried-up bend in the Shebelle river, where a landslide had created a diversion in the water flow, leaving a shallow gulley with a sun-baked crust thick enough to take the pickup's weight. It was less than a quarter-mile off the road, giving us the opportunity of a fast exit if we needed it, so I parked up and left Masse using the tarp again to create a bivouac, while I carefully wiped out any traces of our passing in the soft earth visible from passing traffic.

Sleeping wasn't going to come easy, so I told Masse I was going walk-about to check the area for signs of life and took the AK and the SIG. He was asleep under the tarp before I'd gone twenty yards.

'He'd been stripped clean of any ID . . . I have no idea who he was.'

Walking was a welcome distraction and allowed me to give free reign to the thoughts that came crowding in over and over. I needed to go over what had happened over the past few days and figure out what I was going to do about it. If it hadn't been just the liquor talking, Masse had just admitted to killing Lunnberg's man, McBride. That meant he hadn't left the building and gone into the city at all, but had managed to get close enough to the American to get him to lower his guard, then used his knife. It made what he'd told me about finding him already dead a pack of lies and had me questioning what else he'd lied about. For one McBride must have been carrying some ID other than the barcode, maybe a billfold or passport. Perhaps McBride had figured he was only going straight in and out again, so carrying ID wasn't likely to be a problem. Then he'd run into Masse.

Trashing McBride's face had been a cold-blooded and deliberate act to confuse me or anyone else who happened along. They were about the same size and my expectation was that I would be meeting Masse. Finding a white, dead body of a similar size but unrecognisable would be enough to make me assume he'd run into trouble.

And it had worked.

That led on to something else, too; such as how Ratchman and his team had found me in the hotel in Djibouti. I'd put it down to chance or good intelligence, but maybe they'd had an inside track. Like Masse.

It was possible that he'd gone rogue . . . or had simply lost the plot and saw everything as a threat and reacted accordingly. Like the way he'd killed Ahmed; it had been without remorse or explanation. You don't kill in this business unless you or an asset are facing explicit danger. If Masse could do it so casually, it set me wondering why he hadn't put me out of the picture, too. The only explanation I could think of was that he needed me to get him and the hard drive safely out of the country. We were already up against it with Ratchman and his team chasing us, but Masse's chances of fighting them off by himself would be close to nil.

Whatever his reasoning, out here wasn't the place to go into it. I needed to get him back across the border with the hard drive; explanations could come later.

I circled in a wide sweep, keeping the location of the bivouac a hundred yards off over my shoulder. The ground was rough, but manageable, with a mix of rocks, shale and bushes. We were close enough to the road to hear the occasional hum of passing traffic, but that only lasted until darkness fell. After that, nothing moved. Nighttime travel without heavily armed guards was too full of danger from bandits or other predators looking for easy targets.

I made three tours of the area, stopping at random to take in a little water and eat a couple of the bananas Masse had bought at the roadside stall. It wasn't a great diet but I didn't exactly feel up to anything more complicated, even if I'd had it. There's always a point in an assignment when you just want to bring it to a close and get out of the field; when you want to sign it off as job done. But that's when you can face the maximum danger; when you allow your defences to drop and fail to remain alert to a possible threat.

318

Lucky for me I was in a good position to see movement when it came.

I'd just checked my watch and saw it was nearly 03.00. Sunrise would come anywhere between 05.45 and 06.00, which meant I wanted to be on the move by just before 05.00 to give us time to make the RV before daylight and scope out the land. As I looked up to check the sky, I saw the outline of a figure coming along the edge of the riverbed.

He was bent double and carrying a rifle.

I slid down into the bottom of the dried bed where I was out of sight, and waited. I hadn't been able to see any great detail, but I figured a man with a rifle creeping up on our position in the middle of the night hadn't just dropped by to say hi.

I heard the scuff of footsteps and froze. The sound hadn't come from where I'd spotted the newcomer, but from above my head. Had he crossed to my side or was there more than one? Then the first man appeared. He was still on the far side of the riverbed and heading straight towards the bivouac. He evidently couldn't see me in the shadows, but was focussed on where he was treading.

I turned and looked up. For a second I couldn't see anything. Had the other man gone by me? If so that put him dangerously close to Masse. Then a vague shape appeared against the stars, and he was standing directly above me – so close I could hear him breathing and smell his body odour. He was also armed and staring out over the surrounding area.

Then he looked down.

He made a small sound of surprise and began to swing his gun towards me. I dropped the AK and lunged upwards, grabbing his ankles and pulling him off-balance as hard as I could. He gave a yelp and crashed down alongside me in a shower of sand, and I followed up with a punch to the side of his head to keep him quiet.

He was hurt, but he wasn't down or out – and he was strong. He lashed out with his rifle, which he'd kept hold of. It bounced off my shoulder in a wave of pain, then he threw it aside and came at me with a glimmer of something shiny in his hand.

My gut contracted instinctively. Knives are not as easy to defend against as some so-called experts like to say, especially in poor light and on uneven ground. So forget all the balletic counters you see in the movies. Most untrained knife carriers use a wild slashing motion in a close-up tussle because the adrenalin is high and they've never been taught anything more refined. That makes them very difficult to stop or grab hold of without taking some serious cuts to the hands and arms, or worse.

The AK was out of reach and I knew he'd be on me the moment I moved, so I felt for the SIG. If I had to shoot him that was the way it would have to go. But the SIG had fallen to the ground somewhere, so I reached down and grabbed a handful of sand and stones, and threw them in his face. I followed that up with a kick which sent up another spray. He flailed around with his free hand, spitting out sand and came at me like

320

a windmill, grunting each time he slashed the air with the knife. As I dodged back my foot sank into a hollow. I went over backwards and rolled, picking up more dirt and hurling it at him.

It wasn't pretty and wasn't meant to win any marks for style or technique. Scoring points wasn't the plan – survival was. This guy wanted to kill me and he didn't care how. On the other side, I didn't care how I stopped him as long as I did.

I felt the ground give way beneath me and realised I was close to the centre of the riverbed where the ground was mostly made up of silt. I reached down for something – anything – to use against him again and felt a large, loose rock sitting on the surface. It was the size of a soup bowl and heavy, like a discus. I waited until he was close, stepped to one side and swept it up and across. It connected with the side of his face with a squishy thud, and he went over and lay still.

I wanted to throw up, to sit there and relish still being alive and in one piece. But there wasn't time. I hunted around until I located the AK and the SIG, then ran back along the riverbed towards the bivouac.

I saw the pickup first, with the bivouac to one side. There was no sign of Masse so I figured he was still asleep. But the second man I'd spotted wasn't – and he was within a few paces of the vehicle with his rifle levelled at the door.

There wasn't time to take aim and fire; I was too wobbly with the effort of the fight and running, and likely to hit Masse by mistake, apart from alerting any companions these two men might have close by. Instead I shouted, 'Stop!' I didn't expect it mean anything to the man but he'd have had to be inhuman if he didn't at least turn to see who was there.

It was enough to make him hesitate. By the time he reacted I was close enough to slam into him, knocking his rifle aside and bowling him over. He was small and skinny and smelled of sweat and *alaq*, and hit the ground hard. Christ, he was no more than a kid – but still dangerous if I allowed him to get up. I tapped him with the butt of the AK and he didn't move. He was still breathing so I tore off his *keffiyeh* and used it to tie his upper arms with a couple of loops around his neck. It wouldn't last long but it would give us time to get out of here and away.

I woke Masse, who looked as if he was nursing a mountainous hangover, and told him we were leaving. He began to protest but I wasn't listening. I tore down the tarp around him and threw it into the rear of the pickup, then told him to get behind the wheel. He was holding the remains of his juice bottle, so I took it out of his hand and threw it away as far as I could.

'What are you doing?' he croaked. 'I hadn't finished that!'

'Leave with me or stay,' I told him. 'Two men found us and there are possibly more nearby. Now, get in and drive.' I jumped into the back of the pickup and showed him the AK, and he finally got the message and clambered behind the wheel.

We came up out of the riverbed, the load of

truck parts shaking with every rut. The road wasn't far, and I could see it as a vague outline from my perch on the back. There was no sign of a vehicle that might have brought the two men here, or of other armed men, and I concluded that they must have been loners who had spotted us on their way through the area and had decided to chance their luck.

I gave it a mile or so once we were on the road before leaning down and signalling Masse to pull into the side.

'What now?' he queried, still sore at losing his *alaq*.

'We need to get rid of this load,' I said, and began throwing the truck parts over the side. They had been useful to begin with, but Ratchman had probably identified us by now and we needed as much speed as we could get.

Once everything was gone I climbed in the passenger seat and Masse continued driving.

Forty minutes later he turned off the road onto a rough track which snaked into an area of scrubland and acacia trees, and after ten minutes bouncing over ruts and stones, finally stopped the pickup and turned off the engine.

I looked out at even more scrubland stretching away into the gloom. 'This is it?'

He nodded slowly, nursing his headache. 'The vegetation has grown since I was here last. But yes, this is it.'

I got out and clambered onto the roof, and did a 360° sweep of the horizon. It was flat and featureless, and the lack of light didn't show much detail, but it looked empty enough. I was pretty sure that even with Ratchman's military experience, a couple of SUVs would have stood out, so maybe they'd turned off somewhere or driven right on by. Either was a good sign. So far.

I jumped down and told Masse I was going to check the landing area. He didn't reply but stared out towards the coming dawn.

Thirty-Six

The ground looked even worse close-up, and as I walked along its length carrying the AK, I began to question how Marten was going to land here and take off again. Numerous ruts and fissures showed up as shadows, too big and deep to my eyes to allow any kind of wheeled vehicle to pass over without sinking out of sight. Rocks that on first sight passed as small to middling seemed as big as footballs when standing over them.

I moved a few of the largest stones aside and kicked soil into the worst of the holes. It was too little too late but better than nothing. This place really needed a going-over with a road grader and a gang of men with shovels to make any appreciable difference.

Looking further out I could see that the land here wasn't as flat as I'd first thought. The strip was sitting in a shallow basin surrounded by a range of low hills way into the distance. Most of the terrain consisted of coarse grass and patches of sandy soil dotted with a whiskery growth of shrubs. If it had ever been farmed it must have been too far from the water to have been useful, and must have been eventually abandoned as a dead loss in favour of land closer to the river. Away to the west I could see a spread of flat-topped trees with spindly trunks and branches, taking distinct shape as the sun did its work and flooded them with light. A few black shapes in the upper branches sat motionless like a musical score, until one of them flapped long wings and took off, revealing the gangly flight of a vulture, searching for a thermal to lift it into the windless sky.

I searched the horizon to the north-east, wanting to see a familiar dot appearing over the hills and hear the welcome buzz of an aircraft engine. I didn't know how direct Marten was going to make his approach, but I guessed he would want to take a quick look-see first, to make sure there wasn't the wrong kind of reception committee waiting for him.

Nothing doing.

I walked further out to where a slight rise in the land gave me a few feet of extra height over the surrounding countryside. It wasn't much help visually, but at least I couldn't see anything threatening heading our way, which was a plus. But it didn't last long.

As I turned and walked back towards the pickup, something disturbed the atmosphere.

I stopped, holding my breath and cocking my ears to the sky. I was certain I'd heard a hum. It was distant, so faint I could have been imagining it. But something was there, I knew it. I jogged back to join Masse, who was squatting in the back of the pickup, head hanging down. An empty water bottle lay on the floor by his feet. 'Do you hear that?' he said, and nodded to the south. 'It's coming from that way.'

I jumped up beside him and shielded my eyes against the rising sun. If there was anything out there it wouldn't be friendly; it was either the SUVs or worse. But all I could see was a long stretch of nothingness reaching for several gently undulating miles, dotted with the same scrubby growth I'd seen everywhere else. The only movement came from a couple of guinea fowl a hundred yards away, preening themselves in the new warmth and unfazed by our presence.

I cupped both ears with my hands and closed my eyes, focussing all my attention on the area to the south. Depending on ambient factors such as wind, weather, the movement of vegetation – even one's own pulse rate pounding in the ears – it can extend the hearing potential to a reasonable degree, gathering up sound and movement in the atmosphere and allowing a person to dismiss the unimportant or known trivial and concentrate on the familiar.

Engines. They were a fair way off, but in this flat, windless landscape with nothing to impede it, sound can travel for many miles.

I looked up, half expecting to see the flash of sunlight off a windshield or the telltale puff of dust in the wake of a moving vehicle. Not a thing. But somebody was coming and of all the places they had chosen, it had to be right here.

It could only be Ratchman.

I turned to Masse. 'We haven't got long.'

He scrambled to his feet, the sudden movement making him wince. 'What do we do?' He looked suddenly helpless, as if he'd come to the end of his mental resources, and I wondered how useful he was going to be if it came to a fight. There was only one way to find out.

'We leave the pickup here and find a place to dig in, one on each side of the landing strip. If it's Lunnberg's men they'll come in fast, wanting to get this over and done with. They've got the firepower and the confidence to think we'll be easy targets. But that makes them vulnerable.'

He looked sceptical. 'Won't it be better to stay with the pickup? At least then if we have to run we'll be mobile.'

'We'll also be a bigger target and easier to hit. If they have any sharpshooters on board, all they'd have to do is blow out a tyre and we're done for.'

He shrugged. 'Yes, I see.' Then he looked at me almost slyly. 'I was thinking . . . we could offer to do a trade. The hard drive in exchange for our lives and our silence. It might work. What do we have to lose?'

'Our lives,' I said. 'So forget it.' It was a desperate idea by a man who wasn't thinking straight. 'You think these same men who killed Doney for no reason will let us go free in return for a piece of hardware?'

He looked puzzled by my mention of Doney. Then the penny dropped and I realised that for a moment he'd completely forgotten about the teacher. Was it a case of out of sight, out of mind, or simply a cold-blooded side to his nature? I'd met people with that attitude before and they had always worried me because you never could be certain they wouldn't apply the same attitude to you if things got tough.

'We're not meant to come out of this, André,' I continued. 'Don't you get that? The hard drive and anybody who came near it are meant to disappear so that no questions can be asked. Ever. That means you and me. We're the last loose cannons in the chain.'

He didn't say anything and I could see my words weren't having much effect. Whatever else the *alaq* had done to him it hadn't speeded up his instincts for caution, or his memory for what he had been sent here to accomplish. The fact that he was actively considering the idea wasn't so much him selling out as pure desperation; of thinking he could control the eventual outcome and walk away unscathed.

I let him stew on it and jumped down from the pickup. I picked up the two tarps, which I'd kept from the scrapyard, and tossed one at Masse's feet. It was the one with Ahmed's blood on it, now dried to a brown crust. 'Find yourself a position down at the end of the strip on the right-hand side and dig in. Use rocks, scrub and soil like I did at the scrapyard. Make sure you can see the approach track. They'll be coming up there but they'll probably split up and circle round to come up either side of the pickup, so you'll need all-round vision. Keep your eyes on them at all times.'

'Where will you be?'

'I'll be across from you and down a ways with this.' I slapped the AK. 'That way we'll have them between us. If you have to open fire make sure that they're close enough to hit and that you're not shooting towards me.'

'What if Marten comes?'

'We deal with that when it happens. He'll see

the pickup so he'll know we're here. But he's not going to stay on the ground longer than it takes for us to jump on board, so as soon as he touches down, make a run for it and I'll provide cover.'

Just then I heard a distant hum overlaying the sound of the approaching SUVs, and turned to see a tiny dot in the sky approaching from the north-east.

Marten.

I spun round and checked to the south. The binoculars showed nothing at first, just an empty landscape. Then I saw a flicker of movement. Tiny to begin with, so quick I thought I'd imagined it. A bird, maybe. Then the unnatural shape of a radiator grill and headlights became clear coming along the track from the road, followed by another identical shape just behind.

Ratchman.

I turned and whistled to get Masse's attention. He was down on the far side of the airstrip away from the approaching SUVs. When he looked up I signalled urgently for him to get under cover. He nodded and dropped to the ground, disappearing behind a dried-out shrub. It would do; if I couldn't see him, Ratchman's crew were unlikely to do so either.

Jogging the length of the landing strip, I veered off to the side facing the approach track, choosing a spot giving me a clear all-round view, but in rough ground where the SUVs couldn't simply run over me. Then I threw the tarp over myself and propped it up with a couple of sticks to give myself a field of fire. I broke off more sticks ready to do the same on either side and to the rear.

Where was Marten? I stuck my head out and listened. The drone of the plane was increasing all the time, but not fast enough. At this rate the SUVs would be on top of us well before Marten began his approach run. It was too late to ask him to speed up, but I could try to slow the opposition down a bit. It was risky but the only thing I could think of.

Hell, what was the point without risk?

I rolled out from under the tarp and did a monkey-run towards the track, keeping as low as possible. It was hell on the leg and stomach muscles but I had to get close to the track to be effective. By the time I got there I was breathing hard, my thigh muscles were burning and my gut felt as if I'd been kicked by a horse.

Dropping to the ground in the middle of the track I settled my breathing as best I could to reduce any tremors. By lifting my head a fraction I could see the SUVs approaching, now about half a mile away. They were kicking up a storm of dust and moving at a fast rate, which meant they probably had a clear view of the pickup and knew that the end was in sight.

I turned my head and saw the plane losing height, the buzz of the engine changing its tone as it did so. It looked as if Marten was going for a straight landing rather than making a circuit of the area first, and I figured he must have spotted the SUVs and had decided on risk-all tactics. Maybe it hadn't been as long since his last visit as he'd claimed, and he knew the ground sufficiently well to take a chance.

I checked the AK. Everything was good. I had a full magazine, a decent field of fire and everything to lose if I screwed up. How was that for motivation?

The first vehicle popped up large in the binoculars, churning up a cloud of dust as it bucketed along the track. It had two men standing in the back and holding on tight, assault rifles clearly visible, and they were not slowing down any but coming in fast and head-on. So where was vehicle number two?

I checked off to the side and caught a glimpse of pale bodywork just above the bushes as the second Raptor went across-country towards the far end of the landing strip. It was throwing up twin clouds of soil in its wake, the engine screaming as the driver sought to get maximum revs and forward power. I couldn't do anything about it because it was too far off, but I could certainly throw some serious intentions towards the one approaching down the track.

The AK-47 has a rate of fire of roughly 600 rounds per minute. That's impressive on paper and if you scare easy, but who the hell has that number of rounds at their disposal? I didn't, so I was going to have to be more selective. There was also the question of accuracy. The AK was said to have effective range of between 300-400 yards, but I was going to err on the side of caution because this weapon had seen some action and, reputation aside, was possibly past its best.

I gathered my legs beneath me and sat up facing

roughly two o'clock from the track, which was twelve, with my elbows on my knees. It wasn't as effective as lying down, but I was going to have to present a small target while having the ability to jump up and out of the way if push came to shove.

As I centred the sights on the windshield, driver's side, they saw me. I could tell because the driver began zig-zagging, using up the full width of the track to throw off my aim. But doing that is a bit like a stopped watch; on two occasions it will be accurate. All I had to do was to hold my aim and wait for him to swing back, then squeeze the trigger.

I pumped three shots at him one after the other and saw the glass go crazy, then shatter completely. He could probably see a little through the mess, but only if I'd missed him.

I hadn't.

Suddenly the front wheels hit a rut in the track and spun sideways. The forward momentum was too great to cope and, big as the tyres were, one of them found a deeper rut than it had ever hoped for and tipped the SUV on its side.

I stood up and fired six more shots, seeing glass and bits of jagged metal spinning off into the air. I couldn't see what the internal damage was but one of the doors popped open and a figure tumbled out and rolled into the scrub at the side of the track. He must have been wearing his lucky rabbit foot.

Just then the plane went over my head and I felt the wind of its passing. When I looked up Marten was curving round to make another approach, and I figured he'd gone for the look-see method first. But I was impressed; at least he was staying with us instead of heading for the hills.

I heard something snap past my head and ducked. A figure had appeared down the track on the other side of the Raptor and was down on both knees. He had blood on his face and looked like he'd taken a bad knock. But he was still fighting and therefore dangerous. I aimed quickly and fired off three shots, using the full 300-yard system of aiming for the centre body mass.

He flipped over backwards and dropped the rifle.

I heard a rattle of distant gunfire coming from somewhere behind me, and turned in time to feel the AK ripped out of my hands and take a hit in the shoulder which spun me around and dropped me where I stood.

Thirty-Seven

It hurt. That was my first thought. it hurt like hell. My second thought was that I'd messed up. Damn, how stupid; I'd taken my eye off the other vehicle and paid the price.

I forced myself to my feet, feeling my head spinning with the shock, and started moving towards the landing strip. I could still hear the noise of the other SUV moving in the distance, and figured it was coming round to finish me off. The plane . . . I couldn't tell where the plane had got to; it was still there, buzzing around in the background, but I was having trouble focussing. Was it the plane I could hear or the SUV? And there was another noise out there, too; bigger, heavier, pounding the air and beginning to drown out everything else as it got louder.

I looked up and saw a familiar shape skidding across the sky in a long curve about two miles away, like a pregnant caterpillar. But caterpillars don't fly. What the hell? Then I remembered what Masse had said. '*They had to bring their vehicles, too, and a Chinook would have swallowed them easily.*'

Now it was coming to take them back out. Game, set and match.

Putting one foot in front of the other, something I'd been doing quite successfully all my life, had suddenly got to be a problem, and I knew I was wandering off to the side. I felt one of my legs go and sank to one knee and threw up. Not the thing to do in polite society, but it made me feel better and helped clear my head a little. I looked up and saw a figure coming towards me, and in the background, a large bird coming straight for us, waggling it wings with its feet down like a duck about to land on water. Wait. No water. And not a duck. Marten's Cessna.

Then Masse was pointing at me with his mouth open, and I wanted to ask him why but just then Marten flew right by and touched down, sending up a whirlwind of dust and grass all around us.

Masse stopped pointing and grabbed me by the arm, helping me towards the end of the strip where the plane was turning in a wide circle to face the other way. I just went along with him, wanting to ask him lots of questions but knowing there were better, more important things to be doing right now, like surviving and getting the hell out of here.

We made it to the end of the airstrip where Marten had stopped and was waving frantically at us to get on board. Masse jumped in, then turned to look over my shoulder and shouted a warning.

The second SUV had appeared from the far end of the airstrip and was barrelling towards us with two men firing from the back. Their aim was being thrown off by the unsteady movements of the vehicle, but they were getting closer all the time, their shots kicking up dirt close by and one pinging through the skin of the Cessna's wing. Give it a second or two and a lucky burst and they'd be right on target.

My instincts kicked in and I turned to bring up the AK. A squeeze of the trigger and it would all be over. I'd done it many times before and could do it in my sleep. After all, how hard could it be to hit a Ford Raptor coming at us head-on? Then I remembered dropping the AK somewhere but couldn't think how. Damn, that was dumb. I remembered the SIG Pro. I pulled it out and leaned against the Cessna's fuselage, which was a relief, and began squeezing the trigger. Quick lesson when in desperate straits: point gun at bad guys and squeeze trigger. Repeat until empty. End of game.

Then I heard a rapid snapping sound really close by and looked round to see a figure sitting in the doorway calmly firing an assault rifle with a bulbous end. A suppressor. Cool. I looked back in time to see the SUV wander off-course and the two men in the back were leaping out before it went ass-over. Then the plane was moving and I felt a pair of powerful hands pulling me in through the door and Marten shouting at us to stop fucking about and get our belts on, or words to that effect.

Fade out.

I came to as the plane was coming in to land. I knew that because I could feel the downwards pressure as we lost height. I couldn't see much through the windows because my eyesight was a bit hazy, so I concentrated on looking round inside the cabin.

The first person I saw was Angela Pryce. She was wearing jeans and a shirt and I thought how cool she looked. She was smiling with what might have been relief. She had a nice smile.

The second person was bigger and grinning down at me from the seat next to mine, while holding a field dressing against my shoulder. It hurt, and why he was grinning beat the hell out of me. A sadist, perhaps.

'That was close, matey.' It was a classic piece of understatement if ever I'd heard it, but Doug Tober was British and they're given to that kind of talk. He was also a member of the Basement, MI6's hand-picked team of specialists and the equivalent of the CIA's Special Activities Division. The last time I'd seen him, it was him nursing a bullet wound and we were off the coast of Somalia, close by the border with Kenya being chased by pirates. Slung across his chest was a fancy piece of weaponry I hadn't seen before. It was bulky around the barrel and short, with a curved magazine and some kind of natty scope system.

'You really didn't have to come all this way,' I told him. 'A postcard would have done. What the hell is that?'

He looked at the weapon. 'Oh, this. I was asked to give it a field test. I think it passed, although it felt like it was pulling to the left a bit. Sorry, I can't tell you what it's called, otherwise I'd have to throw you back out the door.'

'Why you?' I meant, why was he here, so far from London? Pryce I could understand; she was in the region anyway and probably hadn't gone far after our last meeting.

'The boss asked for a volunteer to get someone's arse out of a crack. When I heard whose arse it was I told him it had to be me or I'd resign. Just in time, too, by the looks of it.'

'Bullshit. I could've taken them, no problem.'

Trash talk, I know – but it helps in times of stress.

As we touched down I looked across and saw Masse sitting behind Doug. He was looking worried and I remembered a few things that were important and thought about why, and what I was going to do about it.

Things got a little hazy for a while, but after landing I was apparently taken to a military medical facility where the staff were accustomed to dealing with gunshot and shrapnel wounds. For them I was a bystander, drifting in and out of consciousness, only vaguely aware of an array of faces going by, some smiling, most hidden by masks, and hearing a lot of talking which didn't make much sense. But the pain gradually eased off from serious to a dull ache and I was told I wasn't going to lose anything and it had been pretty much only a flesh wound. In other words, suck it up, Sissypants.

The following day things became a little clearer; they told me I'd lost a bit of meat from my shoulder and gave me a souvenir to remember it by. After that they made it clear that I'd received all the treatment I was going to get and they had some inbound casualties so it was time for me to leave but to take things easy for a few days. Doug and Angela showed up full of smiles and got me out of there and into a nice room at the Sheraton. I thanked them probably too many times, until they began to yawn and I got the message and shut up.

'I've arranged a flight out tomorrow morning,' Angela explained. 'Until then we're keeping you here to let some of the dust settle.' The way she said it made me look up.

'Why, what's going on?' It didn't come out quite that smooth; I was having trouble focussing my mouth rather than my thoughts, but the medics had said that was to be expected and I shouldn't plan on giving any lectures.

For an answer she switched on the television. CNN was running a bulletin about the latest air strikes carried out by French forces. But instead of Syria or Libya, it was a bit closer to home – Mogadishu.

> 'Early reports from French sources reveal that drone strikes directed with the assistance of the US military against two targets in Somalia, close to the capital, Mogadishu, have been successful. Unconfirmed sources claim that one of the senior leaders of al-Shabaab in the region, Liban Daoud, who was allegedly planning a series of bomb attacks in the region and elsewhere, was killed along with several of his followers. A bomb-making factory was also destroyed.'

Angela muted the sound. 'The US and France working together again. It was a joint decision. There's a serious clean-up operation going on. I shouldn't tell you this but they're working to bury all talk of any negotiations with terrorists or the Somali government on the question of oil.'

'And burying Daoud is the beginning?'

'Looks like it.'

'They're not playing games.'

'Exactly. I suspect there's a lot of file-cleaning going on in and around Washington and Paris right now, and diary entries being amended to prove they were nowhere near any of the decision-making. Give it a couple of days and it'll be like it never happened.'

'Any news of Masse?'

She looked a bit glum. 'Sorry – we took our eye off that particular ball. He disappeared while we were getting you to the hospital. He hasn't been seen since and we assume he may already have left the country along with his controller, Petrus.'

I wasn't so sure. This was Masse's turf and he would know every bolthole there was. As for Petrus, I was pretty certain he would have orders to stick around until everything was tidied up. Going back too soon and finding echoes coming back to haunt him later would be a real career-killer.

I knew where Petrus was staying, but I didn't want to drag myself out of here unless I had to. I took out my phone and dialled his number from memory, hazy as that was. I got it first time.

'Yes?' He sounded both cautious and professorial at once.

'Is Masse with you?'

It took him a second to respond, and I suspected he was checking the windows of his hotel and getting ready to make a run for the exit. Not that he had anything to fear from me, but paranoia comes free in his profession. 'Portman? Do you have it?'

It. The hard drive. The man was all heart. Straight down to the main business – and he hadn't answered the question.

'No. Masse must have it. I think that puts me out of the frame, don't you?'

He ignored that and said, 'Why would you think this person is with me?'

This person? 'Masse. He's your man, why wouldn't he be?'

Another long pause, then he came back sounding icy calm. 'Portman, I think you are mistaken. André Masse is not and never has been an employee of . . . my company. He is – was – an occasional asset, employed on occasional tasks where his local knowledge proved useful.'

I thought back to the original briefing in Paris. Now I thought about it, Petrus hadn't actually made the distinction but he'd certainly given me the impression that Masse was part of the DGSE. Masse himself had gone along with that, too, talking about needing to complete the job and not correcting me when I mentioned Petrus being his controller.

The truth was he was an asset – a dark one. Unconnected, unaffiliated. And in the end, unreliable. Except that he'd come to believe otherwise. 'That wasn't made clear to me.'

'I regret that. Masse is a fantasist. Yes, we used him for occasional assignments over the years because he knew the region intimately. But that was the extent of our involvement.'

'Like recovering the hard drive.'

'I don't understand. The what?'

So that's how it was going to be: play dumb in case somebody was listening in. 'The hard drive, Petrus. Mogadishu. Liban Daoud. Ring any bells?' I knew I was wasting my time. The shutters were already coming down. This assignment never existed. No speak, no hear.

He confirmed it. 'I'm afraid you have lost me, Mr Portman. Perhaps you have called the wrong number. Good day to you.'

The phone went dead.

Angela and Doug were staring at me with looks that said they'd heard enough to have added the numbers together and figured it out. End of game.

'Is Lunnberg still around?' I said.

Angela nodded. 'Yes. But word is he's leaving today for a hot date in Washington.'

I gave her a look. 'Now, how would you know that?'

She smiled. 'Tom suggested we keep our eyes on all the players . . . which is why we're keeping you here. Lunnberg's got some explaining to do back home, apparently, which won't be fun. There's even talk of a Senate hearing. But he's a slick operator and the less evidence there is lying around, the easier it'll be for him to hold up his hands and play the innocent once he's back home.'

She was right. Nobody in Washington would want to air that particular basket of dirty laundry if they didn't have to. But as one of the people connected to the evidence, along with Masse, that didn't put me out of the woods just yet. I couldn't sit around and wait for Lunnberg to arrange for one of his bully-boys to tap me on the shoulder. I stood up. I was wobbly but mobile.

'What are you doing?' said Doug, grabbing my good arm.

'I have something to prove,' I told them. 'It involves Lunnberg. And I need a witness. Two would be even better.'

Doug said, 'Count me in. Where are we going?'

'The Hotel Kempinski. It's not far.'

They didn't argue or waste time with questions, but got me downstairs and into a cab. The journey to the Kempinski was little more than a few blocks, but I didn't feel like walking and it was clear that Doug had slipped into close protection mode. It made a change for me, being the protectee. Nobody spoke on the way. I think Angela had an inkling about what I was doing, but refrained from asking.

We entered the hotel and checked out the bar, then walked out onto the terrace. I was looking for Lunnberg, but Masse or Petrus would have been a bonus, although from what Petrus had said, that wasn't going to be likely.

'I see him,' Angela said softly. 'Over my shoulder down at the far end.'

I sat down at a table and took a look, using Doug as cover. Sure enough, there was Lunnberg, looking relaxed at a table with a beer in front of him and smiling at a younger man who looked like a gofer. There was nobody else around, least of all anyone who looked like muscle. But on reflection I figured Lunnberg must have used up those facilities already and had run out of men.

It reminded me of a specific question I hadn't asked yet. 'What happened with the Chinook and the SUVs?'

'They got evacced out,' said Doug. 'Smooth operation, too; the vehicles and men, dead and mostly wounded, loaded double quick and disappeared inside the American section of Lemmonnier.'

All part of the clean-up, I reckoned. No witnesses, no evidence, and the remaining men would no doubt surface after a time back home if they didn't do some time in the slammer for unspecified crimes. At least they were off my back, which was good.

I took out my phone.

'What are we doing here?' Angela asked at last. 'I'm guessing it involves Lunnberg and Masse, but how?'

There was still one thing that was bugging me: the telephone number I'd found repeated on Masse's phone. The one he'd called several times. I wasn't certain of anything about this business but there was only one way to find out whether I was right or not. Building a wall with bricks, was what I was doing. And there was one particular brick that would make a lot of sense once I had it.

'I think I was being tracked all the way here and across the border,' I explained. 'I don't mean electronically, but I got the feeling Lunnberg's men were never too far behind me. Somehow he knew a little too much for somebody who rarely shifted from this hotel.'

'Yeah, how did they manage that?' said Doug. 'Getting his men across the border was chancy.'

'He must have had the authority to arrange it. It was risky, but only if he knew there would be no official repercussions from the Somalis.'

'He paid them off?'

'I can't prove it, but it seems likely. I'm guessing the one condition from the contact on the Somali side would have been that no trace remained afterwards; foreign contractors on sovereign soil would have been difficult to explain away. That was why the airlift came off.'

'And the drone attack on Daoud?'

'Part of the clean-up. He knew too much.' I was watching Lunnberg, relaxed and urbane, not a worry in the world, toying with a cell phone and sipping his beer. He probably figured he was safe and that the hard drive had been destroyed and he could talk his way out of any problem back home.

I fed in the number and pressed dial, then pushed the phone across to Angela. I needed her corroboration for this. She picked it up and listened. It was quiet enough where we were sitting to hear every sound on the phone.

Nothing happened. No ring tone, nothing. And down at the far end of the terrace Lunnberg was still talking and sipping his beer as if he had all the time in the world.

Angela looked at me and lifted an eyebrow.

Then I heard a tone and Angela touched the hands-free button. It rang once, twice, three times and she turned the volume down so only we three could hear it. But Lunnberg and his companion were yakking away and didn't look like breaking off anytime soon. I was about to give it up as a bad idea when Lunnberg held up his hand to break off the conversation and lifted his phone to his ear.

'Lunnberg.' His voice was nice and clear. There was a long pause, then: 'Masse – is that you?'

I signalled to Angela to cut the connection. She did so and put the phone down. Lunnberg was scowling at his phone but he didn't look round.

'So Masse was working with Lunnberg.' Angela looked surprised.

'He was playing both ends. He was desperate to get out of the country but he knew he had nothing to go back to. If what Petrus just told me is true, he wasn't on the payroll and he probably figured on trying for a big pay-day so he could disappear for good. I think he'd been out here too long and it had all got too much for him.'

I could see they weren't sure, but the evidence was stacking up. To add to it, I reached into my pocket and dropped something on the table. It was a fragment of lead.

'Is that what I think it is?' said Angela.

I nodded. 'I got hit just as you were landing in the Cessna. The medics at the hospital said it probably came from a nine-millimetre pistol and must have fragmented off after hitting something harder. I remembered the AK being torn out of my hands a split second before being hit, but none of it made sense at the time, there was so much going on.'

'A ricochet,' said Doug, pragmatic as ever. 'It was your lucky day. If it had hit you square on, you'd be dead meat.'

Angela scowled at his bluntness, then looked puzzled. 'What are you saying, Marc?'

'The people I thought must have shot me were the men in the second SUV. But they were still a way off down the far end of the airstrip when I got hit. I think they'd gone round that way to stop the plane taking off. But they were armed with 5.56 millimetre assault rifles, so a nine mil round – and that distance – didn't make sense.'

'Masse,' said Doug. 'He had a Beretta – I saw it when he climbed on board.'

'Yes. It took a while but I finally figured it out in the hospital.'

'But why let you get so close only to try and kill you at the airstrip?'

'Because I was doing what I'd been hired to do: watching his back and getting him there safely. But in the end I was going to be a liability he could do without. I hadn't seen the hard drive or anything on it, but I think he knew I was onto him. He probably figured on striking a bargain with Petrus or Lunnberg once he got back. Either would have done as long as it got him out of the country.'

I saw Angela and Doug look past my shoulder and felt a brush of movement behind me. Then the cold barrel of a pistol was pushed into the back of my neck.

'Do not move – any of you,' Masse said quickly as Doug and Angela began to rise. 'Show me your hands or I will shoot him now.'

Thirty-Eight

'What are you doing, André?' I was trying to sound calm but I didn't feel it. If I hadn't thought Masse was a nut job before, I did now. He'd moved beyond rational thought into the twilight zone. Trying to kill me back at the airstrip had been the actions of a crazy man; if he'd thought about it, he could have kept his cool and got off the plane back in Djibouti and disappeared without me being any the wiser. I hadn't tackled him about any of my suspicions, so all he had to do was make the best deal he could and be gone.

'I want protection,' he said. He was so close I could feel his breath on the back of my neck. He smelled of coffee and alcohol and stale sweat and his voice was stiff with tension. I realised he was kneeling down to use me as a convenient shield in case anything kicked off. It made it tough getting at him without endangering anyone else.

'From who?'

'Lunnberg . . . Petrus. Any of them. I need you to tell them what I went through for this mission.'

'Would that include stabbing McBride in Mogadishu and trashing his face so I thought it was you? Leaving the fake hard drive and arranging for the Somali troops to pitch up just after I'd got there?'

'How do you know—?'

'Come on. You were the only person who knew I'd be there. All it took was a phone call to your contact in their intelligence section. And dumping Colin Doney so Lunnberg's men thought he was in it with you? That was low.'

'*C'est pas vrai!*' he hissed, close enough for me to feel his spit on my skin. 'It's a lie. They came to the bar, yes – but I did not know he was going to be there.'

'Maybe not. Yet you still left him to it and ran. Did you ever wonder what they did to him?' He didn't reply so I said, 'They took him out into the country beyond Ali Adde and wired him on the ground between two trees so he couldn't move. Then they built a fire.'

Angela and Doug were transfixed, staring between Masse and me. Angela's face had gone pale.

'It must have taken a while. When the sticks from the fire were good and red, they placed them on his stomach and chest and waited for him to spill.' I waited but Masse said nothing. 'Of course, he couldn't tell them because he didn't know anything.'

Masse's breathing began getting faster and I felt the pressure of the gun barrel increase on my neck. I wasn't sure what I was hoping to accomplish, but if he gave me a fraction of a chance to move sideways, I might be able to get hold of his gun. The problem was, if I didn't get it right, Angela and Doug were in his line of fire.

'You don't understand,' Masse snapped. 'What I did I did for France! Can you say you ever did anything for your country, Portman? Is that even your real name?'

'Actually, it is. So you killed Ahmed for France?' I looked at the two others and explained, 'A bandit who stumbled on me coming away from Mogadishu. André here stabbed him in the neck while he was tied up and defenceless.'

'He was a threat!'

'What about all the calls to Lunnberg? Was that for France, too? You've been working with him all along . . . and against him. Actually, you've been playing Petrus, too – and me most of all. The hard drive is your ticket back to France – you've made no secret of that. But it has to be you who delivers it, not Petrus and certainly not Lunnberg.'

'Because he would bury it!' Masse croaked. I noticed he didn't say which one of them, but it didn't really matter at this stage; both men were in the same position and wanted everything gone. 'He would hide everything that is wrong about this affair and leave me to take the blame for the failure!' He sucked in a deep breath and I could feel the rage coming off him like a blast of heat. 'All I have ever done is my job, to serve my country. But they . . . Petrus and Lunnberg, they serve only themselves. Petrus would leave me here to rot and destroy my reputation back in Paris. All he cares about is his own career. I would have nothing to go back to – no pension, no job . . . nothing.'

'But you never had one, did you? You're a paid outsider, like me. Only you've kidded yourself that you're part of the team. It was quite convincing.'

352

I couldn't see his face but his silence said everything. I'd have almost felt sorry for him if he wasn't grinding his gun barrel into the back of my head.

'Maybe we can help you with that.' Angela broke the silence, speaking calmly, not moving. Even so, I felt Masse's gun twitch. 'None of this needs to come out.' Angela was looking at Masse without blinking. 'You can take the hard drive and do with it whatever you want.'

It sounded a desperate pitch as arguments go, but something in her voice and face must have been persuasive enough to have hit home, penetrating the tortured mess that was Masse's brain. Maybe he so desperately wanted to fasten onto some kind of get-out, he saw this as his only real chance. Hell, I know I was convinced.

'How?' The pressure of the gun decreased a tiny fraction as he shifted his attention onto her. 'Why should I believe you? I don't even know who you are.'

'My name's Angela. I work for the man who got Marten to airlift you out of Somalia.'

He nodded. 'So?'

'So he's a senior officer in MI6 and has a lot of influence.' She had produced a cell phone while we'd been talking, and held it up. 'I'm sure he could even get you a deal on that hard drive. Cash . . . papers – whatever you want. Wouldn't that be safer than trusting anybody else? I mean, it sounds as if Petrus has cut you loose anyway, doesn't it?'

There was a long pause while he mulled it over. 'How? How will you do it?'

'One phone call. That's all it will take. I can have you out of here this afternoon, guaranteed, on a military flight so nobody can get to you . . . not Lunnberg, not Petrus – nobody. But you'll have to make a statement about Lunnberg. A full statement.'

This time the pause was shorter. Angela's words had been the magic he was looking for. 'Do it,' he said.

She pressed a button and waited. Then she spoke briefly, reciting an ID code number and her surname and asking to speak to Vale. She spoke for fifteen seconds, giving the briefest summary of what was involved, then nodded and smiled. 'Four p.m. take-off? Protection guaranteed? That's a deal. We can keep him safe until then.'

Next to her, Doug Tober wore a look of innocence, but I could tell he was coiled like a spring and ready to go.

'He wants to speak to you, André,' Angela said, and held out the phone. 'His name is Tom Vale. Whatever you do, don't bullshit him.'

I don't think Masse could believe his luck. He took a while to react, then beckoned her forward out of her seat. 'Bring it to me. Quickly.' His free arm was close to my face but he kept the gun screwed tight into my neck. 'No tricks.'

Angela stood up and moved forward, holding the phone out. As he reached out to take it, she stumbled against the table and dropped her hand a fraction, forcing him to make an instinctive grab for the phone. As he did so the tip of the gun barrel slid away from my neck.

'*Move*!' Angela snapped, and stepped forward,

jabbing the phone into the side of Masse's neck. I heard a fizzing sound but by then I was already rolling sideways out of my chair and seeing Doug doing the same.

We were lucky; using a stun device on a crazed gunman with his finger on the trigger is pretty risky. A million-plus volts going through the body can do weird stuff to the muscles. But in the end it's a gamble and no more dangerous than assuming the man won't eventually shoot you anyway. In this case Masse bent double at the waist with shock and dropped the gun. Doug stepped around the table and put his foot on it, while Angela dropped the fake phone and got Masse in a wristlock and held on tight.

As I stood up I saw movement at the far end of the terrace. Lunnberg had seen what had happened and was up and out of his seat, walking away like his feet were on fire. His companion was staring after him, no doubt wondering what the hell was going on.

'Leave him,' I said, as Doug began to move. We had Masse to testify against him, which I figured would put a nasty crimp in his pants soon enough.

'What do we do with this one?' said Angela. She gently slapped Masse's face to make sure he hadn't gone into cardiac arrest.

It was a good question. The answer came back to a simple fact: Masse had played a complex game for his own ends, and in doing so had cost lives. Some might have deserved their fate, others had been caught up in the net of his scheming by chance. Such events are like throwing a stone in a pond, causing ripples that spread ever wider, eventually touching the unconnected and innocent. Like Colin Doney. He'd been guilty of nothing more than being in the wrong place at the wrong time, and of getting to know the wrong person.

I wrestled my phone out of my pocket and dialled Petrus's number.

'Yes?'

I didn't give him a chance to play dumb. 'Masse's down here on the terrace. He's had an electric shock. I know you don't want to acknowledge him, Petrus, but when he wakes up, he's likely to start shouting your name from the rooftops and telling anybody who'll listen what you've been doing here. I don't think you want that.'

He didn't pretend not to know me or to argue the point, but said he'd be right down. He was probably picturing the screaming headlines if a stray reporter happened on the story . . . and what might happen to his own career. What he chose to do with Masse was up to him, but I figured he'd have him on the first plane out of here to somewhere quiet where he couldn't do any harm. Before that happened, I bent down and went through Masse's pockets until I found the hard drive.

'You might want to pass this to Tom Vale,' I said, and handed it to Angela.

She looked surprised. 'Don't you want to deal with it?'

'No point. Masse was right: Petrus will bury it and I don't know who else to give it to. I'm sure Vale will find it useful.'

'Won't Washington have something say about that?'

'I doubt it. Nobody wants to admit it exists. But after all the trouble it's caused, it has to be good for something. Great work with the stun gun, by the way. Sneaky but neat. Thank you both.' I felt the horizon dip and sway, and noticed Doug giving me a quizzical look.

'Portman, are you OK? You look like shit.'

Amen to that. I felt as if I'd gone several rounds with a cage fighter. The excitement had obviously been too much for me. I was about to wave it off when I remembered that our roles had been temporarily reversed and I was the one in need of looking after.

'Say, could one of you hotshots do me a favour and get me out of here? I think I need to fall down.'